DICK CLARK'S SMILE
WENT AWAY.

He said, "Now you're gonna be a good girl, right? Right?"

Good girl? *Good girl?* Mae-mae thought about that one for a minute.

Hell no, she was not. She was damned if she'd be a good girl. Life, man, sometimes you had to just take hold of it, forget about good and bad, just take hold and shake it. He had almost had her—almost lulled her into submission with his tedious cop story and his smile for the camera and his nice blue suit. He had almost, almost, *almost* had her.

But he blew it.

"Sure," she lied. "I'll be a good girl."

Other Avon Books by
Walter Sorrells

POWER OF ATTORNEY

WILL TO MURDER

WALTER SORRELLS

AVON BOOKS ◆ NEW YORK

WILL TO MURDER is an original publication of Avon Books. This work has never before appeared in book form. This work is a novel. Any similarity to actual persons or events is purely coincidental.

AVON BOOKS
A division of
The Hearst Corporation
1350 Avenue of the Americas
New York, New York 10019

Copyright © 1996 by Walter Sorrells
Published by arrangement with the author
Library of Congress Catalog Card Number: 95-94622
ISBN: 0-380-78020-8

First Avon Books Printing: January 1996

AVON TRADEMARK REG. U.S. PAT. OFF. AND IN OTHER COUNTRIES, MARCA REGISTRADA, HECHO EN U.S.A.

Printed in the U.S.A.

RA 10 9 8 7 6 5 4 3 2 1

To Ruth

✉

PROLOGUE

It was the electrolysis, was what it was.

Candy Frank was driving to work, trying to come up with a good reason why she'd been forced to slip a couple shots of Jim Beam in her Ultra Slim-Fast shake this morning. The reason she settled on was the electrolysis.

How it started, she had bought these instructional tapes off the TV. Amazing mental technology—three audiotapes and a workbook, only sixty-nine dollars—that had gave her the ability to quit fooling around, start taking control of her life.

She had this little facial hair problem, see, been bugging her all these years, making her feel like some kind of hormone imbalance freak. Razor stubble all over her chin, God, imagine the embarrassment living with that? The humiliation? But these tapes, see, they'd gave her this powerful mind control technology whereby she'd finally up and took things in hand. She'd visualized herself free of facial hair, and next thing you know, she was on the phone to this nice electrolysist, an Indian fellow name of Mr. Subir Das. Simple as picking up the phone. How come she hadn't thought of that before? Because she had been trapped in the prison of her negative childhood experiential paradigm, that was why. She knew this for a fact; it said so in her tapes.

Candy slid her fingers cautiously, delicately across her chin. There were still all these bumps where Mr. Subir Das had zapped the hair follicles with his electrolysis gizmo. Painful? You want to *talk* about painful. And seven more treatments to go—Lord, give her strength!

So she'd been forced to indulge in a little taste of Jim Beam this morning. Just to take the edge off the pain, see? Just to take the edge off.

She steered her green 1983 Buick LeSabre down Peachtree Industrial Boulevard till she hit the Atlanta city limits sign, turned right at the next light, then swung into the parking lot of a big faded-blue metal building. A plastic sign, PRINTMEISTER, glowed red over the front door. Seven twenty-five and the light in the front office was already on. Mr. Towe must have got in early.

Candy Frank popped a wintergreen Tic Tac in her mouth as she headed for the door of the print shop, pausing in front of the glass to study her reflection. The vertical stripes on her blouse, shoot, they really did the trick. She didn't hardly look like somebody who weighed 182 at all. Well, 179 really, because of the shoes.

Not that she couldn't stand to lose a few, sure. It was just, like Mama used to said, the Franks knew how to carry their weight. Some people couldn't carry their weight. It was because of their bones. That and their posture. The Franks were lucky, good bones and good posture both. It just come naturally.

She went in the door to the front office. The copier was on, the computer was on—everything ready for the day to start. Only . . . the coffeepot was empty. Mr. Towe hadn't made the coffee. That was funny. Usually if he got in first, he made the coffee. Mr. Towe was real particular about his coffee.

Candy considered having another little taste—maybe that peach schnapps she had in her bottom drawer—but decided against it. No, it just wasn't proper, even if that electrolysis *did* make her chin burn like the devil's own fire.

She debated whether to make the coffee now or say hello to Mr. Towe first. Better do the coffee first. Mr. Towe got awful particular. Two bags, extra strong, just the way he liked it. Once she had the pot started, she went into his office to get his special extra-big Atlanta Falcons mug. Mr. Towe's office was a dull paneled room, everything neat and squared away. There was a picture on the wall of Mr. Towe and his partner Mr. Paris in their golf clothes, both of them holding putters in their right hands—Mr. Towe looking stern and squat and bald, Mr. Paris all smooth and smarmy, every one of his blond hairs perfectly in place.

Truth be known, Candy was not so humongously fond of Mr. Paris. Like the good book said, "Though your words be like smooth stones . . ." Now Mr. Towe, you knew where you stood with him. Candy Frank liked that in a man.

She took his special extra-big Atlanta Falcons mug out to the reception area, poured the cup full, stirred in four packages of Cremora—just the way Mr. Towe liked it—then carried the cup down the hallway and through the door into the printing plant.

The plant was a barnlike concrete-floored place, dark hulks of printing machinery scattered across it. Web presses, copiers, lithographs, the whole nine yards. There in the back next to the darkroom, the shrink-wrapper was clanking away . . . but it was empty, nothing in it. Mr. Towe was nowhere to be seen.

Candy walked back to the shrink-wrapper machine, taking tiny steps so as not to spill Mr. Towe's coffee. The darn machine had jammed again and spilled a huge load of shrink-wrapped computer manual inserts on the floor. She bent her knees and gingerly picked up one of the plastic-covered inserts. The machine had gotten ink all over the plastic wrapping.

Funny. It didn't look like any ink Candy had seen

before—a blackish reddish color. It looked more like off the bottom of a pack of chicken thighs, the juice. There was a puddle of the funny ink on the concrete, leaking out from under the pile.

She looked around the plant. Where in the samhill *was* Mr. Towe? In the little boys' room?

That was when she noticed the hand sticking out from underneath the pile of shrink-wrapped computer manuals. Oh, Lord. Oh, *Lord*! She recognized the ring on the little finger, the one with the pretty red stone in it.

It was Mr. Towe's ring.

Mr. Towe's special extra-big Atlanta Falcons coffee mug fell out of her hand and shattered on the floor. The coffee flowed into the puddle of ink that wasn't ink, and for a while all Candy could think about was that peach schnapps in the bottom drawer of her desk—how good it would feel sliding down her throat.

ONE

In celebration of her thirty-fifth birthday, Mae-mae Cosgrove climbed a ninety-foot steel pole in the Cub Foods parking lot over on Jimmy Carter Boulevard— the kind that holds up high tension wires—and stared out at the dark city.

If you had asked her what she was doing, what manner of dissatisfaction had driven her to climb nearly 100 feet in the air, she'd have been hard-pressed to come up with an answer. She knew a woman who'd run a marathon on her sixtieth birthday, another who had left her husband on her fortieth—so in that context, hugging a cold, swaying power pole ninety feet off the ground didn't seem like such a big deal.

It was galvanized steel, tapered, three feet across at the base, and about a foot in diameter up there at the top. Steel climbing pegs stuck out at right angles all the way up. Four big high tension lines hung from slick-surfaced ceramic standoffs that jutted out to one side. The weight of the humming lines bowed the pole, bent it three or four feet off plumb—just enough so that when Mae-mae looked down, it seemed like the thing was about to pitch over on its side.

Off to the west Atlanta's skyscrapers brushed the night sky with a sulfurous yellow light. Car lights snaked

around below her: on Jimmy Carter, on I-85, on Oak-
brook Parkway—red lights one way, white lights the
other. The motion of them made the pole feel loosely
tethered, slack jointed, ready to sling her to the ground.

It was pretty scary. But there was something clarifying
about it, too, nothing but fear and air and the taut, sore
feel of her shoulder muscles as she gripped the cool
steel.

Mae-mae took inventory: thirty-five years old, five
foot six, uncontrollable brown hair, thirteen pounds
overweight, fairly good teeth. Nothing special there.

She was a lawyer, a sole practitioner, who specialized
in tax and financial planning for small businesses and
moderately wealthy people. Damn good at it, too. Which
was ironic: Here she was, fifteen years or so into adult-
hood, and yet she only had a measly $2,609 in savings
and about forty bucks in the checking account. Balanced
against which she had $3,700 and counting on the credit
cards, student loans out the ying-yang, only three grand
of equity against a $111,000 mortgage, and was a little
behind on the rent at her office. On top of which her
1978 Honda Accord had lately been making this omi-
nous farting noise whenever she accelerated. It was great
being a rich lawyer.

Okay, but depressing facts and figures aside, there was
always personality to fall back on: tactless, sloppy, piss-
poor housekeeper, no kind of cook at all. She was a whiz
with numbers, though, and didn't mind a good belly
laugh. That counted for something, surely. Besides
which, she owned every record Tammy Wynette ever
made—including all those great sappy duets with
George Jones. This was not strictly a personality trait,
not *per se*, but hell, it practically made her a walking
advertisement for the American way of life, didn't it?

Relevant, ever-looming fact: Mae-mae was single.
Couldn't leave out single. No man, no sweetie-pie kissy-
face, no decent prospects. Not even a failed marriage
back there that would give some bitter heft and defini-

tion to her life. It all seemed kind of thin and incomplete. Just when everybody she knew was finally getting their lives on track, here she was, single as hell, sitting on top of a power pole to celebrate her birthday. How pathetically phallic.

And yet! The air up there on her pole was *fine*. It had a quality about it that made all this problematic stuff seem . . . not exactly insignificant, but at least tolerable somehow.

About the time she'd decided she was ready to climb down off the power pole, she spotted the police car.

It was a big white Gwinnett County cruiser, creeping diagonally across all the yellow parking lot stripes, till its headlights were shining right on the base of the pole. The policemen got out and stood next to the cruiser, looking up at her with their hands on their hips.

After a minute, one of them took a flashlight off his belt and shined it up at her, holding it on his shoulder like one of those rocket launchers they showed on CNN during the Iraq thing. The adrenaline was singing in her blood.

The cop who didn't have the flashlight cupped his hands around his mouth and yelled, "Doing okay up there?"

"Doing fine," she called back. And suddenly she *was* doing fine. Doing great, thanks, never better. Alive, by God! Alive, oh man, and scared witless.

The cops talked to each other for a minute, probably worrying about whether she was going to jump all of a sudden, make them fill out lots of troublesome forms.

She started climbing down—hand, foot, hand, foot— the cop's flashlight shining on her the whole time. When she had about reached the ground, she heard the cop with the flashlight, a skinny black kid, say, "Damn*nation*. It's a lady!"

Mae-mae grinned at them.

"Mind my asting what you doing up there?" the other

cop said. He was a fat guy with a big hat, no face under it as far as she could make out.

"Thinking," Mae-mae said, jumping down the last six feet. She hit hard, pitched over, blew the knees out of her jeans.

The cops looked down at her and then looked up at the top of the pole. From the ground, it looked like an awful long way up. After a minute the black cop turned off his flashlight.

"Not thinking about jumping, I hope,": the fat cop said.

Mae-mae looked at him, laughed. "You kidding, I was trying to figure out how I could stay up there for-ever."

The two cops glanced at each other, shook their heads.

"Looking at you, lady, I bet you got a couple kids at home," the fat cop said. "What I mean, you can prob-ably give a better speech than me, all the reasons you shouldn't ought to do a damn fool thing like this. I ain't wasting my breath."

The fat cop jerked his head at his partner and they got back in the white cruiser, slammed the doors. They were still shaking their heads when the back-up lights blinked on.

And then Mae-mae was alone, alone with her sore hands and her no-knee blue jeans.

Thirty-five, she was thinking. So this is thirty-five. Well, hell, break out the party favors.

Next morning Mae-mae was sitting in her rented leather chair in her rented law office, preparing for her morning thigh burner workout. The thigh burner workout re-quired that she first sort her mail. The bills that abso-lutely, absolutely had to be paid this month went on the corner of her desk. The bills she planned to pay later went into a stack with the junk mail.

When she was done, she looked around the office: red leather chairs, a big maple veneer desk, a pseudocolonial sideboard, nice Dürer reproductions hanging next to her sheepskin from Emory Law. Problem was, it was all borrowed prosperity, leased, payments due first of the month. Every stitch of it, even the diploma for her law degree—which she would be paying off until somewhere around midyear 2007.

She sighed. Time for the thigh burner workout. She had this new thigh-burning exercise routine, a sport called "bill basketball," which she'd invented when she figured out she couldn't pay her obligations on time anymore.

Like all good sports, bill basketball was simple in its basic concept: You took your excess bills and junk mail and threw them, one at a time, across the room at the gray metal recycling bin. If the bill went into the bin, you didn't pay it. On the other hand, if it didn't go in, you also didn't pay it. This system eliminated any compunction to indulge in the fussy masculine obsession with scorekeeping. The only drawback, it was a little weak in the aerobic department, didn't *actually* do much in the way of thigh burning. Oh, well.

Mae-mae slumped back in her chair and started sailing the mail across the room.

Georgia Power. *Whoosh.* Catch you next month, guys.

Attn: M Cosgrove! You May Have Just Won a Trip to Fabulous Rio de Janeiro!!! Whoosh. The trip to fabulous Rio flew, crazed and batlike, through her open doorway.

Billing Central. Open Without Delay. *Whoosh.* Sorry girls, not today. Billing Central banked off the wall, fell into the recycling bin. Yes! That just might be worth a little high calorie treat come lunchtime.

Just as she was about to try for two ringers in a row with *MM Cosgrove May Already Be a Millionaire!!!*, a pair of pale blue eyes appeared around the door frame.

"Excuse me?" the eyes said. "I knocked but I guess no one heard me."

The eleven o'clock! Mae-mae had forgotten about the

eleven o'clock. She'd pushed the meeting up to ten—and here it was, five till already. What the hell was the eleven o'clock's name? Nora? Cora? Myra? She was married to this tax client, Charles Towe, the guy who'd been murdered in his print shop the week before.

Mae-mae dropped the last piece of junk mail on the desk. "Mrs. Towe?" she said.

The blue eyes belonged to a thin-faced woman, maybe sixty years old, with lightly frosted hair and not much makeup. She had the kind of fine pale skin that you were supposed to keep out of the sun. Wrinkles, fine as hair, looped under her eyes and across her cheeks. She wore a simple dress, navy blue with white piping on small notched lapels. Not expensive, not cheap. She was an attractive woman for her age, but there was something about her that made Mae-mae think vaguely of nunneries and vows of chastity.

"That's right. Myra Towe." The woman spoke haltingly, as though afraid of causing offense.

"Come on in. I'm Mae-mae Cosgrove. Forgive me, I was just . . . organizing my correspondence." Mae-mae held out her hand. From the look of the woman, Mae-mae had expected one of those wimpy don't-crush-the-butterfly handshakes, but Myra Towe surprised her, gave Mae-mae's hand a nice firm squeeze.

Myra sat down, put a tentative smile on her face, tucked her blue clutch in her lap on top of a brick red accordion folder, crossed her hands over the clasp of her purse. And waited.

Oh, boy. Widows were tough. You got the impression, some of these old girls, that they'd never had to make a financial or legal decision in their lives. They were petrified, just waiting around for someone to take them by the hand.

Mae-mae took a deep breath. "First, I just wanted to say how sorry I was to hear about your husband. It's a terrible, terrible thing."

An awful stricken expression crossed the widow's

face and then slowly faded. "Thank you, dear," she said. "That's real kind of you." She had a soft low-country accent, the words stretched out like pieces of taffy.

Mae-mae wondered what it would be like after all those years to lose a husband—but it was, literally, unimaginable.

"Has there been any progress in finding who . . ." Mae-mae wasn't quite sure how to phrase it. Death, there just wasn't a convenient way of talking about it, no words that made it easier or softer.

A thin smile flitted across Myra Towe's face. "Not really. The police believe he was killed by someone who came in off the street and robbed him. They took his wallet and his watch, ran off with the petty cash box. He worked late a lot, sometimes all night on rush jobs. I guess he was there by himself with the door open and someone came in." Myra Towe spoke in a quiet, dispassionate voice, like she was describing something that didn't have anything to do with her own life. She lowered her eyes and stared at the backs of her hands. "There was a hundred and seventeen dollars petty cash, probably no more than five or ten dollars in his wallet."

From the window of her twenty-eighth-floor law office, Mae-mae surveyed the tedious panorama of the city of Atlanta—nothing much out there but trees and power lines. The only real feature of the view was Stone Mountain, a sort of distant gray tumor poking up on the horizon. Mae-mae shook her head sadly.

"So pointless," Myra Towe said, her voice taking on some animation for the first time. "So stupid."

"A human life," Mae-mae said. "For a hundred and seventeen dollars. My God."

"Yes," Myra said, her blue eyes taking in Mae-mae's face. "Only, I didn't mean that exactly. I meant it was stupid of Charles to resist. He should have just given them the money."

"Well," Mae-mae said after an awkward pause. "Did

you bring the records that I mentioned to you?''

Myra Towe wordlessly handed her the red accordion folder, its edges worn soft and flannel-smooth. The last time Mae-mae had seen the folder, it had been in Charles Towe's ink-stained hands, all his important legal and financial records stored alphabetically, little color-coded tags glued on the dividers.

Mae-mae pulled a stack of paper out of the folder, spread the sheets on the table. After Mae-mae had given an overview of the probate process and explained what her role as attorney for the estate would be, she said, ''The estate—of which you're the sole beneficiary—has a few major components that I'd like to go over right now.''

Myra Towe nodded tentatively.

Mae-mae explained about the life insurance, about the house, about the million-odd dollars in investments her husband had left her. And about her husband's business, a company called Printmeister: two mil a year in revenue with a net of about a hundred and a half. Printmeister was fifty-fifty owned by Charles Towe and a partner, a guy named Lester Paris.

At first Myra seemed to pay close attention, but when Mae-mae went back to talking about the tax implications of the probate process, she started to fade: her eyes moved around helplessly, not resting on anything in particular, a sort of dreamy, tired look on her face.

''Now in such instances where your husband held property in his name, that is not jointly with you, that property will have to be inventoried for the purpose of—''

Mae-mae decided to shut up. Myra just wasn't with her. She was looking around again, her eyes not focusing. ''I'm dumping too much on you, aren't I?'' Mae-mae said.

Myra Towe held a thin finger near her cheek, thinking about it. ''I guess—I feel foolish. . . .'' She watched Mae-mae, then her eyes dropped to the floor.

Mae-mae waited. "Go ahead."

Finally it came out. "You're saying I'm a *million-aire*?"

Mae-mae looked out the window again. You sat around talking about half a million of this, four hundred thousand of that all day, you forgot how big those numbers sounded to most people. Mae-mae smiled. "I hadn't thought of it that way. But, yes, you're a millionaire, Mrs. Towe."

Myra Towe's pale eyes widened a little, and her face turned inward, like everything had been erased from her mind. After a moment she shook her head, denying it, as though it were something she didn't want to hear. "I don't understand. My husband . . . I had no idea. I just had no idea."

"Your husband is . . . *was* fifty percent owner in a very successful business."

"I just didn't know that a man who came home with ink under his nails every day—" She held up her hands, stared at them. They were the kind of hands where you could see everything under the skin, all the veins and integuments, like they'd been flayed for a biology class. "I mean we live in the same house that we've always lived in, we don't go on vacations. We don't . . ." One hand moved softly in the air. "I guess I just didn't realize that a man like my husband could be a . . . millionaire." The way she said it—*millionaire!*—it sounded like some kind of magic word, some kind of incantation.

They sat silently for a moment. Myra stared out the window at the trees. Something seemed to be collecting and growing in her face, some unformed emotion taking shape. Suddenly a sound slipped out of her mouth, a high childish giggle. As quickly as it had come, it went away, and her eyelashes glistened, full of water.

"Big money," Myra said. "When I was a little girl I imagined—*Big* Money, you know?—what that would be like. We lived in a little white house with chickens in the backyard. A couple guinea hens, a peacock. I used to have this sort of fantasy, this daydream: I'd marry this rich boy, and then I'd sit on the edge of a huge green lawn, wearing a big white hat and watching him play polo on a beautiful chestnut horse. That was the way I imagined it, lounging around in my big old white hat.'' She paused for a minute, wiped her eye. ''Then I married Charles—we were nineteen and he was going into the service—and I thought, well . . . so this is my life. No millionaires, no polo, no big white hat.'' A tear slipped out, dissipated in the network of tiny wrinkles under her eye. ''And here he has to go and *die* for me to find out I was married to a millionaire after all. He could have at least told me.''

Mae-mae searched for a neutral comment, but couldn't really think of one.

''Look,'' she said finally, ''how about we finish this up another time. The only other thing, if you've got a couple minutes, it might be worthwhile for me to look through your records, see if anything pops out at me.''

Myra's voice: soft, weary. ''That'd be just fine, honey.''

Mae-mae looked through the stack of material from the folder, adding things up in her head. There was one thing that bothered her as she made a last check of the figures. She pointed to the account record of one of her former client's investments. ''Maybe this is nothing, but starting last year your husband started making substantial withdrawals from this fund, the Imperial Balanced Fund Number Two. Around five, ten thousand at a time.'' Mae-mae added up the withdrawals. Seven drafts totaling $62,000. ''There's no record on here of where the money went. Do you happen to know anything about this?''

Myra Towe frowned, squinted at the account records, shook her head. ''That's an awful lot of money, isn't it?'' She still didn't seem to be able to get over the size of all those numbers.

"Did you by any chance bring along the mutual fund drafts? They look like checkbooks."

"These?" Myra said. She was holding a handful of checkbooks bundled together with a fat, ink-smudged rubber band.

"Exactly," Mae-mae said. "If you'd check the stubs for a fund called the Imperial Balanced Fund Number Two . . ."

"Here," Myra said, handing her one of the checkbooks. "You know more about this than I do."

Mae-mae looked in the front of the checkbook on the pages that said *Transaction Register* at the top, tiny lines ruled underneath. There they were, neatly lettered in black ink: checks 101 through 108, dated intermittently from January of the previous year through the current month. Wait, that was eight checks. Mae-mae added them up. Eighty-two thousand. The eighth check was dated April 21st of the current year, made out for twenty grand. That one wasn't on the account record yet. Too recent. All the drafts were described as having been made to "Cash."

Mae-mae stared at the list. Cash. He was withdrawing *cash* five and ten grand at a time? That was kind of strange.

"What day was your husband killed?" Mae-mae said.

Myra Towe looked weary. "April twenty-second. Why?"

"According to this register, your husband may have been carrying a lot of money when he was killed. Did your husband often carry large sums of cash?"

"Like how much?"

"Twenty thousand dollars."

"Twenty *thousand*?" Myra Towe blinked. "I never saw him put more than fifty, sixty dollars in his wallet."

Mae-mae closed the checkbook. "I think the police ought to know about this, Mrs. Towe."

Myra Towe looked away for a minute, staring out the window. She sighed. "I just wish this could all go away.

Police, lawyers, papers, things to decide. It's just so hard." She kept looking out the window. "You know, Miss Cosgrove, I suppose I must just seem like some old worn-out fool, but this is so hard, so *hard*, I just wish I could rest a while." Her eyes were red at the rims, like she might cry again. But then she just sat there, her chin thrust at the window.

Mae-mae studied the woman's face, trying to think what to do. This was the trickiest thing about being a lawyer. You got all mixed up in people's lives. It had seemed like such a clean, simple, by-the-numbers business when she got started. You learned your tax and corporate law, threw in a pinch of accounting and some stocks and bonds, stirred in a little common sense, and you were home free, right? Only it didn't work that way. The way it really worked, money was all mucked up with problems like, *What do you want out of life?*— minor stuff like that. And sometimes Mae-mae couldn't do anything to help her clients until she had slogged around in that muck herself.

"Tell you what I can do," Mae-mae said. "If you'd like, I can look into it for you. It's probably nothing. If the police need to come into the picture, we'll worry about that when the time comes."

"Please." Myra seemed to be trying to summon a smile, but without success. "That would be such a help."

They shook hands and Myra got up to leave. She stopped at the door and looked wonderingly at Mae-mae. "A millionaire," she said softly. "Well. Who'd have thought it?" She smiled a sudden, sad smile. "I guess polo's out of the question."

Mae-mae laughed. "You want my professional advice? Go out and buy the biggest, whitest hat you can find. Then see what happens."

After the door closed, Mae-mae sat in her chair for a while, staring at the last piece of junk mail sitting on her desk. *MM Cosgrove May Already Be a Million-aire!!!*

Bull*shit*.

MM Cosgrove wasn't even solvent. So what was MM Cosgrove doing wrong? She was trying to start a law firm during a recession, that was one problem. She was trying to be a sole practitioner, swimming against the stream in the day of big corporate firms and franchised sleaze bags who advertised on TV. But, no, that wasn't it either. There was something else. Maybe, notwithstanding all her diplomas and Liz Claiborne suits, she was just another dreamy babe waiting for some polo-playing, jodhpur-wearing guy to spirit her off into the glowing nuptial sunset.

Hard to know. But what was the point in worrying about it? Psychologizing just made her irritable and hungry anyway.

She sailed the piece of junk mail at the recycling bin. It whirled spastically through the air, missed the bin by a mile, fell facedown on the floor.

So much for her workout.

TWO

On the way home for lunch Mae-mae stopped by Printmeister, Charles Towe's business. She was surprised by the drabness of the big metal building. There was a red Porsche sitting at the curb, though: this grungy place was cranking out a hundred and forty grand a year, pure profit. Whereas up in her nice office tower with her nice rented view and her nice rented furniture and her nice rented plants, she was barely making ends meet. Didn't seem fair.

The Porsche, she decided, must belong to the man she was coming to see—a guy named Lester Paris, who was Towe's partner.

As Mae-mae went through the glass door and into a bright reception area, a big lumpy woman in a black-and-white polyester pantsuit lumbered out of a doorway on the back wall of the room.

"Can I hep you?" the fat woman said. She was holding her hand over her chin. It reminded Mae-mae of some writer pretending to be thoughtful for a book jacket photo.

"I'm Mae-mae Cosgrove, Mrs. Towe's attorney. I was hoping I could speak to Mr. Paris."

A look of exaggerated horror came over the fat woman's face. She kept holding onto her chin. She moved uncomfortably close to Mae-mae and said in a low voice, "My name's Candy Frank. Office manager. *I* found him, you know. His mortal shell, I mean."

"That must have been horrifying," Mae-mae said.

"Awfullest thing I ever seen," the fat woman said. "I got his *blood* on my *hand*." She took her hand away from her chin finally, waved her fingers daintily in front of Mae-mae's face.

Mae-mae shook her head sympathetically. She couldn't help noticing, now the woman's hand had moved, that her chin was covered with small red welts.

"Electrolysis!" Candy Frank said sharply. She squinted her tiny eyes, laid a moist palm on Mae-mae's wrist. "This facial hair situation? Sister, I'm taking control. Taking control!"

"Ah," Mae-mae said. She managed to keep a straight face.

"Mr. Paris's office, right this way." The fat woman swept off down the hall on a pair of very high white vinyl pumps, trailing a breeze that smelled strongly of overripe peaches.

They entered a large office furnished with trendy bland furniture, lots of white oak veneer, the kind you took out of a cardboard box and put together with a screwdriver. A blond man in a blue suit was sitting on the edge of an oak desk looking at a piece of paper through a jeweler's loupe.

There were lots of pictures on the wall, photographs of the blond guy smiling at Andy Young, smiling at Newt Gingrich, smiling at a tennis player whose name Mae-mae couldn't remember, smiling at a bunch of not-quite-famous people. Without looking up the blond guy said, "These things still a little out of registration here, Donald?"

"Visitor, Mr. Paris," Candy Frank said. Then she hove to and navigated back up the hallway.

The man in the blue suit looked up and smiled apologetically. "Oh, I'm *so* sorry, I was expecting my shop manager." He held out his hand. "I'm Lester Paris."

Mae-mae introduced herself, explaining that she was the attorney who would be handling Towe's estate. Lester Paris invited her to pull up a chair. He was blond, fortyish, with the kind of soft, anonymously pleasant features and general expression of corn-fed goodwill that Mae-mae associated with ministers at prosperous Baptist churches. He wore a reddish mustache that he probably thought made him look older or more virile than he really was.

"Boy, I mean," Lester Paris said. "It's been a terrible blow to us all. Of course losing a business partner— that's nothing compared to Myra. Losing a *life* partner?" He smiled a rueful Baptist minister smile.

Mae-mae allowed that this was true.

Lester Paris leaned back in his chair and said, "So what can I do for you?"

"Well, eventually I'll be needing to inventory and value the estate, so for starters maybe you could tell me a little about the business," Mae-mae said.

"How about a tour of the facility, a little show-and-tell type of thing?" Lester Paris said.

"Sure," Mae-mae said, and Lester Paris sprang out of his chair like there was nothing in life he'd rather do than show a lawyer around his print shop. She had a nagging feeling that he'd end up selling her something if she wasn't fairly vigilant.

They walked down the hall and through a door into a cavernous, noisy space—metal walled and floored with stained concrete.

"Here's our plant," Lester said. "We've got the production equipment in-house to do most normal printing jobs. Twenty-four- and forty-eight-inch web presses, four color lithographs, various binders, color copier, shrink-wrapping, single- and double-side lamination." He pointed out various large, grimy machines.

"Careful, it's a little dirty back here. Don't want to mess up your pretty outfit." Lester Paris winked.

Mae-mae smiled coldly. There was something about this guy that annoyed her, something she couldn't quite put her finger on.

"Back here, this is our crown jewel." Lester Paris pointed to a large green machine that was whirring and clanking in front of them. "This baby prints lithographed stamps, high quality, low cost, all kinds of shapes and sizes."

"Like postage stamps?" She had to shout over the noise.

A tall, thin man in a stained apron was tending the press, hunched over the guts of the machine so Mae-mae couldn't see his face. He seemed pretty intent on his job, ignoring them completely.

"That's the general idea," Paris said. "Modified version of the very same machine used by the U.S. government. Had to buy it in Switzerland. Of course the government prints their own postage stamps. What we produce here is mostly used by direct mail houses. Say, Donald—" He called to the thin man in the apron, "How about handing me one of those sheets."

The thin man turned and looked at them for a moment. He had piercing black eyes, and his skin was patchy and mottled like the hide of a rotten fish. There was a weird asymmetry to his face: one of his eyebrows was missing, eaten away by what—fire, disease, a hole in the genetic code? His lips peeled back from his teeth for a moment. Whatever the expression was supposed to signify, it didn't seem to be a smile.

Without saying a word, the fish-faced man pulled one of the sheets out of a bin on the side of the press, handed it to Lester, then went back to staring into the machine again.

Lester Paris showed the sheet to Mae-mae. "See, this is what I was looking at when you came into the office."

Mae-mae studied the sheet of stamps. It contained about fifty inch-and-a-half-square stamps, each stamp bearing a tiny picture: a swath of neon blue ocean, a stylized palm tree, a garish yellow ball of sun. Over the picture, printed in hot pink letters: *Yes! Send Me to Rio!*

"What's particularly crucial for stamps," Lester said, "is that the printer be able to feed this somewhat sticky paper through at high speeds while maintaining extremely tight registration."

"Registration?"

"See this bull's-eye-looking thing? This is what we call a registration mark." Paris pointed to the upper left-hand corner of the sheet. Outside the area printed with stamps was a design about the size of Mae-mae's thumbnail: a circle with tiny bars coming out at three, six, nine, and twelve o'clock—sort of like the cross hairs on a rifle scope. "When you print a multicolored lithograph, you actually print each color separately. Now if the colors are printed out of whack, the picture comes out blurry. With stamps, because the design is so small, your stamp looks terrible if the registration's off even a sixteenth of an inch. That's the beauty of this baby. Tight registration!" Big smile.

"Great," Mae-mae said, trying to sound enthusiastic.

"Very profitable machine," Lester Paris said. "Now about the business. This was pretty much Charlie Towe's kingdom back here." Paris gestured at the room full of equipment. "He supervised all our production work. A very exacting, meticulous gentleman. But his interpersonal skills, that wasn't his strong suit, if you get my drift."

"In what sense?"

"In terms of selling, administration, people-type activities. That was more my arena. See, our secret, we each brought something totally different to the table. He could print, I can sell. That's what it came down to." He shook his head sadly. "It was a dynamite combination for a while there."

He *talked* like a Baptist minister, too, or a coach at a fundamentalist boys' prep school—earnest, positive, but somehow not completely credible. "Have you thought about what happens next?" Mae-mae said.

"Not really. It takes a little while for something like this to sink in. I guess you hate to even face it." Paris bowed his head, gave it an appropriate moment of silence before leading her back to his office.

Mae-mae sat. "There's just one other thing," she said. "Can you think of any reason why Charles Towe might have been carrying a large amount of cash the day he died?"

Lester Paris's soft face took on a puzzled look. "Large? Large, like how much?"

"Like twenty thousand dollars."

"You're kidding me." Eyes wide. "He was kind of tight with a dollar, you know. Be lucky to catch the guy with ten bucks in his wallet."

"You can't think of something connected to the business that he might have been using it for?"

Paris laughed, shook his head. "This is a credit business. No walk-ins, no cash. We do the job, we send a bill." He studied Mae-mae's face. "Twenty thousand, huh? So what's this all about?"

"I'm kind of wondering that myself," Mae-mae said.

As Mae-mae made her way out of Printmeister, Candy Frank emerged from her office, peering furtively up and down the hallway.

"Miss Cosgrove!" she whispered loudly. "I got something I need to show you."

"Sure," Mae-mae said.

Candy Frank pulled Mae-mae into her office by the sleeve and shut the door. It was a small cramped room, crowded with filing cabinets, stacks of invoices, paper everywhere. The only decorations were a bunch of green porcelain frogs, all shapes and sizes, the kind you could buy at flea markets for three or four bucks. Frogs everywhere.

For a moment Candy's face took on a slack, baffled look. Then she collected herself, leaned forward and said, "You got to appreciate, I'm the only person who really understood him."

Mae-mae cocked her head, unsure what the lumpy woman was getting at. There was that peachy smell again. What was that?

"I don't mean . . ." In the off chance Mae-mae had misconstrued what she was saying, Candy let a little decorous flush drain through her cheeks. "What I mean is, Mr. Towe and me under*stood* each other."

"Ah . . ." Mae-mae said. Peaches. Peaches. What *was* that smell?

"He been under a lot of pressure lately. I could tell. Maybe nobody else could see it. Maybe nobody else cared. But *I* did. *I* cared." Her lower lip trembled like a slice of overripe nectarine.

"Was there something going on," Mae-mae said, "something that you knew about?"

"What I'm saying is that since you're representing Mrs. Towe, I thought—" Candy blinked, then turned suddenly, reached into a swollen pink purse on her desk, and pulled out a letter-sized envelope. She thrust the envelope into Mae-mae's hand. "Here!"

Mae-mae looked at the letter. The envelope had been torn open along the top and was addressed to Mr. Charles Towe. It was postmarked Atlanta, but there was no return address. Mae-mae pulled out a piece of cheap white Xerox paper. It wasn't exactly a letter, just a two-sentence message that said: *Danger? The greatest danger of all is weak follow-through.*

The entire sentence appeared to have been cut from a book or magazine, taped in the middle of a sheet of paper, and then photocopied. Mae-mae didn't know quite what to make of it.

"Where did you find this?" Mae-mae said.

"It was next to his hand." Candy's small wet eyes were open very wide, little pouches of fat pooled up underneath her lower lashes. "When I found him!"

"And you showed it to the police?"

Candy looked at the floor, shook her head slightly. "I guess I forgot."

The cloying smell of peaches had grown stronger. It wasn't exactly peaches, though. Something else. What *was* that awful smell? Mae-mae was getting a claustrophobic feeling in the tiny office. Candy leaned closer. She had Mae-mae cornered between the desk and the wall, her big polyester hips cutting off the angle to the door. Wall-eyed porcelain frogs stared woozily from all points.

"You forgot?" Mae-mae said.

"I didn't want . . ."

Mae-mae waited.

"I didn't want his name dragged through the filth. I mean, if . . ." Candy kept leaning in and leaning in, until Mae-mae could feel her breath on her face. Peach breath.

"If *what*?" Mae-mae was starting to get annoyed at all this beating around the bush. That and the meaty, peachy, winey smell of Candy's lungs.

Candy Frank's damp, cheese-textured fingers closed around Mae-mae's hand. "Take it! Take it!"

Mae-mae threw a desperate hip check and fled the room. She was all the way out in the parking lot, the letter still clutched in her hand, when she realized what that cloying smell had been.

Wasn't it a little early in the day for peach schnapps?

THREE

Seven-thirty that evening. Mae-mae finally gave up, resigned herself to making dinner. Maybe she'd eat Italian.

She went into the kitchen, opened the microwave. The trusty jar of Ragú Chunky Vegetable spaghetti sauce was sitting there, ready for action. She unscrewed the lid, stuck the jar back in the microwave, and turned the machine on high, four minutes. The Roman Meal bread was hidden under a pile of empty rice cake bags. She dropped two slices on a plate, waited for the Ragu sauce to boil. Cooking pasta—too much trouble: Bread was way simpler.

There was no Mr. Pibb in the refrigerator, so she poured herself a few fingers of the gloopy prune juice she had bought during a brief moment of derangement while pushing her cart through the health food section at Big Star. When the Ragú Chunky Vegetable was bubbling nicely in the microwave, she took the jar out with a greasy pot holder and dumped enough on the plate to cover up the bread.

Ah, the simple life.

Once she had her dinner set up, she thought back on the letter Candy had given her. What was up with that?

She took the letter out of her purse, set it down next to her plate.

Danger? The greatest danger of all is weak follow-through.

Was it some kind of veiled threat? Maybe there had been something else in the envelope, something the killer had taken out that would have explained the message. Mae-mae sighed, put the message back in the envelope, and dropped it on her desk.

And what was Candy going on about—getting his name dragged through the filth? What filth? Maybe the police ought to know about this.

She picked up the phone and dialed Myra Towe's number.

After a moment Myra answered. Mae-mae explained about her visit with Lester Paris. "So the bottom line is, no indication as to where that money went. This could potentially be a snag in the probate process, you know, accounting for where the money went and so on."

There was no response on the other end.

"Mrs. Towe?"

"I'm sorry. It's just—" Myra Towe said. "Well, I was just thinking."

"Tell me."

"Oh, I don't know if this is anything, but perhaps you should talk to our son Chris." Her voice sank to a near whisper. "He . . . it's possible his father may have given him some money."

Mae-mae had that prickly feeling that she was getting further and further away from the realm of the law—of probate court and wills and tax consequences—and deeper into the messy netherworld of family weirdness. Not that there was anything wrong with that. It was part of the job and all that. Unfortunately it was also the part she most hated.

"Are you sure you don't want to talk to the police about this?"

"Oh no!" Myra Towe's voice leaped up. "Not yet at

least. I mean, let's not blow this thing out of proportion.'' She paused. ''Just talk to Chris first. I mean if it isn't too much trouble.''

''No no no,'' Mae-mae said. ''No trouble at all.'' At eighty bucks an hour it wouldn't be the slightest problem. Maybe she could milk enough out of this to pay her rent on time next month. It got depressing having to think this way—like every time you looked at a client, you were figuring out how much they could be counted on to chip in for your next light bill.

After she got off the phone, Mae-mae tried to remember whether Charles Towe had ever mentioned his son Chris. That's right, he had mentioned Chris once—said something dismissive about him, something to the effect that he *thinks* he's a musician. She imagined a guy with long hair, tattoos, an angry face—the kind of thing that always ticked the old man off. Of course the guy could be a classical violinist for all she knew.

Mae-mae looked him up in the phone book, noticed that he lived on Barnett, only five or six blocks away from her own house. She was getting ready to dial but then thought, Why not go out for a walk, drop by the guy's house, and see if he's home?

At least it would give her an excuse to get her thirteen-pounds-overweight ass off the couch for a change.

Chris Towe's house was typical of Atlanta's midtown area: one-story brick, built in the thirties or forties, with a tiny, precipitous yard flowing down to the tree-lined sidewalk. A cozy, well-kept place. It was also empty: no one answered her knock.

As she was about to leave, she noticed a piece of paper folded in half and stuffed into the crack between the sill and the door. Surreptitiously she pulled the note out of the door.

It said: *Hi, Clay. Change of plans. I'll be playing down at Club 15 tonight. Come see.* It was signed *Chris.*

Club 15. Wasn't it that overgrown tavern in Little

Five Points? Sure. Last time she was there, she had watched a bunch of acoustic guitar strummers playing on a little stage up front, serious-looking young women who didn't seem to be finding much enjoyment in life.

She'd gone five blocks—might as well go the extra mile and walk to Little Five Points. Go watch the show, catch Chris between sets, find out if Daddy gave him twenty grand last week. It seemed a little unfair, sandbagging the guy like that. Well, she had to do it sometime, might as well be tonight.

Besides, she had a weakness for musicians, bone deep, that went back to sixth grade, when she'd fallen in love with Ringo Starr for three or four weeks. The sad thing was that her taste never seemed to get any better. She never fell for the Paul McCartneys. It was always the Ringos or the Johns—the goofy ones or the screwed-up ones. She'd dated two drummers that she could think of, a jazz singer, and a cellist. She'd even lived with a speed freak guitar hero for one hellish summer in 1982. One disaster after another. It was a weakness—what could she say?

She jammed the note back into the door frame and ran down the concrete steps to the sidewalk.

A sign on the scarred front door of Club 15 said, TO-NIGHT: SINGER/SONGSCRIBBLER CHRIS TOWE. NO COVER. TWO-FOR-ONE PABST BLUE RIBBON. It was a Monday night and Club 15 wasn't exactly brimming with people. There were a few clots of yuppies, a table of grim lesbians, a table of happy lesbians. Up at the bar, a couple guys were posing with their Pearl Jam tour jackets and their longnecks. A very svelte, very trendy little waitress in a tiny black see-through tent dress and combat boots was busy talking to the bartender, ignoring the customers.

Mae-mae took a seat at the bar. At the far end of the room a thin, anguished guy was singing and strumming a guitar. Anguished but cute. Chris Towe, presumably.

Some of the songs weren't bad, but he had trouble with his high notes.

"What'll it be?" the bartender said after a while. He was a kid about twenty-one, twenty-two, with a silver hoop in his nose.

"This two-for-one Pabst deal," Mae-mae said, "you think I could just have one Pabst for half price?"

The bartender held two fingers near his nose ring. "Two . . . for one." Now he was holding up one finger. "That's the deal."

"Guess I better take you up on it then, huh?" Mae-mae smiled. The bartender didn't.

"You want a glass?"

"Does that cost extra or something?"

"Absolutely, totally free." It was hard to tell whether the guy was trying to be funny or whether he was just an asshole. Mae-mae had noticed about people his age that you never could tell if they were being serious or not. Maybe it was from watching too much MTV. Or maybe she was just turning into an old fart, losing her youthful joie de vivre.

The bartender brought out two cans of Pabst, popped the tops, set an empty glass next to them.

"Pouring," Mae-mae said. "Is that free, too?"

The bartender poured, making the beer foam up over the top of the glass, then sidled back to the firm-thighed waitress.

Mae-mae watched the singer. He looked to be about Mae-mae's age, thin, tall, with sandy hair and pale blue eyes. He wore small round wire-rimmed glasses, a white T-shirt and blue jeans, and he had the lean face and arms of someone who ran long distances every day. There was something of his mother in his face, a distant, ascetic look in his blue eyes. No particular resemblance to his father.

In between anguished songs, he made jokes with the people at the tables up front, a bright, impish smile lighting up his face. Then he'd switch back to anguished mode and start singing again. After a certain amount of careful study and internal debate, Mae-mae decided he was pretty attractive.

When his set was over, Mae-mae approached him, introduced herself. "Join me?" he said, pointing to an empty table near the bar. He smiled again, a funny crooked smile. Very attractive. Mae-mae had never gone for the perfect smile, perfect pectorals type anyway.

She brought her two beers over to the table.

"I'm just getting over a cold," Chris Towe said. "Can't quite peg those high notes today."

Mae-mae laughed and said, "I don't want to get started under false pretenses. I was your dad's lawyer. I'm probating his estate." She explained about the missing money.

A cloud came over Chris Towe's face. He took off his glasses, wiped them on his T-shirt, and stared silently off at an empty corner of the bar.

"Your mother thought there was some reason I should bring it up," Mae-mae said. "Any idea why?"

After a minute Chris Towe shrugged, put his glasses back on. "Dad and I never got along real well," he said finally. "Bad chemistry or something." He shook his head slowly. He looked blanched and worn for a minute, like laundry that had been out on the line too long.

"I'm sorry," Mae-mae said. "I shouldn't have ambushed you like this. If you don't—"

"No." Chris Towe's blue eyes met hers briefly, then flicked away. "No, it's okay, I guess." He took a sip of his drink—plain old tap water it looked like. "What I was going to say was that he never wanted me to be doing this, this singing stuff. Never had any sympathy for it. But I can't help it, it's just what I do."

Mae-mae nodded.

"See, it's hard for a songwriter to make a living, just whaling on a guitar, singing songs. You need a band, you need a record, you need equipment, all that." He smiled the crooked smile. "Or you'll end up stuck in

places like this forever. It's damn expensive getting
started. Sound systems, recording costs, paying a good
band. I decided about a year ago that this singer-
songwriter gig was a dead end. Record companies don't
like guitar strummers. They like *bands*—you know, syn-
thesizers, drums, good crunchy electric guitars. That's
what Mom was talking about.''

"I'm not sure I follow."

"The point is I'd been hitting Dad up for some
money, a loan, so I could hire some real professionals,
rehearse them, put together a decent demo tape." His
thin features twisted sourly. "But it never came to anything. He never would agree to it."

"So you're saying the money that came out of this
account, none of that went to you?"

Chris looked at the floor for a minute, then shook his
head.

"That's too bad," Mae-mae said.

Chris's blue eyes flashed at her, a puzzled expression
on his face. "Oh?"

"I just mean—" Mae-mae felt her face get hot.
"You're pretty good. You deserve a break."

"Thanks," Chris said. Then he looked away for a
minute. When he finally spoke again there was a hint of
annoyance in his voice. "So that's it? That all you
wanted to know?"

"Well, one other thing." She opened her purse and
pulled out the letter Candy Frank had given her, set it
on the table. "Know anything about this?"

Chris Towe picked it up, took out the message, read
it, folded it up, then put it back in the envelope. A tense-
ness crept into the muscles around his mouth. He threw
the envelope back on the table, fiddled with his cocktail
straw for a minute.

"Could you excuse me a sec," he said suddenly,
pointing across the room. "I need to talk to somebody."
A compact guy with a ponytail and a brown leather
jacket was gesturing to him from the stage.

Chris walked over to the stage, took a paper sack out of his guitar case, handed it to the ponytail guy. They spoke briefly, the ponytail guy asking questions. He seemed annoyed about something, and after a minute he tried to hand the sack back to Chris, but Chris wouldn't take it. The guy said something in a loud voice, and Chris took him by the elbow, hustled him out the door.

Mae-mae could see Chris through the front window of the club, but the ponytail guy was out of her view. Chris was talking intensely, shaking his finger at the air. He didn't seem to be yelling, but his head was thrust forward on his neck like he was getting pretty worked up about something.

After a moment he stopped talking, shook his head sharply, then stalked back into the bar. The ponytail guy didn't come back with him. Chris didn't have the paper sack anymore.

"Friend?" Mae-mae said when he sat back down.

"Something like that," he said quietly. He lifted his water, took a sip. The glass trembled slightly in his hand.

"So . . . does the letter mean anything to you?" Mae-mae said.

Chris Towe's blue eyes studied her face for a minute. It made Mae-mae feel nervous, awkward. "Let me tell you what I think," he said. "What I think is this. Dad's in the print shop one night. It's late. The door's unlocked. Some psycho crack head comes in and says, 'Give me your wallet.' Dad says no, the crazy bastard pulls out a stick, whacks him a couple times. Period. It's not some kind of complicated Kojak situation. It's just one of these random, screwed-up things."

"Okay," Mae-mae said quietly.

"Sometimes bad things just *happen*, you know? They just *happen*." His voice was strained and weak sounding, like he had been yelling at the top of his lungs all day. "And trying to dig up a bunch of stuff about his mutual funds or his mail or whatever—it won't bring him back." He pulled the cocktail straw out of his glass of water, tossed it sharply on the table. "So is that all you needed to know?"

"Yeah. I guess that's it." She finished the beer in her glass. "Look, I'm sorry, okay. I know this must be a really hard time for you. I'll leave you alone."

After a moment his features softened a little. "Funny," he said, "when I saw you coming over to talk, I thought maybe you were just hot for my sensitive disposition. Or maybe my rugged physique."

"Oh?" she said, and she poured her second can of Pabst into the glass. "Well, I wouldn't rule that out just yet."

Chris let a smile play with one corner of his mouth. "I better get back on the horse," he said. "Any requests?"

"How about a cheating song. Nobody ever lost my attention with a good cheating song."

He went up on stage and sang this old Tammy Wynette tune, "D-I-V-O-R-C-E," in a warbly falsetto, and everybody laughed.

A Tammy Wynette fan *and* a sense of humor. Mae-mae didn't mind this guy, didn't mind him one little bit.

✉

FOUR

"**I** think I'm in trouble, Sebastian," Mae-mae said into the phone. It was eight-thirty the next morning, the sun crashing through the window of her office. Her head felt like it had been squashed in a vise.

"An older man?" Sebastian said. Sebastian was her best friend, her confidante.

"Worse. A musician."

"Oh dear," Sebastian said. "Oh dear dear."

"Also the son of a client."

"You didn't *sleep* with him, did you?"

"Sebastian. This is the nineties. We just had a couple drinks—a *few* drinks, I mean."

"Ahhhh . . ." Sebastian drew the word out into a long, breathy noise, a sigh of high church Anglican proportion. There was a long pause. "Perhaps you'd best join me for lunch, my dear."

"That's a fine suggestion."

Sebastian liked to say that he was Mae-mae's surrogate mother. Maybe it was true.

Her mother had died when she was eleven. Her clearest memory of her mother was the way she used to read stories to Mae-mae, hour after hour on weekends, with Mae-mae sitting in her lap. *Snow White and Rose Red,*

35

Just-So Stories, Hans Brinker—she'd read the stories in her slow, raspy cigarette voice, her arms wrapped around Mae-mae. The sound of Daddy's football games floated out of the other room, and sometimes they'd both drift in and out of sleep. Mae-mae had never felt that safe again, not once in her life. You could spend your whole life trying to get back to a feeling like that: close, safe, warm, taken care of.

Then her mother had been killed when some dumb kid dropped a rock off an overpass and into her windshield. Mae-mae wondered every now and then whether she'd have turned out differently if her mother hadn't died then. Would she have turned out softer, sweeter, easier-going? Would she have learned how to sing, made more friends, gone to the junior-senior prom with some wacky good-looking guy instead of the treasurer of the chess club? Would she be married, have her own kids, fall asleep on weekends reading to them from a big, soft chair?

There was no knowing. Things ended up the way they ended up. Maybe that's what Chris Towe had been getting at the night before when he'd said that bad stuff just happens sometimes.

So her father had had to do the whole thing with no woman around to give him pointers. She supposed he'd done okay, considering. A bookkeeper for a cement company, he used to take her to his office in this building up on stilts where you could watch through grit-covered windows as the huge chutes dumped aggregate and cement and water into the mixer trucks. Daddy would make her add up numbers in her head while she watched the trucks, calling them out to her from his desk. He had never had any schooling past eleventh grade—but he had a head for figures and was a genius at calculating exactly how much material to put in the trucks. They had computers to do it now: you didn't want to make too much cement, or you lost money; you didn't want the trucks showing up to the site too early, or the drivers would sit around adding water and adding water—and then the concrete wouldn't cure properly. Daddy did it all in his head, never even used a pencil.

"Numbers are your friends," he used to tell her, saying it like he was joking—even though he wasn't. And she supposed the lesson had sunk in. She never forgot a single phone number or price tag or an item from the tax code, and could add up huge piles of numbers in her head, hardly break a sweat doing it. That's what had attracted her to tax law—all those numbers. The thing about it, her daddy was a kind of prickly guy, suspicious of people, and she'd never gotten to know him, not really: whatever closeness he had to people, to him it was just a matter of proximity. Had that been a lesson, too, one that she had learned without even wanting to?

Sebastian had lunch laid out in the breakfast room of his turn-of-the-century Ansley Park house—a relentlessly restored heap of gingerbread and porticoes and scalloped shingling. He had trotted out the Irish linen, the silver, the crystal. Grapefruit salad on antique Spode plates. Sebastian was on a campaign to rid Mae-mae's thighs of the thirteen-pound cellulite beast. Hence, grapefruit salad.

"I hate to admit it, but this is great," Mae-mae said. "What's in the dressing?"

Sebastian waved a thin dismissive hand, gave Mae-mae a coy smile. He played his recipes close to the vest.

Sebastian was a historian of common law at Emory Law School—tall, long nosed, fiftyish, with lank graying hair falling over his right eyebrow. He wore an English-cut coat, fawn, over a navy-striped broadcloth shirt, little gold cuff links flirting with the chandelier lights. The paisley bow tie sprouting from his throat looked like fresh celery leaves that had floated briefly in a puddle of pinot noir.

Mae-mae told him about Mrs. Towe, about her husband's murder, about the odd cash withdrawals from his investment fund.

Sebastian shook his head sadly. "Tragic," he said. "Perfectly tragic." Which was the way Sebastian always talked.

Sebastian stared off into the distance for a second, as though he'd forgotten what he was doing, then took the salad plates into the kitchen, came out with more stuff. "*Et voilà!* The jellied salmon with capers, the julienned leeks with ginger, and the rice *à la grecque.*"

"Mmmm." Mae-mae tried the glistening salmon. Fine!

"Very low in fats and sodium. Now"—Sebastian prodded the leeks with his fork—"about this young man . . ."

"Chris."

"Chris, yes. Not another drummer, is he?"

"Not a drummer, no."

"What was that one's name—the one who kept drumming on my Empire taboret? With the long hair?"

"Leo?"

"With the long hair."

"Leo."

"You would have thought it was a bloody snare drum."

"Actually Leo was a stockbroker."

Sebastian pinched his lips together. "Well. Stockbroker, drummer, whatever—he wasn't worthy of you."

Mae-mae laughed. "Yeah, they never are."

"This latest one excluded, I'm sure."

"Chris."

"Chris, yes. Chris." Sebastian tasted the salmon, chewed judiciously. "Attractive, is he?"

"I like him." Mae-mae shrugged. "He's kind of cute."

"Doesn't drum on the furniture or eat with his hands?"

"I can't testify about that one way or the other."

"Well, I'm sure he'll do just fine." Sebastian dabbed his mouth with a linen napkin. For a second he had a faraway look in his eyes. "By the way, my dear, I have a surprise for you."

Mae-mae had never known Sebastian to dismiss a swain with that short a conversation. He usually wanted juicy details—not that there were any. But today he seemed a little preoccupied. "What kind of surprise?"

"I'll show you tomorrow."

"Hey! No fair, Sebastian."

Sebastian smirked into his food.

"Come on. Tell me, tell me."

"It wouldn't be a surprise if I told you, now would it?" Sebastian smiled placidly. "More salmon?"

When she got back to the office Mae-mae called Print-meister, asked the receptionist for Candy Frank.

"Don't know what to make of the letter, Candy," Mae-mae told the office manager. "Is there anything else you can think of that might be helpful?"

"I have been just wracking my little brain," Candy said. "I'm fixing to go out of my nut thinking about it."

"So you're saying you haven't come up with anything yet?"

"No, ma'am. But something was cattywhompus around here, I know it. He'd just been so *nervous*, so high-strung."

"What about that day—did anything unusual happen that day?"

"Not that I can recollect."

"Did he meet with anybody? Talk to anybody? Go anywhere?"

"Let me check his calendar." Mae-mae heard heels tapping off into the distance, then coming back. "Here we go, Miz Cosgrove. Wednesday, April twenty-first. Only one appointment. June and Barry King. That was at five-thirty in the evening."

"Is that unusual—only one appointment?"

"Not specially. Mr. Paris, he does most of the client contact. June and Barry, though, they got so much work here, they just go straight to Mr. Towe."

"Tell me about them."

"June and Barry King? You never heard of June and Barry King? They was on *Oprah* just last fall." It sounded like she could hardly believe Mae-mae's ignorance. "They wrote that famous book *Stop Feeling Like Hell*—you never heard of June and Barry?"

"I guess I don't catch *Oprah* too much."

"Me neither. Lucky for me, my mama taped it on the video out the old folks' home where she's at. Real dynamic show. How to actualize your internal self, that type of thing? That's how come I decided to do this electrolysis I was telling you about. Barry and June, their philosophy is, you don't like your life, change it."

"Can't argue with that."

"First time I seen them on *Oprah*—the video Mama made me out the old folks' home?—I had tears just pouring down my face. Just flat *pouring*. Since then I bought all their home study tapes, the workbooks, everything." She paused. "You really never heard of June and Barry? Motivational Techniques Research International?"

"No, I swear I haven't. Do you know where I could get hold of them?"

"We're gonna lick this thing!' That's their slogan. They're out at Peachtree Corners, one of them office parks out there. You *sure* you never heard of them?"

Mae-mae wrote *Motivational Something-or-other Int.* on the legal pad in front of her, then wrote SNAKE OIL? next to it, with a couple of circles around it.

"How's the electrolysis coming along?"

"Real good. Can't hardly see the bumps," Candy Frank said. "Second treatment tomorrow. We're gonna lick this thing!" Candy tittered.

"Good for you," Mae-mae said. "Good for you."

Thinking, *then maybe you could try AA, see how that goes.*

"I been thinking, maybe I'll nose around the shop here, see if I can find anything else, might be interesting."

"If you find anything," Mae-mae said, "let me know."

After she hung up, Mae-mae felt kind of sad and wished she had been nicer, more positive. *We're gonna lick this thing. What the hell, there were plenty worse brands of snake oil than that.*

Next she called Motivational Techniques Research International and asked to speak to Barry or Jane King. The receptionist wanted to know what this was in reference to, her tone indicating that the Kings were very busy, important, and inaccessible people.

Mae-mae thought about it for a moment. "I'm an attorney investigating a murder," she said finally.

"Oh, goodness!" the receptionist said. This bought Mae-mae a transfer to Mr. and Mrs. King's executive secretary, who finally let on that they were leading a seminar at a hotel down in Buckhead.

"How convenient!" Mae-mae said brightly. "I'm right across the street. I'll just run right over."

"But they can't be disturbed during—"

"We're gonna lick this thing!" Mae-mae said. And then she hung up.

FIVE

The hotel, a big white structure with wavy walls and lots of architecturally pointless doodads jutting out of it, squatted on Peachtree Road next to Lenox Mall. Its panoramic views encompassed several bland buildings with mirrored windows, a six-lane road, two malls, and an impressively large parking lot.

Barry and June King were holding their seminar in a conference room on the third floor. An easel next to a big wooden door announced, RAGE AND PAIN WORKSHOP, 9:00 A.M.–3:30 P.M. Mae-mae looked at her watch. Three twenty-five. Right on time.

Thumbtacked to the easel was a color glossy of a beaming couple, their arms circling each other's waists. He was dark skinned, with a helmet of dark hair and a salt and pepper beard; she was small, petite, green eyed, auburn haired. They both wore white suits, and she was holding a book in her hand that said *I Hurt!*—big red italics splashed across the cover.

Mae-mae peeped through the door. At the far end of the large room was a low dais on which Barry King stood, wearing a dark suit and a shiny red tie, talking into a wireless mike. Seated behind him, one shapely leg crossed over the other, was his wife. A hundred or so people sat at round tables with water pitchers on them.

Mae-mae slipped in and sat next to a man wearing an expensive toupee and a cheap suit.

The Kings looked about the same in person as they did in the picture in the hall—except they weren't wearing those tacky white suits. Hers was green, his was blue. Big improvement.

Barry King's voice was coming out of a small PA system: "... which is why I want you to *explore* the pain ... which is why I want you to *feel* the pain ... which is why I want you to *know* the pain." Heads bobbed happily throughout the room. Mae-mae watched June King, decided she was going a little overboard, blinking her eyes and acting completely enthralled by every word that came out of her husband's mouth.

Barry King held the microphone with three fingers, striding around with his pinky sticking out into the air. He kind of reminded Mae-mae of Jimmy Swaggart: a total phony—but he put on such a good show that if you turned off your brain, it was a fairly entertaining ride.

Barry King glanced at his watch, a heavy gold thing that sparkled with what looked suspiciously like diamonds. "So what I'd like you folks to do when we break tonight is to *visualize* that pain. Visualize it, okay, as a house with many rooms. Then take a mental tour of that house, room by room. You with me?"

The bobbing heads were with him.

"We're gonna do some things with that pain tomorrow, and you're gonna be amazed at the power it'll unlock inside you." He looked over at his wife. "June?"

She stood slowly and looked out at the crowd with her intense green eyes, paused, spoke into her microphone in a soft, sonorous contralto. "I can't wait, Barry," she said. She actually sounded serious. Then she talked for a minute or two.

After she was through, Mae-mae couldn't remember a single word the woman had said, only that it had been encouraging, calm, soothing. Her voice was quiet and a little too well modulated, classical music announcer–style—but with a spooky edge to it.

"Don't forget," Barry said. "Order forms for the tapes and workbooks are available by the door." Then he gave the crowd an irreverent grin, raised his arms, and said, "We're gonna lick this thing!" This whipped the crowd into ragged applause. The Kings clasped their microphones in front of their hearts, bowed deeply at the waist.

As the mob of suckers made their way through the rear door, Mae-mae headed for the podium where the Kings were talking to each other.

"Excuse me," she said.

Barry King turned and looked at her. He was smiling, one of those smiles people give you when they don't really mean it. "Think of the rooms," he said. "If the pain comes from your parents, maybe you could put that in the master bedroom. If—"

"I'm not with the seminar," Mae-mae said. "I'm an attorney. I represent Charles Towe's wife."

Barry and June glanced at each other.

"What a terrible waste," Barry King said. "What an absolute tragedy."

"We were just talking about Charlie," June King said. Still in the hypnotist voice. Did she ever turn the thing off?

"Just this morning," Barry King said. "We were just talking about what a sad person it must have taken to commit such a senseless, brutal crime."

"The rage," June said. "The rage he must have had."

"Or she," Barry said.

"Or she . . ." The Kings nodded, doing their best to look really cut up about the whole thing.

"We saw him that day, you know," Barry said.

"Right," Mae-mae said. "That's what I wanted to talk to you about. You were the last appointment on his calendar that day. I was wondering what you were there for."

Barry and June's eyes sneaked briefly toward each other again.

"You said you're an attorney?" Barry said.

Mae-mae nodded.

"In what capacity?" he said, smiling just enough to show the tips of several white teeth through the hedge of graying beard. "If I may ask . . ."

"I'm probating the estate."

"Uh-*huh*." Barry nodded. June nodded. "And this pertains to . . ."

"A financial matter," Mae-mae said. "Which may or may not have anything to do with his death."

"Uh-*huh*." Barry nodded. June nodded.

"We met with Mr. Towe," June said, "to discuss a printing job he was doing for our company." Her face was calm and open but oddly expressionless. Like she had some kind of emotional valve that let things in but not out.

"Exactly," Barry said. "There was a problem with some brochures they had delivered to us. They were out of—" He snapped his finger twice, trying to remember something. ". . . out of . . . what the heck's the word, June?"

"Registration. The colors were out of registration."

"Registration. Right. It made us look cross-eyed in the pictures," Barry said, "you know, the way the colors were."

"And what time did you leave?" Mae-mae said.

"Oh, six, six-thirty," Barry King said. "Wasn't that what we told the police, June?"

"Six or six-thirty," June said.

"And did you notice anything . . . unusual?"

"Unusual?" Barry said. "Not unusual, no."

"Nothing out of the ordinary," June said.

"That's what was so shocking," Barry said.

"The ordinariness," June said.

"We're there, you know, and everything's the same as always," Barry said.

"And then the next day . . ."

". . . right there in the paper . . ."

". . . a shocking murder."

"Boy," Barry said, making a fist at his solar plexus. "Gets you right there, you know, the closeness of it . . ."

". . . how close we all are to death."

Barry and June nodded again, their heads going slowly up, slowly down, slowly up, slowly down. It was like they were still on stage, showing you what warm and sensitive human beings they were.

"So you might have been the last people to see him alive?" Mae-mae said.

Barry King raised his eyebrows. "Last? Oh, no. Definitely not. His shop foreman was there. What's his name, June?"

"Rascoe," June said.

"Rascoe. Donald Rascoe. Exactly. We met briefly with Charlie, going over the problems, this thing with the registration—"

". . . and Donald Rascoe was there operating the press," June said.

Mae-mae remembered him: the guy with the rotten fish face, the one with the missing eyebrow.

" 'Cause, hey, cross-eyed, that's not the type of thing you can just let slide in an image piece, something you're mailing out to two and a quarter million households, right?"

"And just as we were leaving, his daughter Rachel came in, too," June said. "Remember, Barry, because she was carrying that package?"

"Right," Barry said, putting a hand to his forehead. "Right. It's coming back now. She had a package. A manila envelope really, and she dropped it in the hall-way . . ."

". . . and I tripped over her," June said. "She was bending over and I tripped over her. I remember because she was . . ."

"She was not very pleasant," Barry said.

"No, she was not very pleasant."

"We said something about it in the car as we were leaving," Barry said. "All that rage . . ."

". . . in such a beautiful young woman."

Mae-mae looked at the two of them, nodding and mugging at each other, and said, "You aren't suggesting that Rachel Towe might have had something to do with her father's death, are you?"

Barry gave her a pop-eyed surprise face. "My gosh, no!" he said.

"We all have rage in us," June said quietly. "All of us. A great, great deal of rage. Rage and pain and sadness. That doesn't make us murderers, does it?"

"I just wanted to make sure I was following you."

Barry King said, "See, the trick is channeling that rage, Miss Cosgrave—"

"Cos*grove*."

"Cos*grove*, I meant. Cos*grove*, of course. That's why it's so important for people to attend our seminars."

"Because so much good can come . . ."

". . . from so much bad."

Mae-mae was getting tired of their act, finishing each other's sentences. Talking to them was like playing the straight man in a bad vaudeville act.

"You really should try one of our seminars," Barry said. "I think you'd be amazed at the results of the self-discovery process we'll lead you through."

"Not *lead*," June said. "Guide. Guide. I think *guide* is a better word."

"Have you heard about biovisualization therapy?" Barry added. "It's really an extraordinary mind technology."

"Sounds interesting," Mae-mae said. Yeah, *right!* "And this guy Donald Rascoe—he was still there when you left?"

The Kings looked at each other. "That's what we couldn't remember," Barry said.

"When we were talking to the police . . ."

". . . I was thinking that he'd left."

"But it seemed to me he was still there."

Barry smiled, looked at his watch. It was a gold Ro-lex, studded, sure enough, with big diamonds. "Was there anything else? We need to clear out before the hotel staff start blowing their pacemakers." He turned on the laugh box for a second.

"Just one other thing," Mae-mae said. "You wouldn't know anything about twenty thousand dollars in cash that Charles Towe might have had with him at the time, would you?"

"Cash!" June said.

"Cash?" Barry said.

They both stared at her, shaking their heads.

"Thanks for the help then," Mae-mae said.

"Before you go . . ." Barry handed Mae-mae a shiny brochure that said *Tired of Self-Defeat and Self-Denial?* on the front. "The one-day seminar—call this number, tell the girl to knock thirty-five bucks off the regular price."

"How much *is* the regular price?"

"Okay, okay, okay. Tell her I said knock off seventy bucks. That'll get you down into two figures."

Next stop was probate court, a dull brown building just off the square in downtown Marietta, the county seat of suburban Cobb County. Mae-mae wasn't looking for-ward to this, a late afternoon sit-down with the judge presiding over the Towe estate's probate process.

Mae-mae took the elevator up to the third floor, stood for a moment looking at the fake wood grain sign on the door: THE HONORABLE TOMMY T. PRICE, JUDGE, COBB COUNTY PROBATE COURT. Mae-mae wiped her sweaty hands on her skirt and went into his chambers.

Price was sitting at his desk talking on the phone when she came in. He was a small, neat man with a white pencil mustache and a large bald head that had the somewhat irregular dimensions of, say, a pumpkin. Today his eyes were looking moist and angry. Mae-mae wasn't sure whether to sit down or not. She decided prudence lay on the side of standing.

Mae-mae had an unfortunate history with the judge. Aside from being naturally unpleasant and an alcoholic, Judge Price had a nasty attitude toward female lawyers—somewhere between patronizing and hostile, depending on his current relationship with the bottle.

Presently the judge hung up. Without acknowledging her, he picked up a manila file folder and peered at its contents, eyes narrowed, as though expecting to find something grotesquely offensive on any page. The file had copies of all the financial records she'd been able to dredge up, plus the draft notice of probation and so forth. He had yet to speak to Mae-mae or even direct his gaze in her direction.

"Can I sit down, Judge?" she said finally.

The judge grunted, fingered his mustache. Mae-mae sat down, waited for a long time.

"What we have here," he said finally, "we got a very complicated situation."

"Not *that* complicated. There's a recent will, everything's well documented and in order, and the wife is the sole heir, so I think that from the standpoint of—"

"Hold on, girlie-girl," the judge snapped. "I'm not finished talking."

"Yes, Your Honor," she said.

"Complicated situation. Complicated situation." He pinched his lower lip. "Complicated situation due to the partnership agreement here, codicil to which says on the decease of one party, other party got a right of first refusal to buy up a hunnerd percent interest in the bidness. Am I right? Am I reading this correctly?"

"Yes, Your Honor."

"Well, then!"

"What I was going to say was that Mrs. Towe's preference is to sell the business to Lester Paris, in fact—

assuming of course that they can come up with the right price.''

"The right price! I've heard that one before.'' The judge cackled. "Heard that one time, little ole bidness like this, family bidness, various kinfolks start in to squabbling, whole thing got stuck in probate for five years!''

"I'm sure, but—''

"You'd like that, wouldn't you, honey? Sit around running up the tab on this thing for four, five years, you'd be in hog heaven, wouldn't you?''

"Your Honor—''

"You got any motions pending?''

"Not at this time, no.''

"Good. Good.'' The judge rocked back in his chair, felt around on his large head with a liver-spotted hand. He opened the file again, licking his finger each time he turned a page. Mae-mae sat silently, listening to the hum of the air-conditioning.

It gave her time to think back on the first time she'd dealt with Judge Price. She'd been fresh out of law school, working for a firm downtown. At the time she knew virtually nothing about probate law. She was assisting a partner in a complicated case involving the estate of a very rich man whose children, having been treated less than generously in his will, were merrily suing and countersuing both each other and the estate. Hours before a hearing on an important motion in the case, Mae-mae's boss came down with the flu and Mae-mae was forced to step into her place. She knew very little about the case and less about the law: she'd only had time to skim over the brief for an hour before driving up to the courthouse.

At the hearing, she stumbled and blithered for a while and finally sat down. After the hearing was over, the judge said, "I'm gonna accept Miss Cosgrove's motion. Now all of y'all get out of here. Except Miss Cosgrove.''

When the other lawyers had cleared out, the judge

shook his finger at her and said, "You know what I hate?"

"I'm sorry," she said. "It's just that I was—"

"No, huh-uh," the judge said, smiling fiercely. "It's just that you were sloppy and unprepared, that's what you were. And I hate that. You jeopardized your client's rights in this matter quite severely. If this hadn't been such a good brief, you'd have lost the motion. And I don't have to tell you how many millions of dollahs your client has at stake here."

"Yes, Your Honor."

"Next time I see you jeopardize a client's interests like that, believe you me, young missy, I'm gonna do my best to see you disbarred. We clear on this, honey?"

Mae-mae had nodded glumly.

She had cried so hard on the way home that she almost ran off the road in front of the Big Chicken out on Cobb Parkway.

After he'd finished going through the Towe file, Judge Price browbeat her some more about a few outstanding issues. Finally he instructed her to go away.

As she reached the door, the judge called out to her. "Honey?"

She sighed, turned around. "Is it absolutely necessary for the court to address me as 'honey'? I mean, is that too much to ask?"

The judge glared at her. He was holding up a Xerox of the check register from the Imperial Balanced Fund Number Two. "Why you so touchy, all you people? Touchy, touchy, touchy."

Mae-mae said nothing.

"I just noticed this here twenty-thousand-dollar check. What's this all about? Has it cleared yet?"

Damn. That was the thing about this guy: even when he was drinking, he was as smart as a whip. How had he managed to home in on the one picky little detail that was out of order?

"We don't know," Mae-mae said.

"You don't know *what*?"

"We don't know who he gave the check to. Nobody's cashed it."

The judge raised his eyebrows. "Well, you better find out, young lady. You just better find out!"

SIX

"**S**o it looks like it was either Towe's daughter Rachel or this guy Donald Rascoe who was the last to see him before he was killed." Mae-mae was talking to Sebastian on the phone.

"Donald who?"

"Roscoe, Rascoe, something like that. He's this weird looking guy that works at the printing plant."

"Have you spoken to either of them?"

"Wouldn't hurt, would it? Maybe I'll drop by and see the daughter on the way home tonight."

Mae-mae got around to the real purpose of the call: she had checked the paper and found that Chris Towe was playing that night at a club in Buckhead. "Speaking of tonight," she said, "how'd you like to go see some music?"

Sebastian let some time pass. "Would this be your new friend?"

"Well . . ." Mae-mae grinned into the phone. "It might."

"And would this be rock and roll?" Sebastian said. "It hurts my teeth, you know, all that dreadful noise."

"No rock, no roll. Your teeth are safe. Just a boy and his trusty flattop."

"Some sort of moody Byronic type, I suppose? Full

of angst and woe and sophomoric poetry?"

"Something like that."

"I assumed as much. I'm reminded of something Stevenson once wrote. I don't recall it exactly, I'm afraid—something about young men of three or four hundred pounds a year looking down from the pinnacle of doleful existence while recording at considerable length their lack of fitness for—"

"Yeah yeah yeah." Mae-mae laughed. "I'm sure that's Chris in a nutshell. How's eight-thirty sound?"

After finishing up a memo recommending a tax shelter for a client, Mae-mae drove to Little Five Points, her Honda stalling at every other stoplight along the way.

Rachel Towe's house was a slump-shouldered brick duplex with a tired wooden porch and a weedy yard. Mae-mae knocked. Eventually the door opened a few inches, and a pair of pale blue eyes looked out. It had to be Rachel: she had the same eyes as Chris, the same eyes as her mother. An old R.E.M. record was whining away in the background.

Mae-mae introduced herself, went through her song and dance about probating her father's estate, and the door opened all the way. "Come on in," the young woman said in a flat, bored voice. She looked about twenty-five and had a thin face, all the bones in high relief, no makeup. Her long blond hair was not too carefully combed, and her bare feet stuck out from under a frumpy plaid robe that she held closed by the lapels.

"You want to sit down?" Rachel said, tossing out the words like she didn't care one way or the other.

Mae-mae sat in a cane-bottomed chair, its seat torn and sagging. The apartment was dark and old, furnished with a jumble of split-seamed Salvation Army throwaways and cheap Scandinavian knockdowns. As if the smoky, closed-in atmosphere weren't bad enough, somebody had filled the place with the stink of patchouli. Beer cans, books, CD cases, and overflowing ash-

trays crowded every flat surface. The walls were jammed
with artwork: everything from paintings and original
photographs to pages cut from magazines.

Seated on the floor in the far corner of the room, a
dark young guy was smoking a filterless cigarette, a
sketch pad propped on his knee. He looked at Mae-mae
intently. It was the guy from Club 15, the guy with the
ponytail who'd argued with Chris Towe.

Rachel didn't introduce him. "He's drawing me,"
was all she said. "You mind if we keep going while I
talk?"

"Go right ahead," Mae-mae said.

With that Rachel dropped her bathrobe on the floor.
It was a little disconcerting: she was stark naked. Mae-
mae felt the sting of thigh envy. Rachel had heavy, wide-
spaced breasts; a flat belly; a smooth, dimple-free
bottom.

"You want a beer?" Rachel said, padding into the
kitchen.

"That's okay," Mae-mae said. In the other room the
refrigerator opened with a clatter of bottles. A dull feeling of discomfort started collecting between her shoulder
blades. She could feel the silent young guy looking at
her. "On second thought, yeah," she called out, "I think
I will."

Rachel came out with two cans of Schlitz, handed one
to Mae-mae, then arranged herself on a mat at the other
end of the room, settling into a pose with her torso
leaned back, one leg crossed over the other, one arm
behind her head, face pointed up at the ceiling.

"Like this?" she said.

"Back a little," the guy with the ponytail said.
"Yeah, yeah, right there."

"Well, hurry up," Rachel said in an irritated voice.
"This is uncomfortable as shit."

Behind her Mae-mae heard the scratch of charcoal
pencil. The whole thing felt weird—like she'd walked
into somebody's bedroom. Rachel and the ponytail guy

didn't seem to think much about it though.

Mae-mae explained a little about how probate court worked, omitting any mention of the missing $20,000 check. "So I guess what I'd like to find out is what you saw the night your father was killed."

"Now what's this got to do with probate court?" Rachel said.

Mae-mae hedged. "We're inventorying the estate for probate, and some money was missing from the print shop. In order to know what to do about it I have to figure out whether it's part of the estate or not. Anything you could tell me would be helpful.

Rachel took a sip of beer, then draped her head back again. "I was just there that night," she said to the ceiling. "Same as always. A bunch of presses, all kind of noise. You know."

"Nothing unusual?"

"Nah." Her voice had a tone of adolescent petulance that should have withered away by the time she'd gotten this deep into her twenties.

"Do you remember who was there?"

"Yeah."

Mae-mae waited, but Rachel was going to make her ask. "Well—who?"

"Dad was there. That guy Rascoe was there. Donald Rascoe. Also those people, the Kings. June and Barry. Man, what a couple of geeks. You ever see them on TV?"

"On *Oprah Winfrey*?" Mae-mae said.

"No, those infomercial things, like at midnight on cable. They pretend like it's a talk show, only it's really just a long commercial for the twenty-nine-dollar miracle videotape that's gonna change your life or whatever."

"Yeah, I heard about that," Mae-mae said. She was trying to ignore Rachel's body, but it felt awkward talking to a naked stranger. A bunch of the photographs on the wall, the nudes, were pictures of Rachel. You couldn't get away from her perfect thighs even if you wanted to.

"Are you a model?" Mae-mae said. "I noticed the pictures. . . ."

"Trying to get into it," Rachel said. "Modeling's on the side. I should have started when I was a kid cause I'm kind of over the hill now. My regular job, I work in a record store."

"I see."

"Real bogus," Rachel added. Mae-mae wasn't sure if she meant the Kings, the record store, or modeling. Or life in general for that matter. "Anyway, they were there, the Kings. They got kind of pissed off cause I was kind of listening in on their conversation. They came out the door and I had to pretend like I'd dropped something on the floor. That woman, whatever her name is—"

"June?"

"Yeah, her. She bangs into me coming out the door and gets in a big hissy fit." She laughed softly, her face not changing expression particularly.

"What were they talking about?"

"Oh, just the usual. What's-his-name, Barry, he was pissing and moaning about these brochures. Kept saying how the pictures made them look cross-eyed."

"Anything else?"

"Not really."

Mae-mae thought back to what the Kings had said about Rachel earlier. She was full of rage. They might be snake oil salesmen, but they had gotten that one right. She was sure pissed off at the world about something.

"What about Donald Rascoe?"

"What about him?"

"Did he do anything while you were there?"

"I think he . . ." She looked at Mae-mae for a moment, a puzzled expression on her face. "You know, I have this feeling that he left while I was there. But I just can't remember."

"And what time was this?"

"When I got there? It wasn't dark yet. Maybe seven? Six? I can't really remember."

"You mind my asking why you were there?"

"Just to talk about some stuff." Hesitation. "We had a fight."

"About what?"

She stared up at the ceiling, the perfect breasts rising and falling. "I don't want to get into that," she said finally.

"Are you sure?"

Behind Mae-mae the ponytail guy spoke for the first time. "She'd rather not get into it," he said softly. "Didn't you hear her?"

"Hey!" Rachel yelled at him. "Draw your stupid picture and shut up."

"I will if you'd quit moving," the voice said.

"I mean it was no big deal," Rachel said to Mae-mae. "I just don't feel like talking about it right now."

Mae-mae waited, hoping if she gave Rachel time to think about it maybe she'd just blurt something out. She didn't. Behind Mae-mae, the charcoal pencil continued its scratching.

"So you have no idea who killed your father?" Mae-mae said finally.

Rachel shrugged. "Some crack head. Just some asshole crack head. For a couple bucks—I mean, who else would do something like that?"

"It's hard to figure, isn't it," Mae-mae said.

"I'm tired of this," Rachel said. She slumped down on the floor, elbows resting on the faded cotton mat, breasts sagging against her belly. She didn't seem to show the slightest inclination toward modesty. She picked up her beer, took a long pull, rested the can on her flat stomach.

"Do you have any reason to think your father had a large amount of money on his person when he was killed?" Mae-mae asked.

"Like how large?" Rachel was staring blankly at the wall like the whole subject was boring her.

"Like a check for twenty thousand dollars made out to cash."

That got her. She turned and looked at Mae-mae. "Twenty thousand! You got to be kidding. Dad never had enough cash on him to pay for a milk shake. He was like the ultimate cheapskate."

Mae-mae couldn't think of anything else to ask. "I'm really sorry about your father," she said.

"Yeah. Me too." Her tough-girl face evaporated and a kind of empty, dazed look replaced it. "Me too."

Behind her Mae-mae heard the young man make a snorting noise. There was a slap—paper against wood— as he tossed his sketch pad on the floor. His footsteps thumped against the floor, disappearing into the kitchen.

"Hey, you can go to hell!" Rachel yelled at the receding footsteps. The back door banged.

"Who's the guy?" Mae-mae said softly.

"Clay. My boyfriend. *Supposedly* my boyfriend." Her voice was suddenly high and tremulous.

Rachel put her hands against her face and began to cry, folding up into a small, naked ball. Her spine traced a knotty ridge up the middle of her back.

Mae-mae had an urge to go over and stroke her hair, pat her on the back, something—but naked, no, it was just a little too weird. "It's a hard time, isn't it," she said.

"Yeah," said Rachel's wet voice. Then after a minute, "You think you could bring me my robe?"

Mae-mae left, found the kid with the ponytail smoking out on the dark front steps. She sat on the step next to him.

"Clay, right?"

Clay nodded. His cigarette ember glowed and died in the dusk.

"What was that all about?" Mae-mae said.

Clay shrugged, like it was someone else's problem.

"Her father just died, for Godsake. She's really vulnerable," Mae-mae said, suddenly angry.

"Yeah, well, we're all vulnerable, aren't we?" Clay said. He had a strong accent, a kind of redneck twang. Not Georgia redneck, though. Texas, Oklahoma, someplace out there.

"Is that some kind of excuse?" Mae-mae said.

The young guy sucked on his cigarette, blew out a slow trail of smoke, then threw the butt on the sidewalk. It glowed orange for a moment, faded. He ground it into the concrete.

"So I didn't like her dad much. I could play hypocrite, pretend I thought he was a hell of a guy and everything, but I just don't choose to do that. Is that okay with you?" Clay didn't raise his voice, but there was a slightly menacing quality to it.

"What about her? Do you feel sorry for her?"

"Yeah." He thought about it, shrugged. "Yeah, I do. I guess I fly off the handle when the subject of her dad comes up."

"What was wrong with her dad?"

He stared out into the darkening trees across the street. "We didn't get along, that's all."

"What, he didn't think you were son-in-law material?"

"Son-in-law material." Clay laughed a little. "I don't know that I'd be such great son-in-law material either."

"So what was it then?"

"You want to know the truth? You really want to know?"

"Yeah. I really want to know."

"I didn't like the way he treated her. Her or her mother either one. That's reason number one."

"How *did* he treat Rachel?"

He made a sour face.

"Okay," Mae-mae said after a minute. "How about reason number two?"

"Reason what?"

"Number two. You said just said 'reason number one.' There must be a reason number two, right?"

He shrugged again. "Just a figure of speech."

From the look on his face, he was probably lying. But whatever his other reason was, she could tell she wouldn't get it out of him. His eyes were guarded, not giving anything up.

"Okay, humor me. Back to reason number one."

"He treated Rachel's mom like she was a domestic servant, for one thing. I don't go for that."

"And Rachel?"

"Oh, he was just your typical stupid father that works too hard, doesn't have time for the kids—and when he does have time, he expects them to be these perfect little dolls."

"Anything else?"

"He was screwing around, getting a little side action—which I guess isn't the biggest thing in the world—but he didn't even seem to care who knew. Been going on for years, the same woman."

"You know her name?"

"Colleen. I forget her last name." He patted his pockets, looking for cigarettes, then turned to look at her, up and down, the same way he'd looked at her when she walked in the door of the apartment. "You ever modeled for anybody?" he said.

"Oh, please."

"No, I'm serious."

"What—having Miss USA in there isn't good enough?"

"You draw her, what do you get? A picture, looks like it ought to have staple marks through her navel from tracing it out of *Penthouse*."

"I thought that's what men liked."

"Maybe to look at. Not to draw, though. I like somebody who's got a little more mass, a little more character.'' He cupped his hands, about a yard apart, waggled them.

''More mass? Oh, yeah, that's pretty flattering, Clay. Why don't you just come right out and say it?''

''Say what?''

''That I've got a fat ass.''

He squinted at her. ''Fat ass? Why does every woman in the world think she has a fat ass?''

SEVEN

Mae-mae came into the club, spotted Sebastian sitting over in the corner looking stiff and uptight. It wasn't his kind of place. Sebastian's idea of popular music was fairly limited: watching Bobby Short sing "Lush Life" at the Café Carlyle in his velvet dinner jacket—that would be about the limit.

Chris was already onstage in his leather jacket and his T-shirt and his cowboy boots. Looking pretty good, all in all. His voice sounded stronger than it had the day before.

"Sorry I'm late. I was held up," Mae-mae said, sitting across the table from Sebastian. "What do you think?"

Sebastian took a delicate sip of his martini. "He *is* attractive," he said finally.

Mae-mae laughed. "I meant his singing."

"I wouldn't cast him in *La Gioconda*, counselor, if that's what you're driving at."

"It wasn't. But that's okay."

After the first set was over, Chris came straight over to their table. "Join you?" he said.

Mae-mae hadn't expected that. She didn't even think he'd noticed her in the audience.

"Please," she said. She introduced him to Sebastian.

63

After they had talked for a while, Sebastian excused himself. "Must run," he said. "Early class tomorrow."

"Who's the guy?" Chris said after Sebastian disappeared through the door of the club.

"Just an old friend," Mae-mae said quickly.

"He is . . ." Chris hesitated, not wanting to come right out with the word.

"Gay? Yeah. He's gay."

"Okay, just wanted to be straight on that."

"So to speak."

"So to speak." Chris smiled a little. "He came up before the show and told me you'd be here. Said under pain of death I better come over and talk to you after I finished the set."

Mae-mae blushed. "*Did* he? I'll kill him. I was trying to be subtle about this."

"Subtle? You know, I figure once you break thirty, subtle goes out the window." Chris grinned. "Subtle's okay at the senior prom. But not when you're playing for keeps."

Playing for keeps. Mae-mae filed that one away. Was she playing for keeps? It was hard to know. "You're probably right. What was that last song you played? It was nice."

"No title, really. It's just another morose my-girlfriend-just-dumped-me song. It's funny, I'm actually a pretty cheery guy, but it seems like I only write when I'm depressed."

"I wish I could write songs. Or do something like that." It made her nervous talking about it. "Creativity—I guess I always felt kind of weak in that department."

"There's not much to it really. All I do is wait for something depressing to happen in my life, cut the thing down to three verses and a chorus, slap on four chords, and it's done."

"So . . . that last song . . . did your girlfriend just dump you or something?" Never hurt to probe a little.

You didn't want to catch them on the rebound. That was always a recipe for disaster. Mae-mae had a checklist by now: no rebounders, no married men, no bisexuals, nobody living with Mom, no management consultants, no bodybuilders, nobody with a codependency book on the coffee table. Any of that stuff showed up on the list, it was time to pay the tab, say "Nice knowing you," and head for the door. No sense bothering.

"Nah. Nobody's been wearing my varsity jacket for quite a while." Chris's smile disappeared. "Actually I wrote that song right after my divorce."

"Married, huh?" Divorced was *not* on the list. If it were, there'd be nobody left.

"Yeah. Got a six-year-old girl, Lisa." A bitter look crossed his face. "Thanks to the infinite wisdom of our court system, I almost never get to see her. The other day when I saw her, you know what she called my ex-wife's new husband?"

Mae-mae shook her head.

"She called him Daddy." Chris took off his glasses, pinched the bridge of his nose with his fingers. "Daddy. Closest I've come to freaking out in a long time. My father's funeral included." He shook his head. "But what could I do? I haven't been able to see her in six months."

"You didn't get visitation rights?"

He shook his head sadly. "She was real bitter, made up all kinds of crazy stuff about me. Got injunctions against me, you name it. After that they wouldn't let me come near her. Or Lisa either, for that matter."

"Like what kind of crazy stuff?"

"Let's see. Bad provider, no help around the house, drinks too much, the usual stuff. All of which, I admit, was at least intermittently true." Chris Towe didn't say anything else for a minute. He had the kind of angry, disbelieving look on his face that you might get if somebody hit you in the head without any warning.

"She also said I threatened to kill her . . . and Lisa. That's where the injunction came from."

"And did you?"

Chris looked off into the distance, put his glasses back on. "No. No, sir. I never said a word against that woman in my entire life." He laughed suddenly, his blue eyes lighting up. "Not up to that point anyway. Since then I've written . . . oh . . . fifty, sixty really mean, spiteful songs about her."

Mae-mae laughed softly.

"You ever married?" Chris asked.

"No. I lived with a guy for a long time, though."

"How long is long?"

"Close to five years."

"That's longer than I was *married*."

"He was a lot older than me—a professor of mine in law school. I was stupid enough to think he'd marry me eventually."

"So what happened?"

"Midlife crisis, what else? I was too inexperienced to realize that a forty-year-old guy living with a twenty-six-year-old woman is a bad sign in the first place. Hell, I was *in luuuuv*." It was Mae-mae's turn for the bitter laugh. "Everything was going along smooth as glass, and then I started noticing all these car magazines around the house."

"Like *Car & Driver*, you mean?"

"Yeah. *Road and Track*, right." Mae-mae smiled. "I mean here's a guy whose idea of a good time was drafting briefs about marshland rights-of-way—a guy who wouldn't know a V-8 engine from a clutch plate. Well, I didn't really think anything about it. At first."

"And then?"

"And then one day I come home from work and there's this damn red Porsche in the driveway."

Chris laughed. "That's a bad sign."

"Real bad sign. I mean, it's like this . . . this muscle-bound, this . . . hunchbacked, this . . . blood red *thing*.

The paint's so shiny it still looks wet? It was a 928, 911, I forget—the kind with the big doohickey on the back?''

''A spoiler?''

''Yeah, I think that's what you call it. He was so proud of that goddamn spoiler. Shows me the spoiler, shows me the engine back where the trunk's supposed to be, you know, makes me smell the leather. Then he drives me around like ninety miles an hour, cutting off all these people out on the interstate.'' Mae-mae thought back to that moment when she'd driven up in her old Plymouth Valiant, the dead feeling she'd had in the pit of her stomach when she saw that red Porsche parked next to the house.

''How long did it take?''

''After that?'' Mae-mae smiled brightly. ''Took him exactly seven weeks to work up enough courage to throw me out of his house. Kind of depressing, isn't it? If I'd lost out to another woman, that'd be one thing. But a *Porsche?*''

Chris shook his head. ''My wife, it was a hammer, a ball peen hammer, the kind with the little knob on the end. I came home one day and she was out on the back porch with this brand-new ball peen hammer, banging nails into the wall. I said to her, 'What you doing?' because I'd never seen her lift a finger to do anything like that before in her life. She says, 'What's it look like? I'm fixing the screen door.' '' Chris took a sip of his water. ''Fixing the screen door. She'd been after me to fix the hinges on this door for like six months, finally figured out she could do it herself. I guess it had never occurred to her before. I told her, 'It'll hold better if you countersink it and use wood screws.' She just looked at me. I'll never forget the look on her face—coldest thing I've ever seen in my life. So I said, 'Besides, you should have bought a claw hammer. Ball peen hammer, that's intended for sheet metal work.' ''

''You probably should have kept that to yourself.''

''So I learned. It tipped her right over the edge, man.

The fact that she could do something on her own, it was such a big revelation to this woman, she moves into the guest bedroom the next day—just to see what it was like, I guess. Didn't take long before she brought some guy back there, figured she'd find out how the springs on the guest bed held up under strenuous use.''

"Ouch."

"Uh-huh." He made a face. "So I took her ball peen hammer, broke that damn screen door right off the hinges, burned it up in the fireplace. You should have seen the look on that poor guy's face, coming out of the bedroom zipping up his pants, and I'm standing there in the living room, I've got the hammer in one hand, bottle of Jack Black in the other.'' He had a funny, scared look on his face, thinking back. ''That was what she later embroidered into the thing about me threatening to kill her and Lisa.''

"Well. Sounds like it'd make a good song, anyway."

"You think I didn't notice?" Chris said, laughing. "Second tune in my next set."

"What's it called?"

Chris looked around vacantly. "I never really give them names."

"How about 'Ball Peen Hammer Blues'?"

He leaned toward her, looked into her face. There was a warm light in his blue eyes. "See? Writing songs, there's nothing to it. All you need is a little inspiration.''

The room seemed kind of warm suddenly. Mae-mae changed the subject.

"Well," she said. "I went by your sister's house today.''

Chris Towe leaned back sharply in his chair. He was still looking into her eyes, but the warmth seemed to have drained out of his eyes. "Oh?" he said.

"This missing twenty thousand," she said. "I thought since your sister was there that night—maybe she'd know something.''

Chris didn't say anything for a minute. Finally he spoke, his voice tight and bottled up. "I talked to Mom yesterday. She told me how much money Dad left her. We had no idea he had that much money. No idea at all."

"She's pretty well provided for."

Chris nodded. "That's exactly my point. So there's a missing twenty grand? Maybe he gave it to somebody. Maybe it was some sort of business expense." He spread his hands. "But who cares? Mom's got more money than she knows what to do with."

"Twenty grand is a lot of money," Mae-mae said.

"Who cares! Who cares! It's gone. Dad's dead. Somebody killed him and he's dead, he's planted, he's history. And if they stole some money from him while they were at it, who cares? It could be ten bucks, it could be twenty grand. It doesn't matter. So why don't you just let it be? Let it lie. Let us get on with our lives."

"I know it may seem like a minor technicality to you," Mae-mae said. "But the probate judge is pushing like hell to get this thing resolved."

This didn't seem to satisfy him.

Mae-mae watched his face. There was a hooded look in his eyes, like there was something he wasn't saying. "Look," she said quietly. "I know this is a hard time for your family. But I have professional obligations. I have a fiduciary duty—"

"Fiduciary duty! Give me a break, okay. Don't people's feelings count for something?" He shook his head angrily, stood suddenly. "Look, I got to start the next set."

He walked back up onstage, put his guitar around his neck, leaned his head toward the microphone. There was scattered applause as he strummed a few chords. "Got a new song I'm working on," he said. "Y'all bear with me while I try out the chorus?" Then he sang in his silly Tammy Wynette voice:

> *Mae-mae Cosgrove,*
> *She was a cutie.*
> *Got carried away*
> *With her fiduciary duty.*

I don't need this, Mae-mae was thinking. I don't need this one bit. She threw a five-dollar bill on the table and headed for the door.

"What do y'all think?" Chris smiled blindly into the lights.

Someone called out, "Don't quit your day job just yet."

When she got home, the message light was blinking. She pressed PLAY. "Mae-mae, hi, it's Lester Paris. I don't want to make too big a deal about this, but I spoke with Barry King this evening and he mentioned that you had been asking him a number of questions about Charlie's death, et cetera. Now, again I understand your professional obligations relative to Myra, but I'd appreciate it if you'd clear it with me before you start contacting our clients, putting ideas in their heads. I'd appreciate your being sensitive to that." There was a long pause. "I think it's in everybody's best interest, okay?"

The machine squealed, rewound. What was *with* these people? You'd think they were glad he was dead.

EIGHT

First thing the next morning, Mae-mae got a call from Myra Towe. "You remember that twenty-thousand-dollar check?" Myra said. "I called Charlie's broker about that. The check still hasn't been cashed."

"Oh, really?" Mae-mae said. "That's odd. And you haven't found it in his records?"

"No."

"And they haven't found it at Printmeister either?"

"Not that I'm aware."

"You know," Mae-mae said, "we really ought to notify the police about this."

Myra Towe grudgingly admitted it probably wouldn't hurt and then gave Mae-mae the name of the detective in charge of the case.

The homicide detective's name was Dick Clark. A plastic sign on his desk said THIS IS NOT AMERICAN BANDSTAND. Mae-mae sat down in the folding chair. They were in a big room full of green desks. Nothing much seemed to be happening.

"What can I do you for, Miss Cosgrove?" Dick Clark was a carefully dressed guy, forty-five or so. Neat gray-flecked hair, starched white shirt, blue necktie with small red dots on it. He was a completely undistinctive guy,

71

except if you knew his name. In which case you might admit that, well, he *did* look a little like the Dick Clark on TV—at least when he smiled. His blue suit jacket hung on a plastic hanger hooked to his out box.

"I usually go with *Ms*. Cosgrove. For what it's worth."

Dick Clark's bland smile didn't flicker. He seemed to be looking at something about six inches over her left shoulder.

"As I explained on the phone," Mae-mae said, "I'm an attorney representing Charles Towe's estate. After he was killed I reviewed his financial records and there appears to be a peculiar pattern of cash withdrawals from a mutual fund he had invested in."

She went on to explain about the missing draft.

Dick Clark took out a notepad, wrote on it for a while with a ballpoint pen. When he was finished he said, "Twenty thousand, huh?"

"Right."

"This mutual fund have a name or something?"

"Imperial Balanced Fund Number Two. Managed by the Jefferson Group."

"And this draft—it looks just like a check?"

"Pretty much."

"Any distinguishing number on it?"

"It was numbered one oh eight. The fund account number was six oh five oh seven nine nine nine three. Payable through Chemical Bank. That's all on the face of the draft."

"You got a good head for figures, remember all that," Dick Clark said. He wrote some more, then looked up and smiled his American Bandstand smile. "Anything else?"

"He had a letter in his hand. Or it was on the floor near his hand anyway—when he was found." She handed the envelope to him that had been given to her by Candy Frank.

Dick Clark took the paper out of the envelope, read

it, copied down the words in his notebook. "This wasn't there when I arrived at the crime scene," he said.

"Apparently Candy picked it up and then forgot to mention it to you."

"This mean anything to you?"

"No."

"How many people have touched this since the murder?"

"Maybe four, five people."

Dick Clark shook his head, annoyed. "So much for the fingerprints." He put the letter back in the envelope, tossed it across the desk. "Anything else you need to bring to my attention?"

"Not really," Mae-mae said, tucking the letter back in her purse.

"Great," Dick Clark said. He closed his notebook and set it on his desk. Big smile. "Anything comes up, we'll notify Mrs. Towe."

Mae-mae waited for something else to happen.

Dick Clark kept showing off his American Bandstand dental work. Finally he clapped his hands, once. "Well," he said. "That's it then."

"Wait a second," Mae-mae said. "I just gave you information that he may have had twenty thousand dollars stolen from him and that somebody may have threatened him and all you say is, 'Great, that's it then'?"

Dick Clark looked at her for a minute. "If you like, I could say it again, counselor," he said.

"Why is it," Mae-mae said, that it seems like nobody wants to find out what really happened to this guy— including you?"

"Always seems that way," Dick Clark said. "Always seems that way."

Mae-mae glared at him.

Dick Clark did a couple of paradiddles on the desk with the tips of his fingers. "Let me be totally honest here, totally frank. Right now the evidence indicates that someone—probably a stranger—came into his office at some time between six o'clock and midnight and attempted to steal money from him. They struggled; the attacker hit Mr. Towe a couple times in the head with a blunt instrument and killed him. After that the perp grabbed his watch and his wallet, ransacked the office where the petty cash was stored, and took off with it. That's what the evidence we have indicates. If the perp also took off with a check for twenty grand, he'll try to pass it pretty soon. When he does, we'll catch the guy and that'll be the end of it.'' Dick Clark looked her in the eye. ''Okay? My perspective, that's where we're at with this case.''

''What about the letter?''

''What about it? 'The greatest danger is weak follow-through'? That could mean anything.'' Dick Clark shrugged. ''Or nothing.''

Mae-mae thought about it. ''I don't know,'' she said finally. ''Something just doesn't feel right about this thing.''

''You're saying you think somebody he knows killed him. That's what you're saying, am I right?''

''I guess so,'' Mae-mae said.

''And you also think maybe you can kind of snoop around a little, turn something up, right?''

''Snooping, isn't that your job?''

''Hon,'' Dick Clark said, ''I gather your experience isn't in the field of criminal law.''

''More like tax and estate planning.''

Dick Clark leaned back in his chair, put his hands behind his head. He had a kind of theatrically sober look on his face, like he was about to give her a speech he'd memorized and told to a lot of people. ''See, *Miz* Cosgrove, there's a lot of ways to solve a murder. You can solve a murder with science, spend all kind of taxpayer time and money on fiber evidence and DNA and X rays and fingernail scrapings; you can solve a case with ass kicking—bust down some doors, take a short piece of hose to some pimp in the bathroom of a strip joint down on Stewart Avenue. You can use psychology. You can use surveillance, hell, whatever. Million ways to solve a case. *De gustibus non est disputandum.* Benefit of a Catholic education, that's Latin for one man's meat is another man's poison. But most cases, the way you solve them is you get a call, you drive up, and there's some poor fool sobbing over the dearly departed, got a bleeding steak knife in his hand. He's going, 'I didn't mean to do it! It was all a big mistake!' Whap! Case closed. Eight, nine times out of ten, that's all she wrote.''

''So what's your point?''

''Point I'm making, the other couple cases, boy, it gets real tricky. Takes a lot of time, money, effort—and sometimes after all that work, you just never know. You just never find out. I got about a dozen cases I'm working on in some capacity right now. None of them simple, none of them easy. Plus I got another hundred open jackets lying around that I'll probably never solve. So I have to parcel out my time to the cases where I think my effort's going to pay off.''

''You're saying it's a lost cause.''

''I'm saying if this one's gonna get solved at all, it'll probably solve itself. I might could turn over every rock, every stone, still decide after it's all over that it was just some freak off the street, some guy I'm never going to find. Or the guy might try to pass the check in some pawn shop over in Mississippi somewhere. Pawn shop owner knows this basehead shouldn't be carrying a twenty grand check, calls the local authorities, they call me, and it's all over with.''

''So I should just forget about it.''

''I'm saying that if this was TV, I'd be telling you to leave it to the professionals, getting all huffy about you trespassing on my territory. But this is real life. I don't got the time or the inclination to turn down any help I can get. If you think something else is going on, well . . .'' He shrugged. ''I happen to think you're wrong, that's all. But if you want to keep poking around, hey, don't quote me on it—but be my guest.''

"I'm no detective," Mae-mae said.

"And I'm no tax lawyer. All this stuff you're telling me, mutual funds and bank drafts, that don't mean a whole lot to me. But if you think somebody killed Charles Towe because of his mutual fund, you probably got as good a chance finding it as I do.''

Mae-mae studied his face, trying to see if he was serious or if this was just a slick brush-off. She couldn't tell one way or the other. "Okay," Mae-mae said. "I'll keep looking." She picked up her purse, stood to go.

"All seriousness, I appreciate your coming forward with this information," Dick Clark said. Then he pointed at her with his index finger, squinting over it like he was aiming a gun at her head. "You find anything else out, though, I better be the first to know."

On the way to the door Mae-mae thought of something. "One last question," she called to the detective. "You say he was killed with a blunt instrument. What do you mean by that?"

"Hard to say," Dick Clark said. "Could be a stick, could be a poker, some type of equipment out of the print shop. Could be a hammer. Could be a lot of things.''

NINE

When she got back to the office, there was a call from Candy Frank on Mae-mae's answering machine. Her voice was breathy and excited. She needed Mae-mae to call as soon as possible.

Mae-mae called.

"It's about Mr. Paris," Candy said. Her voice was low and whispery, like a seventh-grade girl about to spill a secret.

"What *about* Mr. Paris?"

"Can't talk now," Candy whispered loudly. "He might *hear* me!"

"Do you want me to come by Printmeister?"

"No! No! We have to meet somewheres."

Mae-mae looked at her watch. "I've got an appointment this afternoon. What about right after work?"

Candy named a place to meet, a barbecue joint off Roswell Road. "Don't worry," Candy stage-whispered. "It'll be *safe* there!"

Mae-mae put the phone down and had a good laugh.

Garry Hull didn't seem like an advertising guy, but that's what he was. No loud necktie, no sixty-dollar hair-cut, no Italian shoes. He was just a short guy with Einstein hair and thick glasses that made his eyes look like

huge, wet rubber balls. His suit was made of exceptionally shiny blue polyester.

The idea was that he was going to put together some
kind of great ad campaign, and she'd get buried in new
clients, and that would be the end of her money problems. Every sleazeball lawyer in town was advertising—
why not her? When he wasn't talking, Garry Hull
hummed show tunes through his nose. The funny thing
was, he was actually supposed to be really good at what
he did.

Garry Hull was saying, "Ten grand, yeah, that'll get
your foot in the door." Nnnn-nn-nn-nn-hmmmmm-nn-
nn-nn-nn-nnnn. He was humming, if she wasn't mistaken, "I'm Gonna Wash That Man Right Out of My
Hair."

"Get my foot in the door?" Mae-mae said. "I was
thinking I could do this for two, three thousand."

"Sure," he said. "You could write your own solicitation letter, type it up yourself, print it on some Korean
War surplus mimeograph machine, stuff the envelopes
yourself, send out a nice purple letter to six, eight thousand households."

Hnnnn-hmmmmmmmnnnnnnnn. "Misty"? "Embrace-
able You"?

Mae-mae said, "Only it'd be a piece of crap."

"Only—right—eight thousand carefully chosen people would flush it down the john." His huge, wet eyes
blinked once.

"Do me a favor, break down the pricing if you don't
mind," Mae-mae said.

"Here's the economics." Garry pulled an envelope
out of his pocket, tossed it on the table. "This is a typical piece of junk mail, came to my house today."

Nnn-mmm-nnn-nnnnn-hn-hn-nnnnnn. "My Funny
Valentine."

It was a letter-sized envelope, government brown, that
said IRS Distribution Incorporated in the top corner. Underneath that was a seal with an eagle in the middle.

Mae-mae picked it up and looked at it. "So the gimmick here is they try to make it look like an IRS refund so you'll open it?"

"Sweet concept, huh?" Garry Hull said. One huge eye didn't seem to track—like it was transfixed by something on the wall, couldn't tear itself away. "Kind of a frontal assault on your intelligence."

Mae-mae opened the envelope.

"Envelope, custom printed," Garry said. "Eight cents."

Mae-mae pulled out a letter and two three-by-five cards. The second card had small gold labels gummed on it that said, *Stick it and Win!!!* You were supposed to take the gold label off one card and stick it on the other card. There seemed to be no good reason for you to do this—other than the fact that they told you to.

"Double-sided letter, two colors, nine cents," Garry said. "Mail-in card, four cents. Figure—two, three percent response, postage for mail-in card, averages out to less than a penny apiece. Stickers—thirteen, fourteen cents. Fulfillment, ten cents."

"Fulfillment, what's that?"

Bnnnnnnnnn-hnnnn-nnnn-nnnnnnnnnnnnnnn. "Bess, I'm Yo' Man."

"Lickers and stickers—the mail house. They stuff the envelopes, meter the mail, pass it on to the post office."

"Fulfillment. I never heard of that."

"Creative—assuming, say, a hundred thousand pieces—could be anywhere from a penny to a quarter. Say, a nickel for creative. Mailing list, six cents. So how much has this whole thing cost you?"

"Fifty-five cents. Not bad."

"Good," Garry Hull said. "But wrong. You missed the single biggest expense in a piece like this." He tapped the top right-hand corner of the envelope with a stubby finger.

"Postage."

"Postage. First class Zip Code pre-sort, still costs you

thirteen point two cents. More if it's heavier than an ounce. Everything else you can economize on to some degree. But postage . . ." He smiled broadly, hummed a couple of bars through his teeth, something Mae-mae didn't recognize. "Postage you're stuck with."

"So it's looking like seventy cents per?"

"More. In your case, creative is getting amortized across a fairly small number of pieces. Maybe a buck a shot. If we're lucky."

"Ten thousand pieces, huh?"

"Anything less, it's hardly worth the effort. Creative eats you alive."

"That's thirteen hundred bucks in postage alone."

"Sad but true. Postage never goes away."

Ten grand. She didn't have anywhere near ten grand. Where would she get ten grand? From her dad? No, he'd start saying things like, "You know so much about people's money, how come you never have any?" She couldn't deal with that.

"You know, Garry, I honestly don't know if I can afford this."

Garry forced some music through his adenoids—a phrase or two of "In a Sentimental Mood"—before he said, "Advertising sucks, doesn't it?"

The barbecue place was almost empty. Mae-mae was five minutes early, and Candy hadn't showed up yet.

There was one table full of women at the far end of the dining room, a couple more women working behind the long Formica counter. Everybody in the place could have been Candy's twin: middle-aged, forty pounds overweight, their credulous eyes peeping out from under lids caked with various girlish shades of pink and blue.

A fly buzzed languidly across the room, bumped into the glass door, settled on top of a blob of some unidentifiable, greasy substance. Above the counter hung a white plastic menu, a couple of degrees off kilter—the kind that had horizontal slots with plastic letters stuck into them. The food was spelled out in blue plastic letters, prices in red. The shredded pork plate cost four ninety-five, including tea, baked beans, slaw, and your choice of cornbread or biscuit.

"Can I hep you, honey?" the woman behind the counter said. She was about fifty, her hair dyed the same tired shade of brown as Garry Hull's shoes.

"That pork plate looks good. The shredded, not the sliced," Mae-mae said. "With sweet tea and a biscuit."

"Dessert?"

"I shouldn't . . . but sure. The cherry cobbler."

"Now you got the cutest little figure," the woman said. "You could eat that stuff all day, not gain a pound hardly."

"I don't know," Mae-mae said, slapping her thighs. "I've got thirteen pounds right here I'd sure like to get rid of."

"I got thirteen pounds there I could do without myself," the woman said. "Lot of other places I got thirteen pounds I could stand to get shut of." She hooted and handed Mae-mae a sixteen-ounce Dixie cup full of iced tea. "Honey, you just go ahead, set down. I'll brang your plate out soon as the beans come up."

Mae-mae sat down and waited for Candy Frank. Over in the corner of the restaurant Candy's twin sisters talked about a church retreat their children had gone to up near Dahlonega. There had been a certain amount of drinking and carrying on, against which the youth minister had not, apparently, taken sufficient precautions.

Mae-mae let her mind wander, thinking about this situation with Charles Towe. One of the things she had wondered was where Towe had gotten all his money. It wasn't impossible that he'd saved it up from his work. But it seemed somehow improbable. His business had netted a hundred and forty grand last year—which would have been split more or less evenly between himself and Lester Paris. That meant pre-tax he'd made about seventy thousand a year. Even if you added in a smallish salary and maybe a car lease, some other stuff buried in the business—even then, it would have been hard to save two million dollars.

Mae-mae looked at her watch. Candy was already ten minutes late. She wondered what Candy was going to tell her about Lester Paris. There was something slippery about the guy. And it didn't help that he drove a red Porsche.

Whatever dirt Candy had stumbled on, Mae-mae didn't exactly picture him as a murderer, though. But then what's a murderer like?

The waitress brought out her plate, piled with meat and beans, called Mae-mae "honey" a couple more times. The chopped pork was *fine*—real pit barbecue, tender, with a nice smoky flavor. She could feel pig grease sluicing into her veins, congealing in her hips and the arteries around her heart. Magnificent!

Twelve after. Where was Candy Frank anyway?

Over at the table in the corner one of Candy's twins suggested that the youth minister, in fact, may have been involved in a certain particular incident himself. Another twin said she wouldn't blame a girl for fooling around with him, the youth minister being a right healthy and attractive young man.

But getting *caught* at it, one of her friends rejoined, *that* was the point. A congregation wouldn't stand for that—no how, no way. Discretion was the key, see, because you wouldn't last too long a-tall being a minister if you didn't have sense enough to keep your mouth closed and your bedroom door shut.

This point was given general agreement.

When Mae-mae was finished eating, it was six twenty-seven. No Candy Frank. A fly dive-bombed Mae-mae's head a few times, then meandered back toward the kitchen. She went out and stood in the dusty parking lot for a while. Cars flew by on Roswell Road.

No one answered when she called Printmeister from the pay phone bolted to the brick wall of the restaurant.

Mae-mae hung up, sat on the curb for a while. There were an unusual number of orange drink bottles and Goo Goo Cluster wrappers scattered across the weedy, cracked tarmac. There was not much else to notice, though, not much else going on.

At six fifty-four she gave up, got into her old Honda, had to crank it three times before the engine caught for good.

TEN

Next morning at the office Mae-mae poured herself a cup of coffee and opened the *Atlanta Journal*. On page three she noticed a photo of a wrecked car, the front end mashed up into what had once been the driver's seat. Above it was a two-column story with a headline that said, FIERY CRASH CLAIMS ATLANTA WOMAN.

Investigators had identified the charred body of Atlanta resident Candy Rose Frank, forty-three, in the wreckage of her scorched 1983 Buick LeSabre. Besides *scorched* and *charred*, the writer had also managed to slip *melted, blistered, crushed, twisted,* and *ravaged* into the four inches of copy. The story went on to say she'd run off the road and collided with a parked Caterpillar D-10 tractor sometime around six o'clock P.M. An unnamed city of Atlanta traffic inspector was quoted as saying, ''We have not ruled out the possibility this was an alcohol-related type of situation.''

''Jesus *Christ*,'' Mae-mae said to the empty room.

When she managed to stop staring at the awful picture, she got up, taped a note on the door saying she'd be gone for forty-five minutes, and headed for the elevator.

* * *

Lester Paris's red Porsche was sitting in the Printmeister
lot when Mae-mae arrived ten minutes later. Mae-mae
walked through the front door, past the smiling receptionist, and straight into Lester Paris's office. He was on
the phone, talking in his pleasant salesman voice.

"Not elaborate, no," Lester was saying. "Simpler.
Right. What was the one you said before? Not the, no,
not the hand-rubbed bird's-eye maple. Not the Imperiale,
no. Right. Right. That's it, the Noblesse. That's the
cheap one, right?"

He gestured at a chair and said, "I'll be with you in
a sec, Miss Cosgrove." He smiled faintly and went back
to his conversation.

Mae-mae sat down, looked at the pictures on the wall.
In one of the pictures, he and Charles Towe were standing next to each other on a golf course. Towe was a
squat, balding guy, stiff and uncomfortable looking in
his lemon yellow shirt. Paris was smiling like he was
about to do you a good turn, maybe discount something
down to wholesale as a special personal favor.

Lester kept talking on the phone, staring off into
space. Or not into space precisely; he was staring at
Mae-mae's chest.

Ah-ha, that was it! She had known there was
something besides Lester's general insincerity that had
been bugging her about him. He was one of those jerks
who stared at your boobs the whole time they talked to
you. Jesus, if he wanted to glance at them now and then,
fine. But give it a rest, for Godsake.

When Lester hung up the phone, Mae-mae tossed the
Journal on his desk. "Did you know about this?" she
said.

He looked away from her chest long enough to take
in the story. He nodded slowly. "I was just on the phone
with the funeral home. She doesn't have any close rel-
atives except a senile old mother in a nursing home. I
had to identify the body. My Lord . . ." He wiped his
dry eyes. "I've never seen anything like it before."

"Do you know why this might have happened?" Mae-mae said.

Lester Paris nodded gravely. "I think I do," he said.

Mae-mae sat up straighter. She hadn't expected him to say that.

"Yeah," Lester said. "We were afraid something like this was going to happen."

"Why?"

Lester ran his hand through his razor-cut blond hair, squinted at her boobs like he was doing some profound thinking. "She'd been . . . drinking very heavily," he said. "I mean, I hate to say it, because we all loved her to death. But the truth is, she had a little . . ." He cleared his throat. ". . . drinking problem."

"She was drinking yesterday?"

"Yesterday. Day before. She'd been drinking a lot since Charlie's death." He had a funny look on his face.

"Why?"

"Well . . ." Lester made a noise with his teeth. "She kind of had a thing for old Charlie. Kind of had a crush on him. We used to joke about it behind her back. Not me, I mean, but . . . some of the fellows around the plant. You know how that kind of thing is."

"I'm not sure I do."

Lester Paris dismissed this comment with a stoic shrug. "She had a little too much fondness for the bottle. Always had. But up until Charlie died it had pretty much been in control—at least as long as she was at work."

"But not yesterday?"

"Not for the past couple weeks." Lester Paris looked at her, his face settled in a sad-faced mask. "Real, real sad thing," he concluded. "Real sad." He stared dolefully at Mae-mae's left breast.

"I'm just a little curious, though," Lester said after a moment. "Any particular reason you should be interested in Candy? She's not a client of yours, too, is she?" He smiled like he was joking—but putting some edge in his voice so she'd know where he was coming from.

"No, as a matter of fact she's not. She did call me yesterday and ask to meet with me." Mae-mae watched Lester Paris's face. His preacher expression didn't change at all. "She said she had some very important information to give me. Something about Printmeister."

"Uh-huh." Lester Paris ran his tongue slowly across his lip. "And did she say what this information was in regard to?"

"No," Mae-mae lied. "She sure didn't."

"Isn't that puzzling." His eyes still pinned on her breasts. "Isn't *that* strange."

"Isn't it," Mae-mae said. She kept her eyes on his face. There was a flicker of something in his eyes. Fear? Anger? Hard to tell. "Any thoughts, Lester? Any idea what she might have wanted to talk about?"

Lester shook his head. "Boy, that's a tough one. That's a toughy. Like I say, she's been real distraught. Only thing I can think, she's started getting funny ideas in her head." He paused. "Because of the drinking, I mean."

"What were her duties?"

"Oh, usual office manager type of thing. Invoicing, filing employment stuff with the government, paying the bills, answering the phone now and then. Keeping the books."

Mae-mae crossed her arms, covering her breasts. Lester Paris's gaze floated slowly up to her face. Did he have to be so obvious about it? "I don't suppose you'd mind my taking a look at your books? On behalf of Mrs. Towe, of course."

"They might be a little confusing to you," he said, smiling.

Mae-mae smiled back, gave him some southern girl sweet-pea bullshit—blinking and smiling vacuously. "For what it's worth, I'm not only a lawyer, I'm also a CPA." She abruptly turned off the blink-and-smile routine. "Besides, I don't confuse easily."

"You wouldn't mind my calling Mrs. Towe," he

said, coming back with a nice, patronizing smile, wrinkling his nose a little. "Just to get it from the horse's mouth."

"Not a bit," she said. Damn. She hadn't said anything about this to Myra. "I'll speak to her if you'd like."

Lester Paris just winked, then picked up the phone and dialed. "Myra!" he said. "How you holding up, girl?"

Jesus. He was going to pull a big snow job, convince Myra not to let her look at the books.

Lester told Myra Towe about Candy, going into that for about five minutes, talking about the price of caskets and the different kinds of flower arrangements you could get and then asking about the kids and the house and a lot of other stuff before he got around to popping the question. "Listen, Myra," he said. "I've got a little lady here, the girl that's probating Charlie's estate—now she's expressed an interest in taking a crack at our books down here at the print shop. Right. Right. Course I've got nothing against that . . . in principle. Thing is, with Candy and Charlie, all the bad luck we're having, we're stretched real thin right now. Right. Right. Sure, but my point is, if we'd had a little more advance notice—"

He shut up for a while and listened.

"I understand, but . . . I understand. I understand, but . . . okay, okay." He paused, listened some more. "Well, if you say so." He hung up sharply.

Mae-mae smiled and said, "Lead me to 'em, Lester."

Lester looked at her for a minute. "This casket, the Noblesse," he said, showing her a picture from a funeral home brochure. "The cheap one. You think I should have gone with something a little classier?"

Mae-mae took a stack of computer disks back to her office. All the Printmeister financial records were kept on an accounting program that operated as a Lotus 1-2-3 template. She cranked up her computer, loaded the disks, fiddled around with the program for a while.

Everybody does their accounting a little differently, so it took a while to get her bearings—but once she did it was pretty simple stuff: payables, receivables, both of them linked to a balance sheet and an income statement. Easy as pie.

Okay. Two things: First, find out if there was anything goofy, screwed up, or suspicious in the Printmeister books. Second, compare Charles Towe's personal numbers to the Printmeister numbers—see if they jibed.

Mae-mae stared at the green numbers on her screen. The income statement was pretty simple—basically just a cash flow record minus depreciation and a couple of other noncash items.

Mae-mae took out the file of material that Myra Towe had brought the first day. According to the printed income statement in Myra's file, the company had netted $142,567 last year.

The computer came up with a different number: $179,412. After hunting through the depreciation schedules and some other noncash items, Mae-mae found the missing numbers. What happened, some of the parts of the spreadsheet weren't linked correctly, so a couple of noncash items had to be reconciled by hand. False alarm; the numbers balanced.

Of the $142,000 profit, $94,000 had been paid out to Towe and Paris in the form of dividends—forty-six grand apiece. A couple thousand more had gone to Christmas bonuses for the staff. The rest was classified as retained earnings. The company also paid salaries to both Lester Paris and Charles Towe. Towe was paid forty-five grand; Paris forty. So that meant Towe's total pre-tax compensation last year had been almost exactly ninety thousand.

Mae-mae dug through her filing cabinet until she found Charles Towe's IRS 1040. Good old line thirteen—income reported on Form W-2—said that Charles Towe had a taxable personal income of $212,000.

What?

Two hundred and twelve thou. Not including dividends, capital gains, AFDC, spousal income, any of that crap. Earned income, period. Mae-mae started doing the math in her head.

What it came down to was that *in addition* to the ninety grand in salary and dividends he'd made at Printmeister, Charles Towe had earned $167,000 during the previous year. How in the world did he do that? She looked for a copy of the W-4, but there was only one—from Printmeister—listing the forty-six grand.

Mae-mae had just gotten to the end of the IRS statement—not really looking at the numbers but just trying to get the flow of it, dividends, partnership distributions, Schedule C—when it hit her: Schedule C? That was self employment. Why would he file a self-employment statement when he was a paid employee of his own company? It didn't make sense. If he'd been a sole proprietor, sure; but he wasn't a sole proprietor. Printmeister was a limited partnership that paid him a salary just like it did any other employee. The only extra money he made from Printmeister came in the form of dividends—$46,000 last year—which was reported separately on Form 400. Therefore he shouldn't have filed self-employment . . . should he?

She turned to Schedule C. There it was: according to the form, he'd grossed an extra $174,000. Somehow. All of it outside the printing business. There were a couple of trivial expenses that were deducted from that number—some rent, some T&E—leaving $167,000 in Schedule C income.

There was no indication on the form as to what he did to earn all that money. She scanned the form to see what number he had put in the little box that said *Occupation Code*. He'd filled in the number forty-nine.

But what did forty-nine stand for?

Mae-mae rummaged around in her desk, looking for instructions for the tax forms. She was a tax lawyer, wasn't she? So she had to have some spare tax forms.

Wait, there it was, underneath the Golden Buddha take-out menu.

She turned to the self-employment form directions. Occupation code. There was a long list of them divided into sections. Forty-nine. It was under the *Business, Other* section. Next to the number forty-nine: *Consultant.* Great, that was a big help. Consultant for whom? About what?

Mae-mae stared at the little number, forty-nine, then stared out the window at her nice view. It was too hazy to see Stone Mountain. Consultant, she was thinking, gimme a break.

It had the odor of some kind of tax dodge. But if it was a tax dodge, it didn't make any sense. After all, *she* was supposed to be the person dreaming up all his tax dodges. But here he was paying taxes on nearly every cent of the money he got from this "consulting" business he seemed to be running on the side—income he had never disclosed to her. If he were trying to bury income, hide it from the IRS, it would have made more sense to bury it at Printmeister. Or in some kind of off-shore corporation. Anything but this.

But if there wasn't a tax angle, where could this money be coming from?

Mae-mae thought back on her memory of Charles Towe. A square little guy, balding, with an abrupt manner and green eyes. His hands had been short fingered, ink stained, strong. He was countrified, but not in that expansive, pleasant way most people associate with rural southerners; instead he was closed in, every word labored, a cloud of disapproval hovering in his eyes. He hadn't been a client for all that long; in fact, he had only come to see her three or four times. She hadn't liked him much.

He didn't exactly fit her idea of a highly paid consultant. Consultant, you think of some slick guy in a custom-made suit and a Hermés necktie—which, for sure, wasn't Towe.

Mae-mae picked up the phone, dialed Myra Towe's number.

It was a short conversation. "Consultant?" Myra said. "What do you mean, consultant?" As far as she knew, her husband had never been a consultant to anyone in his life.

After she got off the phone, Mae-mae double-checked everything, trying to find out if there was any record of where the money had come from. At the bottom of the pile of material, she found a small stack of invoices with Charles Towe's name and home address printed at the top. The invoices went back about three and a half years.

All the invoices looked pretty much the same. The latest invoice was dated a month and a half earlier. There was a typed notation at the top: *Consulting Services.* Under that it claimed 150 hours had been worked, with the number of hours billed being multiplied by an hourly rate of $100 per hour. Amount due: $15,000 and no cents. What a conveniently round number. Mae-mae flipped through the stack. Some of the invoices ran as high as thirty, forty thousand dollars. All fees payable to Charles P. Towe.

The only other thing on the invoices was the name of the client. It was listed as Janus Print Enterprises, N.V. The company's address was in the Netherlands Antilles.

Janus Print Enterprises, what in hell was that? One thing was for certain, nobody in the Netherlands Antilles was hiring Charles Towe as a consultant. The only thing they printed in the Netherlands Antilles were the names of dummy corporations. The Netherlands Antilles, a couple of dinky islands in the Caribbean, was the international headquarters of slippery money, barely legal financial scams, bogus tax shelters—the reason being that it was nearly impossible to get financial information out of the place. She'd set up a couple shelters there herself. It was like Switzerland—only modestly corrupt. The deadest of dead ends.

Question. What looks like a tax shelter, swims like a tax shelter, and quacks like a tax shelter?

Answer. Mae-mae drew a blank. It all pointed to shelters—except for the fact that Towe had been paying his thirty-eight percent straight to the tax man.

Mae-mae dialed Printmeister, asked to speak to Lester Paris.

"Satisfied?" Lester Paris said. "You happy now?"

"The books look fine," Mae-mae said.

"I told you they would. Sorry I was a little short with you. It's just things are pretty rough sledding down at the shop right now."

"Sure," Mae-mae said. "Look, I've got another question for you, Lester."

"Fire away."

"Does the name Janus Print Enterprises ring a bell with you?"

There was a short pause. "What was that name again?"

"Janus. Print. Enterprises."

Long pause.

"Hate to do this to you," Lester said. "I just got a call coming in on line two, something I been expecting all morning. How about I get back to you?" There was a warbly, panicky sound to his voice.

Mae-mae didn't hear any line two calling—no ring, no click, no beep, no hoot, no squawk. "Line two my ass," she said.

But by then line one had gone dead in her hand.

ELEVEN

Mae-mae had just gotten home for lunch, popped the top on a can of Mr. Pibb, and thrown Wynnona Judd's new disk on the CD player when the doorbell rang. She looked through the peephole. It was Sebastian, grinning. Which was odd because Sebastian wasn't the drop-in type. Or the grinning type, either, for that matter.

Mae-mae opened the door.

"My surprise," Sebastian said. "As promised." He patted a rectangular package under his arm. She had never seen him looking so gleeful.

Sebastian came in the front door, surveyed the vista of Budget Gourmet trays, magazines, general junk. "You *really* must get a maid," he said. "It gets worse by the day."

Mae-mae ignored him. "What's in the package?"

It was flat, rectangular, wrapped in brown shipping paper, roughly two by three feet and six inches deep. "Have you considered a feed trough?" Sebastian said. "They're quite inexpensive, I'm told."

"Sit!" Mae-mae could only take so much needling about her housekeeping. After a while it rankled.

Sebastian sat. He held his brown package gingerly against his chest, the way schoolgirls carry their books

94

to class. A look of barely suppressed glee teased at the corners of his thin mouth. "Guess."

It was bound to be some kind of artwork, maybe an etching. Probably from the seventeenth century. She started with the easy part. "Seventeenth century?"

"Good."

"English?"

"Good."

"Etching?"

Sebastian shook his head. "Better than that."

"Painting?"

"Not that good."

Mae-mae was stumped. Not an etching. Not a painting. What the hell was left that was flat and rectangular?

"Tapestry? Cartoon?" Mae-mae said. "I don't know, I give up."

"You're so, *so* feeble," Sebastian said. The grin was eating at the edges of his mouth again.

But then he slid his fingers underneath the tape that sealed his package, tore it gently, slowly, without ripping the paper. His fingers trembled a little. Underneath the shipping paper was a cardboard box. This, too, was painstakingly opened. Then a rough wooden frame, for protection in shipping. Then foam peanuts, then tissue paper. Finally a white framing mat. His eyes gleaming, Sebastian held the mat so Mae-mae couldn't see what was on the other side.

"Okay, okay!" Mae-mae said.

Sebastian slowly turned the mat around. On the other side was a small sketch, a charcoal bust of a man wearing a gigantic hat, elaborately curled hair spilling out from under the brim. His face was a perfect oval, with small budlike lips and round eyes. There was something about the stately calm of his face that changed the atmosphere of the room, filled it with a still and cool and ancient air.

"Oh, man," Mae-mae said. "It's beautiful! Fox-worthy?"

"Better."

"Parham?"

"Better."

"Not a Closterman?"

Sebastian smiled triumphantly.

"A *John* Closterman?"

"By his own hand. A study for his portrait of Cecil Tremayne, fourth earl of Northumberland, dated 1681. The final product, the oil, is mentioned in several places, but apparently no longer exists. Burned during the nineteenth century." Sebastian smiled sadly. "This is all that is left."

John Closterman was a leading British portrait painter in the late seventeenth century—tragically flawed, Sebastian liked to say, by his twin addictions to gambling and to sucking up to the rich and powerful. Both of which, then as now, could be fairly expensive and distracting propositions. Sebastian had been in love with Closterman's work for as long as Mae-mae had known him.

"It's exquisite," Mae-mae said.

"Yes," Sebastian said softly. "Yes. Yes." He couldn't take his eyes off the picture.

Mae-mae tried a joke: "You're sure this one's real?"

Sebastian's face turned sour for a moment. "Not funny," he said. "Not funny at all."

A couple years earlier he'd paid seventeen grand for a counterfeit painting that was supposed to have been by someone in the Gainsborough school—but turned out to have been painted by a Polish art student in Brooklyn whose trouble obtaining a green card had forced him to be fairly ingenious in finding employment for his talents. It was kind of a sore subject with Sebastian, so Mae-mae tended to bring it up after he had made one too many cracks about her housekeeping.

"The provenance has been very carefully scrutinized. I've been over the piece itself with a fine-tooth comb." Sebastian sniffed. "And as you know I've made a point of learning a bit about counterfeiting over the past few years.''

"May I?'' Mae-mae said.

"Of course. Of course!'' Sebastian handed her the drawing, then took a magnifying glass out of his pocket and offered it to her. "The real thing. See for yourself.''

"That's okay,'' Mae-mae said. "Nothing I could see with that would mean much to me anyway.''

Sebastian pursed his lips and put the magnifying glass back in his pocket. Mae-mae propped the picture on her knees and looked at it for a while. The fourth earl of Northumberland smiled sweetly, politely back at her. He was elaborately groomed—lacework cravat, extravagant wig, high-shouldered frock coat, plumed hat. But overshadowing his aristocratic foppery was a heaviness in the cheeks, a somberness in the eyes.

Mae-mae studied the picture for a long time—the melancholy black eyes, the reluctant smile—and it seemed suddenly that she knew Sebastian better than she had before. "It suits you, Sebastian,'' Mae-mae said finally.

Sebastian looked on solemnly. "I know.''

So they talked about the picture for a while, Sebastian lecturing about drawing techniques and history and provenances. After Sebastian wound up his lecture, the conversation drifted away from old pictures and moved toward the death of Charles Towe.

Mae-mae told him about the missing $20,000, about the phone call from Candy Frank.

"You don't know what she was going to talk to you about?'' Sebastian said.

"It sounded like she had some kind of dirt on Lester.''

"Like what?''

"No clue.''

Sebastian picked up his drawing, held it at arm's length, sighed contentedly, set it back down again.

"If it weren't for that weird letter Candy gave me, I'd

dismiss this whole thing," Mae-mae added. "But it seems like a kind of veiled threat."

"Maybe a second brain would help," Sebastian said.

Mae-mae dug through her purse, pulled out the envelope Candy had pressed on her. "Be my guest."

Sebastian pulled the letter out, perched it on his sharp knee. "*Danger? The greatest danger of all is weak follow-through,*" he read, then he didn't say anything for a while. "Not much, is it?" he said finally.

"Not much."

He held it up to the lamp next to his chair, pinching it delicately by the corners with his long, thin fingers. "Common watermark," he said, squinting up at the light. "I suppose there *might* be one or two drugstores in the country that don't sell this brand."

Mae-mae laughed humorlessly.

Sebastian folded the letter and put it back in the envelope. Then he lifted the envelope with his fingertips and gave it the same kind of scrutiny he'd given the letter. His eyes narrowed suddenly.

"Do you have a thirty-two-cent stamp?" he said.

"I guess," Mae-mae said.

"Go get it, would you?"

Mae-mae went back to her spare bedroom, rummaged through her desk, finally found a roll of thirty-two-cent stamps squashed under a notebook full of pre-1986 tax code commentaries. She threw the notebook in the trash, carried the stamps out to the living room, handed them to Sebastian.

He took out his magnifying glass, looked through it at the stamp in his hand, then at the stamp on the envelope, then back at the one in his hand. When he looked up from the letter, a triumphant smile had blossomed behind the magnifying glass.

"There's your answer, my dear," he said.

"Where's my answer?"

"Look." Sebastian said. "Carefully." He handed

Mae-mae the envelope, the stamps, the magnifying glass.

Mae-mae peered at the stamp on the envelope, then at one of the stamps she had brought from the bedroom. They had little pictures of American flags printed on them. The one on the envelope looked funny, the red stripes not lined up quite right with the blue patch in the corner. "This one's out of registration," she said, poking the one on the envelope.

"And . . ."

She looked some more. "The color's a little different, too."

"As is the finish on the paper."

She looked up at Sebastian. He was smiling broadly. "Are you saying . . ."

"The stamp on the envelope," Sebastian said, "it would appear to be a fake."

The big green press at Printmeister, sheaf after sheaf of stamps piling up in the bin—they'd been having trouble with the registration.

"Why would one bother, though?" Sebastian said.

Mae-mae thought about Garry Hull explaining the economics of direct mail in his cheap suit. "Suppose you worked for one of these companies that sends out junk mail. They call them fulfillment houses." She waved the bogus stamp in front of his face. "A shopping bag full of these little dudes could save you about fifty grand a month in postage."

"Good God," Sebastian said quietly.

Mae-mae dropped the envelope on the coffee table. "Janus Print Enterprises. I think I'm beginning to see where that money was coming from."

"Ah, yes. Janus," Sebastian said. "The god with two faces."

TWELVE

When Mae-mae got back to work, she tried to put things together. A counterfeit postage stamp. A vaguely threatening letter. A missing check for twenty grand. An inexplicable pattern of cash withdrawals from a mutual fund. An offshore company funneling money back to Charles Towe.

It had to fit. It's just that she didn't have enough information to make the whole thing hold together.

So where could she go next? She was sure that Lester Paris was involved in something—counterfeiting postage stamps, maybe—she could tell it from his voice. But what then? It wouldn't accomplish much to go up and ask the guy. He'd just laugh at her and that would be the end of it. She tried to figure out another avenue, but nothing seemed to present itself.

Call the cops? And tell them—what? That she had found this letter with a funny looking stamp on it?

The phone rang. It took a few rings before Mae-mae picked it up.

"Cosgrove and Associates," she said.

There was a pause. "Hi, it's Clay."

Clay. Clay. Clay?

"Clay?"

"Clay Wilder," the voice said. "Rachel Towe's friend. From the other night?"

"Oh, right," Mae-mae said. With the ponytail. "The boyfriend. Sorry, I was kind of spacing out."

"I was calling," Clay said, "because of what we talked about the other night."

"I haven't reconsidered," Mae-mae said. "I'm just not the model type."

"Oh . . . that," Clay said. "No, that's not what I meant. I meant about the girlfriend—Charles Towe's girlfriend. Remember I said her name was Colleen? It just came to me her last name, it was something Italian—Mastronunzio, Mastrantonio, something like that. She used to come around the print shop when I worked there. She worked for one of our suppliers. In sales, I guess."

"Mastrantonio."

"Try Mastronunzio first. N-u-n-z-i-o, something like that. Can't be too many names like that in the phone book."

Mae-mae wrote down the name. It was worth talking to her, what the hell. "Thanks, Clay," she said.

"No modeling, huh?" he said. "You wouldn't even have to take off your clothes."

Mae-mae looked at the stack of bills sitting next to her computer. "How much you get paid for this kind of thing?" Mae-mae said.

"Hmm," Clay said. "Maybe I could pop for six, eight bucks an hour."

She laughed. "I could do that all week and barely have enough to cover the phone bill."

"So maybe you ought to cut down on long distance calls," Clay said. Then, without saying anything else, he hung up.

Clay was right. There was only one Colleen Mastronunzio in the phone book. She had a throaty voice, like someone who smoked too much, with the kind of take-no-shit edge Mae-mae associated with people who grew up in Brooklyn or South Philly. She didn't have the accent, though—just the attitude. Mae-mae imagined her to be a slightly over the hill, slightly overdone Italian beauty: black hair, black eyes, long fingernails, big chest.

Colleen Mastronunzio said she figured, yeah okay, it would be alright for Mae-mae to drop by her house— like the whole thing was a pain in her neck.

"You gonna come in or you gonna stand there?" Colleen Mastronunzio said.

Mae-mae had driven to her apartment after work.

Mae-mae was wrong on all counts—except the hair, which was black. No big tits, though, no long fingernails. Mastronunzio, that's what had thrown her off: it must have been a married name. She should have paid attention to the first name, a good Irish name.

Colleen Mastronunzio had the build of an athletic twelve-year-old underneath a black party dress, size two. Her skin was so fair you could see blue veins snaking beneath the surface, and her eyes were a muddy green— like algae in a stagnant pond. Her face had an eerie, skeletal quality.

Mae-mae came through the door. The apartment was done in cold, monochromatic modern. Black-and-white photographs lined the walls—stark pictures of rocks and mountains. No magazines scattered around, no TV dinners. The room was lit up like a stage by two of those zillion-watt halogen lamps.

"Drink?" Colleen Mastronunzio said.

"Thanks, no."

They sat down across from each other on matching black leather chairs. A white fur thing lay on the floor between them, a white on white carpet underneath it.

"So," Colleen said. "Let me get this straight, you're a lawyer?" It was hard to connect the huge voice with the tiny body.

"I was employed by Charles Towe prior to his death. Tax and estate planning. Now I'm looking into a couple things related to the probating of his estate."

"I *see*," Colleen Mastronunzio said. She looked at Mae-mae stonily, then stood up and went into the kitchen. Ice clinked and clattered. After a while she came back with a clear drink in a very thin highball glass.

Mae-mae said, "The reason I came to see you—"

"The reason you came to see me," Colleen said, "is you got word somehow that Charlie was banging me." She raised her eyebrows in wordless challenge. "Yes?"

Mae-mae looked down at the white fur thing on the floor. She couldn't identify what kind of animal it had once been. Wolf? Dog? Faithful Shep, the throw rug? Actually it looked more like a goat than anything else.

Colleen shrugged. "I was banging Charlie, Charlie was banging me." Colleen smiled remotely. "We had a relationship."

"Okay," Mae-mae said.

"But here's the thing you really want to know," Colleen went on. "You want to know—let me guess—you want to know was old Charlie dishing out his long-suffering wife's inheritance to his backdoor squeeze?" She crossed her arms, looked at Mae-mae. "Well, that's none of your goddamn business." She smiled again, not showing any teeth or even any particular emotion. "Anything else?"

Blindsided. She had expected to tiptoe around a while before she got to that question. And now there it was, out on the table before she had a chance to get ready. Mae-mae tried to figure how she should play this one. It was tricky. Confrontional people were always tricky. Sometimes the best negotiating ploy when you were dealing with people who thought they were smarter and tougher than you was to pretend to be dumber and weaker. The right fish, it worked like a charm.

Mae-mae smiled and blinked once or twice, made a

pert circle with her lips. "Gosh!" she said. "I hadn't even thought of that." Too transparent? Laying it on a little thick maybe?

Colleen Mastronunzio gave her a muddy green stare.

"Actually what I wanted to know was what state of mind Mr. Towe had been in," Mae-mae said. "Before his . . . demise." Demise, now that was an excellent word. Excellently dumb. If you could say *demise* with a straight face, nobody would take you seriously. Nobody.

"State of mind?" The tiny woman said it like she had never heard those words before.

"I mean was he unusually happy, unusually sad . . . I don't know."

Colleen thought about it. "Why?"

"I think he was murdered," Mae-mae said.

Colleen stared for a minute, like she couldn't believe what a nitwit she was talking to. "No shit. I mean, is this some kind of news flash?"

"No," Mae-mae said patiently. "I mean, there's a reason to think he wasn't killed by someone who just wanted to steal his watch or rip off the petty-cash box."

"Like who?"

"That's what I was hoping you could help me with."

"You're talking in circles," Colleen said sharply. "If there's reason to think that, then you already know something. If not, you wouldn't be here in the first place, would you?"

Mae-mae nodded. "I guess you're right. Mr. Towe was sent a threatening note right before he died. Also there are some financial irregularities."

"Like irregular how?"

"He received money," Mae-mae said. "And we're unable to trace the source of these funds. Now this may or may not have any connection to the murder, but it's important that we find out where the money came from in order to accurately project income for the estate this year." This was not an out-and-out lie, but it was pretty close.

Colleen set her drink down on the black stone table in front of her. She drew her knees up to her chest, wrapped her thin arms around them. Suddenly she looked like a very young girl. Her big voice spoiled the illusion. "Okay," she said. "Yeah, he was acting a little funny lately."

"Funny how?"

"Like, nervous. Spooky." The muddy green eyes watching her. "I mean, he's a pretty even-keeled guy. Was. Then all of a sudden lately he started getting jumpy."

"Any idea why?"

Colleen didn't say anything for a minute. "Something at work, I think." She shrugged. "I didn't ask. We never talked about that kind of thing."

"I thought you were in the printing supply business or something."

"Ink. I sell ink."

"And you never talked business?"

"I'm not real obsessed with ink. Ink is ink. It's a job."

Mae-mae watched the hard woman's face on the child's body. She didn't seem too sad about the guy being killed. But maybe it was just a facade.

Colleen smiled suddenly, flashing a mouth full of teeth, her face lighting up. As quickly as it had come it was gone—as though she had replayed some private joke in her mind and then suddenly forgotten it. "I know what you're thinking," she said. "I look like some bitch that didn't give a damn, just squeezing this old guy for his spare nickels." The muddy green eyes, staring again.

Mae-mae shrugged, noncommittal.

"Well, it's not like that. He wasn't the love of my life or whatever. And I wasn't his. But we did okay together. He was pretty generous with me, and I did what I could to make him . . . comfortable." She looked vacantly up at one of her black-and-white pictures for a minute. "That's all it was. We helped each other. He was ill at ease, you know, one of these guys who just never has a real good time. And I'm . . . well, I don't know what I am. Anyway, we got along okay, helped each other through some stuff." She trailed off.

Mae-mae absorbed this speech. Somehow it didn't ring true.

Colleen looked away. There was something going on in the aquatic mud of her eyes, a sign for the first time, of some kind of emotion. The mud seemed to swirl as though it had been covered by a runnel of water.

"We've gotten this far," Mae-mae said. "You might as well tell me."

Colleen looked away for a while before she finally spoke. "Okay, so it's true. He gave me money. Big fucking deal. It's a free country."

"Why did he give it to you?"

Colleen rallied and the swirling disappeared from her eyes. She picked up her tall glass, clinked the ice around. "Why? I asked him for it."

"Any particular reason?"

"I wanted it." She stared into her ice, shook the glass again.

Mae-mae waited.

Colleen said, "I wanted it because . . ." The muddy swirling thing happened again in her eyes. She took a big pull on her drink, set the thin glass down, wiped her eye with the back of her hand. "I see you don't have a ring either," she said.

"A wedding ring?" Mae-mae said.

"Right."

"Nope."

"Been married?"

"Nope."

Colleen smiled for a moment. It was a sad smile. "I got married, nineteen years old, living in Paramus, New Jersey. Guy named James D. Mastronunzio. Jimmy D.—

that's what they called him. Good ole Jimmy D. He was just what you'd figure a guy named Jimmy D. would be like. Union house painter, thick as a brick, stoned out of his mind about ninety percent of the time. Hardly ever worked 'cause he was on the union shit list all the time. He just hung around the house watching TV, or him and his buddies, they'd go down to Atlantic City or the hack track in Cherry Hill or whatever. I stayed married to him for ten years, tripping over his bong all the time, putting up with him drinking and all his dickhead house painter friends coming around to watch Kung Fu movies on TV, throwing up in the kitchen sink. It was a total joke. When I divorced him, he goes—looking back, I still can't believe this—he goes, 'Baby, I been so good to you. I never even hit you. Not once.' " She laughed for a minute. "You believe it? 'I never even hit you.' Like this makes him a prince among men."

Mae-mae didn't say anything.

"So there I am, twenty-nine, living in Paramus, New Jersey, I got no trade, no nothing. I've pissed away ten years of my life to this loser, and I realize, hey, I'm totally smarter than this guy. Better than him in every way you could imagine. I could just walk away, be somebody different from Mrs. Jimmy D. Mastronunzio. But, baby, the clock's running." She held her drink up to one of the halogen lamps, studied it for a minute. "So I came down here to the sunny South, got a job, went to night school down at Georgia State, I'm hustling like crazy. Self-improvement, sweetheart. Getting rid of that damn Paramus accent; learning about the difference between intaglio and screen printing; reading, you know, all these books by people I'd never heard of before; finding out about straight-line depreciation and the conjugation of *pouvoir*. All this stuff I never knew existed. I never even *knew*! And so five years later, running like hell, I've got a degree in business administration, minor in industrial graphics, a job selling ink. Whoopdee-fucking-doo. I'm doing okay for myself. But now I'm thirty-four, and the clock's running faster and faster and I still don't know what I'm looking for.

"So then I meet Charlie, you know, making a cold call one day. I don't know how it happened. Don't know why. But we did something for each other. Me—I'm young, decent looking, know my way around. He's steady, treats me with respect. Mostly. I mean, sometimes he was an asshole but at least he never threw up in my kitchen sink. I don't know why exactly, but it worked okay." The swirling thing happened in her eyes for a minute and she had to wipe them again with the back of her hand. Mae-mae started to feel a heavy, leaden feeling, like something was pressing down on her chest. "Only problem, he's married.

"It started out as just a lark for me. Marking time. Like, while I got nothing better to do? But then it starts dragging on. A year. Two years. Two and half. And I'm starting to feel like, hey, what the hell is going on here? Cause, baby, that clock's just *going*. Going and going, so you can't hardly see the hands moving around." The New Jersey accent had started to surface, twisting her Rs, thickening the vowels.

"Couple white hairs showing up on my head. Even this skinny little body of mine not holding up the way it used to. Can't do a Chinese split, can't stay underwater in the YWCA pool for a minute and a half at a time anymore." She held up one of her pale, blue-veined arms and stared at it for a while. "So I went to him one day and I said, 'Charlie, you've got to decide. Divorce her and marry me—or forget it. Right now.' "

She stared up at the bright ceiling, shook her head vaguely, her tongue probing delicately at the inside of her cheeks.

"And he said no," Mae-mae said.

Colleen smiled bitterly. "Oh, you better fucking believe he said no, sweetheart. 'I can't leave Myra,' he says. 'It would be wrong.' Myra! Imagine that. He chooses *Myra* because it would be *wrong* not to! It would be *wrong*!'' A flush had spread into her high cheekbones. "And I say, 'Alright, so be it.' I get in my car and drive home. And when I get back here I start shaking. Just shaking, you know. Not crying or anything like that—I don't know why the hell I'm telling you this—just shaking, like I got some kind of a fever. So I get under the covers and I still can't stop shaking, and I'm thinking the worst things in the world about him.'' She stubbed out her half-smoked cigarette.

"Didn't sleep a wink that night, thinking about the things I'd like to do to him, the things I'd like to do to his wife. Terrible things. Thinking, you know, knives and guns and snakes and poison and all this shit. And underneath it all there's this horrible fear. I'm thirty-seven years old and the clock's ticking, and I got nothing. *Nothing*, sweetheart.''

She paused, took a breath, went on. "The next day I couldn't get out of bed. I mean I was so afraid, I literally . . . I couldn't stand up. My legs were just so shaky, I got up—I'm serious—I tried to get up and I fell on the floor. And there was no way out. No way out. No solution. No solution but to call him up and say I'd been, you know . . . like, rash or something. Can you believe I said that? I told him I'd been *rash*. You imagine using a dumb, weak pushover of a word like that?''

Colleen picked up her thin glass. The ice had all melted. The halogen lamps threw shards of light through the drink, scattered them against the wall in trembling, luminescent threads. Colleen set the drink down again without putting it to her mouth.

"Tick tick tick tick tick.'' She clicked out the noise with her tongue.

"I know what you mean,'' Mae-mae said.

They sat there for a while, doing nothing in particular. Colleen got up, went into the kitchen, made some ice cube noises, and came back with another drink.

"Let me ask you something,'' Colleen said. "You go to the grocery store and you see all these glowing faces—you know what I mean?—these glowing faces on these women, they've always got this little boy in the little seat on the little grocery cart, and he's asking to get some kind of cereal and she won't get it because it's got too much sugar or whatever, and the kid's whining, and she's pregnant, her stomach's all poked out to here, and she's wearing this dress, this big tent, like a Laura Ashley or something? And she looks like the happiest goddamn woman in the world? You know these women I'm talking about?''

Mae-mae nodded. She knew exactly.

''I mean who are these people? Who are they?'' Colleen's green eyes were wide, uncomprehending. ''Cause I sure as hell don't know any of them.''

''I don't know,'' Mae-mae said softly. ''I've been wondering that a lot lately myself.''

And then they were both laughing. Laughing and laughing until it hurt, until they had to grab themselves to keep from popping something, and still they were laughing, and the warm tears were running down their faces. They laughed for a long time.

And when they were done, Colleen said, ''When is this gonna stop?'' And she didn't have to explain to Mae-mae what she meant by *this*.

Mae-mae knew. This sense of incompleteness. This sense that something was missing. This sense that something—something just outside the periphery of her vision—was working on her, pulling at her, laying its cool hands on her. But every time she turned around to see what it was, that nameless thing was gone.

Colleen pulled out another cigarette, set it down on the huge obsidian ashtray but didn't light it. After a while Colleen said, ''I didn't have much when I was growing up. Mom worked at this grocery, the Acme, union cashier for thirty-five years. Dad, sometimes he was around, sometimes not.''

''So when you went back to him, you asked Charles for money,'' Mae-mae said.

After she'd thought about it a minute, Colleen said, "Sure. I asked him for money. I told him if he was going to have my life, if he was going to buy it, he'd buy it with cold, hard cash. Cause the excitement of dating a fifty-five-year-old bald guy had about worn off."

"And over the course of the past year or so," Mae-mae said, "he gave you about eighty thousand dollars in cash. Would that also be true?"

Colleen looked up, squinted. "How much?"

"Eighty-two thousand is the exact number as far as I can tell."

"Uh-uh." Colleen shook her head. "Sixty-two thousand is the exact number. Not eighty-two. *Sixty*-two."

Mae-mae studied her face. She didn't look like she was hiding anything. "You didn't get a check from him for twenty thousand dollars the day before he was killed?"

"No. I didn't see him that whole week."

"One last question. What do you know about postage stamps?"

Colleen frowned, looked puzzled. "Postage stamps? You go to the post office, you pay thirty-two cents, they give you a stamp. What else is there to know?"

"What about counterfeit postage stamps? Know anything about that?"

Colleen was still squinting at her like she was missing something. "Counterfeit? Why would somebody do that?"

"Save themselves the thirty-two cents, I guess."

Colleen snorted, shook her head like it was the dumbest thing she'd ever heard of, then glanced at her watch. "Look, I have to run." She hesitated. "I've got a date."

"Yeah?" Mae-mae was surprised. Two weeks after her lover dies and she's already out on a date. And yet somehow it felt like the right thing. "Nice guy?"

"Thirty-seven. Divorced. Stockbroker. Drives a Lincoln. I met him a couple months ago. He asked me out a couple times, but I didn't say yes until this week."

"Yeah, but is he a nice guy?"

The muddy green eyes looked at the ceiling for a minute. "Honestly? He's kind of a nerd. Bow ties, for chrissake?" There was a pause, then a girlish little smile, a look of surprise around the eyes. "But, now you mention it, yeah, he's kind of sweet."

✉

THIRTEEN

So. Sixty-two grand accounted for, twenty grand still missing in action. And no closer to finding out about the counterfeit postage stamp or this offshore company, Janus.

Colleen had said that Charles Towe had acted nervous during the last few months. What was the other word she'd used? Spooky. Did that mean something or not?

Mae-mae was driving home, thinking so hard she overshot the turn from Monroe to Virginia and ended up sitting at the Ponce de Leon traffic light before she noticed where she was. She smiled. Her unconscious mind was telling her something, telling her to drop in on Chris Towe.

When the light changed, the left turn green arrow came on, pointing the way to Chris's house. Must be a sign, right? She flipped on her blinker, headed up Ponce toward Chris's place.

The porch light was on at his house, and the curtains were open in the front window. She got out of her car and walked up the steep concrete path.

When she got up to the porch, she could see Chris sitting in a chair talking to someone. He was leaned forward, his back to the door, making some sort of emphatic point, punching the air with the knuckles of his right hand.

Mae-mae paused on the front stoop, wondering if maybe now was a bad time. The front door was open. Chris's voice floated out through the screen door.

"I'm just wondering how could you let him do that to you?" Chris was saying.

"Hey, whoa, hold on," a second voice said. It was a flat female voice. "You just hold on, man. It was my decision, okay? Mine."

It took Mae-mae a second to recognize the voice. It was Rachel.

Chris's voice again: "Well then, it was a bad decision."

Rachel said, "Why is it that my whole life story is me doing things and then having men tell me I made bad decisions? Why is that, Chris?"

"Give me a break, Rachel. Okay? Don't make this into some man-woman issue, because it's not."

Mae-mae kept standing there. Should she go ahead and knock? Should she just go away? Should she keep listening? She decided to take the moral low ground, eavesdrop just a little longer. Hell, she couldn't help herself.

"Chris, I'm tired of your patronizing attitude," Rachel said.

"Well, I'm tired of cleaning up after you."

There was a long pause.

"What the hell is that supposed to mean, Chris?"

"I don't think I have to explain."

"Maybe you should."

It was frustrating listening to the conversation. She had missed the beginning and so she had no idea what they were discussing. Maybe it had something to do with their father's death.

Chris said, "Let's not get into it. I've made my objection. I think the guy's just using you. I mean, I know he can be a nice guy and all that, but I don't think he's good for you."

"Oh, I see. I should go out and find me a nice lawyer, is that the idea? Some boring jerk in a suit?"

That one stung, just a little.

"Look, Rachel," Chris said. "It so happens I know some things about him that you don't know. I'm not going to make a big deal about it, I just don't think he's the right guy for you?"

So maybe it was Clay they were talking about.

"What do you know?" Rachel said. "What do you know about him?"

"Look, it's not that big a deal, okay? I just don't think he's the right guy for you."

"Come on, spit it out."

There was no response from Chris. Mae-mae knew she ought to beat a silent retreat, but she couldn't make her feet move.

Rachel spoke again. "I know what you're going to say, so you might as well say it."

"Do you?"

"Yeah. You're going to tell me that Clay is a bad boy, that he's been in prison. Well, big deal. He doesn't make any secret about it. What he did was a long time ago, when he was just a kid—and now it's over with."

Prison. She knew there had been something about that guy that made her nervous. What had he been in prison for? That might be an interesting thing to do a little research on.

Chris didn't say anything for a while. Finally he spoke, his voice sounding a little sullen. "Well, anyway that's not the point. The point is he's exploiting you."

"Jesus, Chris, listen to yourself. Listen to yourself. You sound just like Dad."

"In spite of what you might think, that's not the worst thing in the world," Chris said quietly. Mae-mae could barely hear him.

Alright, Cosgrove, Mae-mae said to herself, get your ass off the porch.

Chris's voice said, "You know there's nothing I wouldn't do for you. Nothing." He sounded tired, drained out somehow.

"I know that," Rachel said after a minute. "I know that."

Mae-mae tiptoed down the concrete path, down the concrete stairs. By the time she reached the level of the street, she'd been swallowed up by the dark.

I'm tired of cleaning up after you. What had he meant by that?

FOURTEEN

"**T**rash!" Sebastian exclaimed. "You expect me to scrabble through the *trash*, to root through a *stinking* dumpster like some kind of flea-bitten *rodent*?"

They were in Sebastian's Volvo, driving to the gallery where he was going to have the Closterman framed. Mae-mae had spent the past twenty-four hours trying to come up with a way of finding out about the counterfeit stamps, about Janus, about the missing $20,000. And not coming up with much. Her only bright idea, such as it was, was to try hunting through the trash at Printmeister. Maybe there would be something there—an invoice, a letter from Janus, a sheet of stamps. . . .

"You don't have to help. Just drop me at Printmeister, take the Closterman to the gallery, come back and pick me up."

"What do you expect to find in the trash?"

"I'll know when I find it."

"Why not just go straight to the police?"

"Here's my thinking on what's happened," Mae-mae said. "Lester Paris and Charles Towe have been printing counterfeit stamps for a couple years, maybe longer. In any case, for several years they've been funneling the money they're making on the deal through this Janus outfit in the Netherlands Antilles, which channels it back

117

to them in the form of bogus consulting fees. And—putting aside my tricky ethical relationship to the situation as legal representative of the estate—I have zero evidence. No bags of cash, no IRS infringements, nothing to take to the police.''

"Except for the stamp on that envelope.'' Sebastian headed up Lenox, peeled off onto Rockbridge.

"Yeah, but what's that prove?''

"Well, what about the murder?'' Sebastian said. "Where does that fit in?''

"You know what I think? I think they got into a fight over their split of the profits. I think Lester killed him.''

"And Candy Frank, too?''

Mae-mae stared out the window at the dark trees streaming by. "I don't see what else could have happened,'' she said. "She calls me up, says she had found out something about him . . . and then six hours later she's dead.''

"You think he overheard her talking to you?'' Sebastian's thin face glowed red, reflecting the taillights of other cars.

"He must have. Then he probably ran her off the road.''

Sebastian drove for a while, his cheeks tense. "You have no business doing this, you know. You should take this to the police.''

"Bear with me,'' Mae-mae said.

The Volvo swung north through Buckhead, turned onto Peachtree. Neither of them said anything until they could see the big Printmeister sign in the distance.

"This makes me a bit nervous,'' Sebastian said. "I'm not much of a man of action, you know.''

"I told you, just pick me up when you're finished at the gallery.''

"My dear, you underestimate my chivalrous impulse if you think I would abandon you in the middle of the night to do mortal combat with a reeking, rat-infested dumpster.''

As they turned into the parking lot, Mae-mae pointed to a spot at the far end of the lot and said, "Okay, then park over there, turn your lights off, and wait for me."

There were two other cars in the lot, a Porsche and a tired-looking tan Dodge. A green dumpster hugged the back wall of the building. Mae-mae opened her door and said, "If somebody comes out and heads back toward the dumpster, honk your horn."

"Marvelous idea!" Sebastian exclaimed. "Then perhaps after he's brained you with a piece of printing equipment he'll come out and thrash me to death, too."

"You got any better ideas?"

"I'll come with you."

"What—in *those* clothes?"

But before they could resolve the issue, a light came on in the front room of the building and the silhouettes of two men appeared in the glass door.

"Wait!" Sebastian said.

One man came out the door. The second man flicked off the lights and followed him into the parking lot.

"That's Lester, the guy locking the door." She pointed at the second man. "The other one is a guy named Donald Rascoe. Their foreman." The parking lot was now bathed in darkness.

"Isn't *he* a lovely man."

"Yeah."

The two men spoke briefly, went to their cars. Lester dawdled around his Porsche, checking the tires. Rascoe hopped in the Dodge and sped away. As soon as Lester Paris was alone, he hurried back to the door of the shop, unlocked it, went inside.

"What do you think he went back for?" Mae-mae said.

Sebastian shook his head.

The glass door opened and Lester Paris appeared. This time he was carrying a briefcase. His face was bluish in the distant light of the street lamp near the road. He looked apprehensively around the parking lot, locked the door, and hurried back to the Porsche.

After he got in the car, Mae-mae said, "You know what I think?"

Sebastian didn't say anything.

The Porsche's back-up lights blinked on, then the car jerked into reverse, spun around, and headed for the road.

"New plan," Mae-mae said. "Forget the trash, let's follow him."

"My dear—"

"*Follow* him!"

Sebastian muttered disapprovingly, then started the Volvo and drove out onto the street.

"This is alright!" Mae-mae said. And suddenly it was kind of fun—that vertiginous, just-on-the-edge-of-falling sensation you got on the roller coaster. Or maybe clinging to a cold power pole ninety-five feet in the air.

Sebastian shifted into second, following the taillights of the Porsche—which were rapidly disappearing into the distance.

"Come on. Give it the gas."

"This is a Volvo," Sebastian said primly, "not some fire-engine-red scooter designed for men writhing in the throes of their second pubescence."

"That's exactly my point," Mae-mae said.

Sebastian sighed and gave it the gas.

The Porsche headed erratically down Peachtree, then turned south onto the 75/85 corridor. Sebastian was dropping back.

"Come on," Mae-mae said. "He's getting away."

"He's also going eighty-five miles an hour."

Soon the bright towers of downtown Atlanta were receding behind them. They passed the Fulton County Stadium on the left, then downtown was gone.

As they came over the top of a long hill, Mae-mae saw the distinctive red taillights of the Porsche swooping

down a long access ramp onto the Lakewood Freeway.
Sebastian followed. Far ahead of them the Porsche was
sweeping off the freeway and onto the Sylvan Road exit.

They were into South Atlanta now, both sides of the
highway: housing projects, tired old A.M.E. churches,
fried chicken restaurants, rundown factories and warehouses. They couldn't see that alien turf from the interstate—but they could feel it, miles and miles of it
stretching out in all directions.

"Sylvan Road?" Sebastian said. "I hope you know
where we're going."

"Never been here," Mae-mae said. She could feel her
heart beating hard, her palms sweating. This wasn't her
neck of the woods. Not by a long stretch.

"We can always go back," Sebastian said quickly.

Mae-mae hesitated. "No. Not yet."

At the bottom of the turnoff, they saw the red lights
of the Porsche turn left and duck under a bridge. A black
woman in a hair net and cutoff jeans stood under a
streetlight talking to an old, yellow-eyed guy in a Bud
Lite T-shirt. They stared at the Volvo as it stopped next
to the scarred concrete bridge. Sebastian turned left, followed the Porsche through a stoplight, past a cinder
block VW repair shop with a high chain-link fence
around it. At the bottom of the hill, the Porsche turned
right onto a street that fronted a huge prisonlike brick
warehouse surrounded by a twelve-foot razor wire—
topped fence. It seemed like there were fences around
everything.

They drove slowly down the road, past the dark hulks
of unused industrial buildings, until the Porsche turned
left into a gravel lot next to a small mud-colored building with bars over the windows and over the smudged
glass door. An illegible cracked plastic sign hung from
a tilted pole next to the road.

"Drive past and then turn your headlights off and
stop," Mae-mae said.

"My dear," Sebastian said. "I *have* read Raymond Chandler."

Mae-mae laughed as he turned off his lights and pulled over to the side of the road. Around them everything was dark. There was no traffic on the road. On one side of the mud-colored building a rusty railroad siding ran diagonally across the road. On the other side was a big fenced-in lot, full of dark shapes that might have been old cars or pieces of construction machinery. It was hard to tell. The whole area seemed to have been abandoned, given up for dead.

Lester Paris hopped out of the car with his briefcase, went up to the door of the building, and banged on it with his fist. A short black man opened the door. He wore a squashed train engineer's hat and had a Sherlock Holmes pipe wedged in his teeth.

Lester talked to him for a minute. When the black guy drew on the pipe, an orange glow spread over his features and his eyes seemed to expand, like they were going to pop out of his head. After they had talked a while, the black man took the pipe out of his mouth, tapped the crooked stem gently in the middle of Lester Paris's chest, then went inside. Lester stood next to the door, looking around nervously.

After a minute the man with the pipe came back out the door and handed Lester a white paper bag. Lester looked inside the bag, put it in his briefcase, and jumped back in his car. The man with the pipe stood for a moment, watching, then closed the glass door, securing it with a dead bolt. His eyes expanded as he pulled on his pipe. The glow of his pipe faded; his face disappeared.

The Porsche threw up some rocks, sped off, its engine snarling as it accelerated through the first bend in the road.

Sebastian, under his breath, said, "Driver, follow that car."

"You catch on quick," Mae-mae said.

The Porsche retraced its steps, driving a little slower

now, ending up back on I-85 North. They passed through downtown again, the Porsche eventually turning onto the ramps that led to the Buford Highway and Monroe exits. It was a three-tiered maze of concrete, the interstate passing over four access lanes that, in turn, looped over the underpass for the turnoff.

They followed Paris to the Monroe exit. As they made the turn, they saw the Porsche sitting near the bottom of the exit ramp, pulled off on a flat concrete surface at the side of the road. Lester Paris had turned his flashers on and was getting out of the car.

"Damn!" Mae-mae ducked down in the seat so he couldn't see her. "Just drive by and turn right," she said.

"Aye-aye, Cap'n Bly."

Sebastian stopped at the bottom of the hill next to the Porsche, rolled down his window.

"What the hell are you doing?" Mae-mae hissed.

Sebastian smiled out the window. "Problem?" he said.

"Thanks, no," Lester's voice came back. "Just a little, um, adjustment."

"So glad to hear it," Sebastian said breezily. He rolled up the window, signaled a right turn, eased off the clutch.

"You trying to give me a heart attack?" Mae-mae whispered, still crouched as close to the floorboards as she could manage. "What's he doing?" Her heart was clunking around inside her ribs.

"Can't really tell," Sebastian said as he made the turn. He drove a couple hundred feet, turned off his lights.

Mae-mae sat up.

They were underneath the interstate now, in a bleak, dirty, concrete world. Huge cylindrical pylons extended forty feet into the air, supporting the twelve lanes of interstate highway, the murky concrete sky. A few tiny trees had tried to grow up out of the concrete, ruined and dwarfish twigs that sprouted only the occasional brownish leaf. The place was dead, moonlike. Sebastian turned off the ignition. A steady rising and falling hum, like the grumbling of giants, enveloped them: cars and trucks tearing by over their heads.

They were hidden from Lester Paris now, cut off from his view by a row of pylons. Mae-mae jumped out of the car, skirted the row of pylons, peeked out at the space next to the off ramp where Lester was parked.

Evidently satisfied that he was alone, Lester had set his briefcase on the hood of the car, taken out the white paper sack, and was dumping its contents onto the sidewalk. It was hard to tell in the dim light what was in the bag. The surface of the concrete pylon was cool and rough against Mae-mae's cheek.

Lester dug a small plastic bottle out of the Porsche, opened the top, and squirted some kind of liquid on the stuff he had dumped out of the sack. When he finished with the liquid, he lit a match and tossed it on the pile. It blazed immediately into flame, lighting up Lester's face. The flames threw a huge, wavering shadow of Lester against the concrete underpass.

Lester stared at the flames. After a moment they receded. He squirted more lighter fluid on the pile. The fire climbed up the stream of fluid, and Lester waved it around like a wand of flame. The fire kicked up, and Mae-mae could see Lester Paris grinning, talking to himself, the flickering yellow light gleaming off his teeth and eyes. She couldn't hear anything though, with the thunder from the interstate above her. He threw the bottle of lighter fluid down next to the blaze, walked slowly back to the Porsche, and got in. The lights flicked on. Lester backed up, dropped the Porsche into first, and the tires howled as he jumped the curb, climbed back onto the ramp, and disappeared onto the interstate.

"This is it!" Mae-mae yelled, waving her arms to Sebastian.

He fired up the Volvo, made a careful U-turn, and

drove up next to her. Mae-mae jumped in and Sebastian pulled around and parked next to the little fire. They got out of the car and stood next to the fire, staring at its flickering core.

Sebastian leaned toward the fire, his hand over his face. "It appears to be paper."

"Stamps! It's got to be the stamps," Mae-mae said. It was hard to see. She picked up a Mountain Dew bottle off the ground and prodded the fiery mound, singeing her hand. The ashes shifted and through the flames she saw a sheaf of paper. They were stamps alright, but they were facedown so she couldn't see what was printed on them. She kicked the flaming mound, knocking over the bottle of lighter fluid and throwing several sheets of paper free of the fire. She grabbed a couple of them, blew out the fire that had started on one edge, and walked across the road where a streetlight would let her see better. Sebastian followed.

Stamps—two sheets of them. An American flag waving over Mount Rushmore. Thirty-two-cent stamps.

She handed one to Sebastian. "What do you think?" she said.

Sebastian peered at the tiny prints and said, "They did a better job on these, didn't they?" He folded the sheet into quarters and slipped it in the pocket of his jacket.

Mae-mae was about to agree, but before she had a chance to say anything there was a soft noise behind them, like a child falling into a swimming pool. They turned and looked for the source of the noise.

It was the Volvo. Or rather it was underneath the Volvo. A large puddle of flame had gathered under the car and was spreading into the street.

"The lighter fluid," Mae-mae said.

"I forgot to close my door. It's going to get in the car."

She ran around to the other side of the car, but it was too late. The falling child noise—it had been the sound of the lighter fluid bottle exploding. Burning fluid had been hurled into the car, and the front seat was on fire. Acrid black smoke was starting to fill the interior of the Volvo.

Mae-mae looked at Sebastian helplessly. Under the hood, something popped and a second wave of flames spread under the car.

"Damn it. I think it hit the fuel line," Sebastian said.

"What do we do?" Mae-mae said. Inside the car, the fire was brighter, the smoke thicker. Flames licked six or seven feet into the air.

"My Volvo," Sebastian said in a choked voice. "My beautiful Volvo."

"Maybe it'll burn out in a minute," Mae-mae said. It didn't show any sign of that, though.

Sebastian approached the car, circled the fire, staring helplessly. There were more popping noises and still the burning liquid under the car continued to spread. At the front of the car, the flames were shooting six or eight feet in the air, the paint blistering and peeling on the doors.

"Oh my God," Sebastian said suddenly. His gaunt face had suddenly gone a sick white. "The Closterman."

"The Closterman?"

"In the trunk!" Sebastian stared at the flames, horrified. "The Closterman is in the trunk."

Mae-mae had forgotten about the portrait.

"The Closterman! The Closterman!" Sebastian was almost screaming now. He pulled his car keys from the pocket of his jacket. "I've got to get it!"

"Well, hurry up," Mae-mae said, eyeing the flames. The whole front of the car was engulfed now. A long flame darted out from under the rear. "Wait!" Mae-mae grabbed his arm as he started to run toward the burning Volvo.

Sebastian was stronger, though; he broke free easily and ran straight toward the fire.

"Sebastian, no!"

But Sebastian wasn't listening. A fierce, concentrated look had spread across his face. Aside from that first lick of flame, there had been no fire coming out from under the trunk—but the air writhed around it, heat rising from under the Volvo. Maybe he still had time. Sebastian reached the car, fumbled at the trunk lock with his key.

A loud bang reverberated through the concrete space as one of the front tires exploded. The whole car shuddered and Sebastian stabbed at the trunk lid with his key, holding one hand in front of his eyes to keep the heat away from his face. Evidently the heat was so intense that he couldn't see. A loud puffing noise cut through the night, and one of the front windows shattered. A plume of fire shot out where the glass had been.

"Don't, Sebastian, don't!" Mae-mae screamed. But she could tell that Sebastian didn't hear. The Closterman was the only thing that mattered. "It's too late!"

The key finally made it into the lock, and Sebastian threw open the lid. Smoke was pouring out from under the rear of the car. He bent over, scrabbled around inside the trunk, trying to move something that he must have wedged on top of the portrait.

Another window shattered. Another plume of flame shot into the air and a gout of black, oily smoke poured out from under the car, obscuring Sebastian from view. For a moment, Mae-mae could see nothing but smoke and flame. Even from thirty feet away she could feel the heat on her face now.

A loud bang hammered her eardrums and there was more flame—this time from the rear of the Volvo, the place where Sebastian stood. Mae-mae couldn't stand it anymore. She started running toward the car. An oppressive wave of heat rolled toward her, searing her face and making it almost impossible to breathe.

Just as she thought she could go no farther, a shape burst from the smoke: Sebastian, the brown parcel containing the Closterman clutched to his chest. As he staggered forward a halo seemed to form around him, illuminating his torso and head. His eyes were lit up with a blind ecstasy, his face flushed and shining—like a crazed ascetic medieval saint.

At first Mae-mae thought the halo was an optical illusion of some sort, but once he cleared the smoke, she saw what it was. It was no halo: Sebastian was on fire, his coat and pants alive with dancing flames. The flames leaped and spurted, and then the Closterman was burning, too.

"Save it!" Sebastian screamed. "Save the Closterman!" A sheet of flame raced up the surface of the packing that surrounded the portrait.

Mae-mae grabbed the picture, flung it to the ground, then grabbed Sebastian and yanked him down onto the concrete, too. "Roll, Sebastian," she said. Sebastian started to crawl toward the Closterman. His back was on fire. "Roll, Sebastian. Roll over, damn you!" But he just kept crawling toward the dark package on the ground. Mae-mae planted her foot on his hip and heaved, rolling him over onto his back. He righted himself immediately, his wild eyes still intent on the Closterman.

The fire on his back had gone out, though. His jacket and pants smoldered fitfully. He would be okay.

Sebastian reached the picture, grabbed it with both hands. It, too, had ceased burning, the fire put out when Mae-mae threw the package on the ground. Sebastian sat up, turned the picture around. The packing paper had burned off entirely, but miraculously Closterman's drawing seemed unharmed.

Sebastian stared at the picture for a long time, his body heaped on the concrete, knees and elbows pointing in all directions.

"Are you okay, Sebastian?" Mae-mae said.

Sebastian stared at the sad, ancient face of the earl of Northumberland.

"Sebastian! Are you alright?"

Sebastian turned and smiled a bright, startling smile. His face was burned red, smudged with smoke, and his eyebrows and eyelashes had been singed off. He looked as happy as she'd ever seen him.

"Yes," he said. "We're quite fine."

Then he seemed to forget her entirely, and his gaze swung slowly back to the picture. Across the centuries the man in the big hat smiled sweetly, sadly back at him.

FIFTEEN

"It was just a freak accident," Mae-mae said.

"Sure, counselor. Freak accident," Dick Clark said.

He was chewing on a Bic pen, looking at her with his eyes narrowed, his detective shield dangling from his belt. The sign on his desk still said this wasn't American Bandstand. Now that it was nighttime, the big room was full of detectives, full of bedraggled life. Most of the people in the station looked dismal and unhappy, talking in high voices and having to be calmed down, or else mumbling, not talking loud enough for the detectives to understand them. A couple people had blood on their faces or their clothes. Witnesses, people under arrest—they all sort of looked the same here.

"We stopped to look at this fire that Lester Paris had set on the side of the road," Mae-mae said. "Then this can of lighter fluid blew up and caught the car on fire."

"You're saying Lester Paris stopped under a bridge, set him a little bonfire, and drove off."

"Right," Mae-mae said.

"And what did he set fire to?"

"A big pile of thirty-two-cent stamps."

Dick Clark nodded soberly and looked up at the ceiling, his jaw working on the Bic pen. It looked like a huge, foolish cigarette sticking out of his mouth.

"Are you writing this down?" Mae-Mae said.

"After I get the whole story, sure." Dick Clark paused, did his American Bandstand smile. "If it merits writing down, I mean."

"You didn't have to say that," Mae-mae said. "You could have just played along, you know, pretended like you were going to pay attention."

Dick Clark yawned. "I suppose you're right," he said. He took the Bic pen out of his mouth, pointed it vaguely around the room. "You get used to all these people lying to you, wasting your time, then you start getting a little too slow to listen every now and then." He stuck the pen back in his mouth. "You know why Mr. Paris was burning a bunch of postage stamps under the interstate—please go ahead, tell me. I'm real interested to know why he would do this."

"They were counterfeit. He was burning the evidence."

Dick Clark nodded again. He seemed to be working hard to keep from having any particular expression on face. "Counterfeit postage stamps. What'll they think of next?" Then he turned on the American Bandstand smile for a minute.

"You don't believe me, take a look at this." Mae-mae opened her leather purse, rummaged around for the stamps she'd saved from the pile. "They're here," she said hotly. "I know they're here." Only she couldn't find them. Where the hell were they?

She poured the whole contents of her purse out on the desk. Tampons, old laundry tickets, a grocery list, two tubes of lipstick, a pair of Ray-Bans with one ear piece held on by a paper clip, a small bottle of contact lens solution, assorted change, two Trojans—oops—a monstrous rubber band, and half a dozen bobby pins. Also a yo-yo, the kind that lit up when you played with it. Where had that come from? There were no thirty-two-cent stamps, bogus or otherwise.

Dick Clark chewed patiently, the pen bobbing up and down in his mouth. "Yo-yo?" he said.

Mae-mae looked bleakly at the pile of worn ephemera, swept it brusquely back into her purse. "I don't know," she said. "I had them in my hand not even an hour ago."

Dick Clark asked her some more questions; Mae-mae answered. But somehow, the way he asked them, it made everything she said sound inadequate and stupid. Did they train these guys to be that way? She felt all bottled up and tight inside suddenly, like she needed to yell at somebody. What had happened to those damn stamps? It kept bugging her, running through her mind: if she just had the stamps, he'd take her seriously. What had happened to them?

When they had about wrapped up the question-and-answer session, Dick Clark said, "Well anyway, looks like your friend's okay. Just some superficial burns and a little bit of shock."

"Good," Mae-mae said.

As she got up to leave, Dick Clark said, "Oh, the EMTs said your friend kept saying somebody's name when they were taking him down to Piedmont Hospital. I checked in the phone book, information, unlisted, everything, couldn't locate the guy."

"What was his name?"

Dick Clark licked his finger, opened his notebook, and stared at the page for a minute. He took the Bic pen out of his mouth and looked up at Mae-mae. "You ever heard of a guy by the name of John Closterman?"

After she left the police station, Mae-mae drove back and parked under the interstate. It was well past midnight by then, as dark and bleak and lonely as it had been before, but the thunder of wheels continued above her, nonstop, a deep, jarring noise that she could feel in her chest.

It wasn't a fun place down there, not at twelve twenty-five at night. Not when you're a soft hundred and thirty-one pounds and completely alone. But she had to find those stamps, just had to.

Mae-mae got out of her Accord and walked over to the wet, greasy black patch of concrete where Sebastian's Volvo had ended its days. They'd put the fire out and hauled the burned hulk away already. Everything on the black patch had been burned completely to ash—or else washed away by the firefighters' spray.

There was no trace of the stamps.

The dark desert of concrete, the brooding rumble of the interstate, the forest of massive concrete pylons—man, it was spooky. To her left the dark underpass leading to Monroe intersected with the access spur of the highway; above her, twelve lanes of concrete interstate. To her right, a few hundred yards away, there were a couple of warehouses, a gas station, a deserted road. Behind one of the dark buildings, a man was scrabbling through a dumpster.

Mae-mae thought back to what had happened earlier that night, went over it step by step in her mind.

She had taken the stamps across the street to look at them more clearly. Then the can of lighter fluid had blown up. Then she had gone over to try and shut the door, retreating as the fire spread. Then Sebastian had gone over to the trunk to get the Closterman. Did she still have the stamps at that point? She couldn't remember. She must have dropped them.

Where had she been standing? Across the road, right under the streetlight. She walked back across the road, stood in the yellow sodium glow, looked around. No stamps. She felt very exposed, like somebody was watching her. But there was nobody behind the pylons, nobody under the bridge, nobody hanging around her car.

Down the street, though, walking toward her, she saw the man who'd been hunting through the dumpster—a great big guy with a long beard and a floppy, shambling walk. He carried a large garbage bag and wore a wretched looking cowboy hat and a see-through plastic rain slicker with flowers printed on it.

Find the damn stamps and get out of here, Mae-mae was thinking. Close encounters with street people, that ain't on the agenda. Not this time of night.

Okay. Okay. She'd crossed the street, looked at the stamps, gone back to the car . . . then what?

She had yelled at Sebastian. Then Sebastian came out with the painting. He was on fire and he was holding the Closterman. She grabbed the drawing and threw it on the ground.

That was it! She must have thrown the stamps down at the same time she threw down the picture. But there were no stamps on the sidewalk, no stamps blown up against the streetlight pole. On the other side of the sidewalk was a wasteland of scraggly grass, stony dirt, broken bottles, and trash, massive pylons rearing up here and there to meet the concrete sky.

Mae-mae climbed clumsily over the low metal guardrail—what fool had invented high heels anyway?—and looked around. Smashed Styrofoam cups, bottles of Night Train and MD 20-20, twenty-four-ounce Colt 45 malt liquor cans. But no stamps. She kept looking, circling out and out from the street lamp. Maybe the wind had blown them somewhere.

"Hey!" a loud voice said. "Looking for something?"

Mae-mae turned around, heart jumping. Damn. There, standing at the guardrail directly between Mae-mae and her car, was the guy in the cowboy hat and the flowered plastic slicker. He was even bigger than he'd seemed from a distance. A slice of hairy white belly stuck out of his stained shirt, and a wet glistening trail of . . . something . . . ran down the side of his beard. His eyes were open too wide, and he didn't take them off Mae-mae's face, not even for a second.

"Oh, hi," Mae-mae said weakly.

"What you looking for?" the cowboy said insistently.

"Stamps," Mae-mae said softly.

"What?"

"Stamps. I lost some postage stamps here earlier to-day."

The big man ran his hand through his beard, then wiped his hand on his pants. "It was a big ole fire here, man. Hell of a big fire." The giant cowboy smiled, showing off his ruined teeth. "Maybe they got burnt up."

"They did get burned a little," Mae-mae said. "They got burned around the edges."

"Uh-huh. Uh-huh. Fire, man," the big man said, "whole world end in fire." He adjusted his beat-up cowboy hat, sitting it straight up on his head. He was still staring at her.

Mae-mae edged slowly toward the guardrail. The big man moved, too, keeping between her and the car.

"Stamps." He grinned again, then the smile went away. "I knew a girl once, died in a fire. Looked a lot like you, too." He squinted at her. "It could happen to anybody, man. Burn up, disappear, they never see you again."

Mae-mae looked around, hoping a car might be coming from somewhere.

Nothing. The whole place, deserted.

The big man opened his bag, hunted around in it, pulled something out. She couldn't see what was in his hand. He closed the bag, holding his hand behind his back.

Mae-mae climbed over the guardrail. The big man was sitting on the trunk of her car now, the big loose grin pasted to his face.

"I got something for you," he said.

"What do you want?" Mae-mae said. "Just get off my car, I'll give you whatever you want."

"Ee-ternal life," the man said. He pushed up the brim of his hat. "You give me eternal life?"

Mae-mae walked toward the car. The big man edged

around onto the sidewalk. She could smell him now, the rancid, fatty stink of absolute poverty.

"Sure. I'll give you eternal life," Mae-mae said. "If you let me get in the car."

The man stopped smiling. "You think I'm some kind of asshole, huh?" he said. "Some kind of out-of-touch-with-reality fool? You think I forgot to take my goddamn Thorazine!"

"No. No. I don't think that." Not knowing what to say, just wanting the guy to get out of her way, let her get in the car.

"I got news for you, I had enough of reality. I have. There ain't a god*damn* thing I like about reality. It's all heartaches, frustration, people making a fool out of you."

Mae-mae's muscles didn't want to move. Her bladder seemed bloated and full all of a sudden.

"Hey, I'll give you a little something you might like." The foolish grin went on then off, on then off. The eyes were still open too wide, staring.

"That's okay. Just let me get in the car."

The big man took his hand out from behind his back. His fist seemed to be about the size of Mae-mae's head. Something in his hand caught the light. A knife? She couldn't tell.

"Five bucks," the big man said. "Give me five bucks, help tide me over."

Tide him over till *what*? Mae-mae had a cold, paralyzed feeling in her knees that started moving up her legs. Her heart was straining, not happy with the situation. "My purse is in the car."

"Why, hell, maybe I'll just get it myself," the cowboy said. He opened the door, scrabbled around in the car, came out with her purse. "Five bucks. Five bucks. Square deal. Fair price. Five bucks." The man was mumbling, taking things out of her purse. He took out the condoms, Jesus Christ, waved them around. The cold feeling in Mae-mae's knees had crept up into her spine.

"Lubricated, shit yeah." The guy was grinning, waving the condoms. "Don't mind if I help myself to a couple, do you, sweetheart? Ain't gone lubricated in years."

Mae-mae couldn't make her voice do anything.

He stuffed the Trojans in the pocket of his stained pants, started going through the purse again, came out with her red wallet, unfastened the catch, took five dollars out, then stood there beside the Honda, staring into the wallet.

"Can I go now?" she said. Her voice sounded high and funny.

"You got a bunch of money in here," the man said.

"Take it. I don't care."

The man looked up at her with his wild eyes, smiled. "That's mighty white of you," he said, and took out the rest of the money—seven dollars in ones. There went her gas budget for the week. He dropped the wallet back in the purse, handed it to Mae-mae, moved out of the way. Mae-mae took the purse, staggered past him, and fell into the car. She dug into the purse, trying to get at her keys.

"Hey, lady?" the man said.

Mae-mae ignored him. Where were the goddamn keys?

"Lady!" Angry now. She found the keys, looked up to see a huge, threatening fist coming slowly through the window. The smell of the man was overpowering.

She turned the key and the old Honda made a noise—*whack-a-whack-a-whack-a*—but wouldn't catch.

"Hey, lady!"

Whack-a-whack-a-whack-a-shiiiink-a-whack.

"Lookee what I got, man." The fist was right up against her face. There was a white-rimmed sore on the back of the big hand.

Mae-mae looked into the big man's face. "What!" she said. "For Godsake, what?"

The hairy fist opened, inches from her eyes. Inside the

fist, crumpled, burned on one side but recognizable . . . a wad of stamps.

She stared for a minute, smelling the guy.

"Square deal," he said amicably.

Mae-mae hesitated, took the stamps from his hand, uncrumpled them. American flags waving over Mount Rushmore. Thirty-two cents.

"Well . . . thanks," Mae-mae said, her heart rate dropping a notch or two. She turned the key and the Honda cranked right up. The radio came on, Alan Jackson doing "Here in the Real World."

"Hey, man," the big guy said, "I sure do love that song."

"Kind of depressing though," Mae-mae said. "I like 'Chasin' That Neon Rainbow' better."

Then she jammed the Honda into first gear, screeched through the red light and up the on ramp. In her rearview mirror she saw the giant in his flowered rain slicker, his face glowing crimson from the stoplight, staring after her as she drove away.

He was playing air guitar and mouthing the words to "Here in the Real World," the ruined Stetson sitting straight up on his head. It was a sad song. The chorus told about how real life wasn't like the movies where everything worked out neat and happy and squared off. The big man was singing the part about how when real hearts got broken, it was real tears that fell, words to that effect.

When Mae-mae got back to her house, she found a small bouquet of red roses shoved into the handle of her door. The note taped to the green tissue paper wrapped around the stems said: *Sorry I was such a jerk the other night. I guess this whole thing with Dad has got me wound up a little tight. Can I apologize over dinner soon?*

The note was signed by Chris.

Mae-mae slumped against the door frame. Too much stuff happening tonight, she thought vaguely. Too much.

SIXTEEN

The next morning Mae-mae drove by Printmeister with the bogus stamps in her purse. When she walked into the reception area, Donald Rascoe, the guy with the rotten fish face, was pouring himself a cup of coffee.

He looked at her for a long moment, just enough to make her uncomfortable, then said, "Need something?"

"I was hoping to see Lester Paris."

"Not here."

"You know where he is?"

Donald Rascoe shrugged dismissively. "Calling on customers, most likely. You can talk to me, I guess, if you want to. Pretty much everybody else around here's dead." He didn't seem all that broken up about this fact.

"That's okay," Mae-mae said. "I'll catch him later."

Donald Rascoe took a sip of his coffee, grimaced. Without saying another word, he turned and walked out of the room.

Back at the office, Mae-mae tried to get hold of Dick Clark to tell him about the stamps, but he wasn't at the station. When she'd gotten a meeting out of the way— an earnest young couple who seemed disproportionately anxious about setting up a trust so as to meet the cost of putting their as-yet-unconceived child through Choate and Harvard—she called the detective again. He was still out.

After lunch she went to see Sebastian at the hospital, but he had already signed the forms and gone home.

At two she had an appointment at Garry Hull's office to go over some ideas he had for a direct mail piece. When she got there, Hull was up on top of his conference table, dancing.

"A remake of *Singing in the Rain*," he said, striking a pose. "What do you think?"

Mae-mae watched Garry shuffle around on his big table a little more before she said, "I don't think Broadway's quite that desperate yet."

"Sadly, you're probably right." Hull pretended to wipe away a tear and then jumped off the table. "Okay, here's what we've got for you. Couple different concepts, absolutely gonna knock your socks off." He pulled a sheaf of sketches out of a briefcase, set them one by one down the length of the table.

"Concept one," Hull said, pointing to a picture of a beach sketched in various neon shades of colored pencil. A triangle of gray cardboard stuck up out of a slit cut in the blue water. At the top of the page, big pink letters said, *The Best Defense Against Sharks? Dry Land.* "Get it?" Garry Hull said. "Safe haven kind of thing. Avoid the sharks—you know, sleazy stockbrokers, dishonest insurance peddlers, blah blah blah, by hiring an independent legal adviser, someone who could put everything in perspective. That's you. Down here it says: legal and tax experience, no commissions, no conflict of interest, et cetera."

"Dry land?" Mae-mae said. "I'm supposed to be *dry land?* That's a fairly lame metaphor, don't you think?"

"Yeah, but check this out," Hull said. "Audience participation kind of thing." He reached down and pulled on a small cardboard tab extending out of the bottom of the page. The gray shark fin bobbed up and down. Hull raised his eyebrows and grinned. "Neat, huh?"

"How much?"

"Oh, buck fifty, buck seventy-five a piece, tops. Plus a little labor for assembly, sticking the shark fins in the hole."

Mae-mae made a face. "I thought we were trying to keep this under seventy-five cents. For the whole package."

"True," Hull said. He looked disappointed. "Kind of lacks that lawyerly stateliness, too. Just thought I'd run it by you anyway." He wadded up the page, shark fin and all, lobbed it at a wastepaper basket across the room.

"Concept two?" Mae-mae said, looking at the next drawing. There was a cartoon of a man holding a gun to his own head. Scattered on the floor around him were pieces of paper that said 1040. "Hmmmmmmm," she said. "Kind of downer, huh?"

Hull didn't say anything, just wadded it up, tossed it at the wastebasket. It banked off the wall and rolled to a stop at Mae-mae's feet. Mae-mae picked it up, threw it straight into the trash.

"Nice shot," Garry Hull said.

"Junk mail," Mae-mae said. "It keeps me in practice."

"That sure gives me a shiver of professional pride." Garry pointed to the next sketch. "Number three."

"This one's cheap?"

"This one's cheap."

Concept three was a single piece of paper. At the top a headline said: THIS IS THE LAST TIME YOU'LL BE IN-VOLVED IN A LEGAL RIP-OFF! Underneath that were some wavy lines that were supposed to represent snappy ad copy. At the bottom of the paper was a dotted line with a coupon underneath. At the top of the coupon it said: *RIP THIS OFF . . . and get a FREE half hour of tax or estate law consultation!*

Mae-mae said, "I was kind of thinking of something more . . ."

Garry Hull looked at her for a minute. "Staid," he said.

"Conservative," Mae-mae said.

Hull wadded up concept three, threw it at the wastebasket. "Moving on," he said, "to our final effort."

Mae-mae picked up the last piece, a simple trifold brochure. On the outside was a pencil sketch, a smiling family standing in front of a big house. Underneath, lettered in Spencerian script, the copy read:

> You're smart.
> You're educated.
> You're well-paid.

She opened to the next page. It said:

> SO WHY AREN'T
> YOU IN CONTROL
> OF YOUR MONEY?

Mae-mae closed concept four, tossed it on the table. Boy, did that tell the whole depressing story? Car payments, house payments, vacation, clothes, throw in some day care and some Pampers if you had a kid—and come the end of the month, the checkbook was always racing down toward zero. The piece was right smack on the money.

"I wouldn't exactly call it conservative," she said.

Hull's face fell. "You don't like it."

"How soon can we get it in the mail?" Mae-mae said.

Hull looked at her for a minute, his Einstein hair floating dreamily around his face. "You like it?" he said finally. "You really really like it?"

"Throw in some copy about, you know, legal ways of sheltering money from taxes, a little about the importance of estate planning for high net worth individuals, it'll be great."

Hull did a little soft shoe thing. It was like being around a precocious, weird ten-year-old. Mae-mae grinned, couldn't help herself.

"Let's talk money," she said.

"Always gets down to that, doesn't it," Garry Hull said glumly.

Mae-mae nodded. She had an urge to mention, while they were on the subject of money, that she didn't have a clue how she was going to pay for all this stuff. But, what the hell, there'd be time to worry about that later.

They talked about ways of saving money, types of paper, mailing lists and so on. When they were done, Hull wrote down some numbers on the back of an envelope, added them up, and said, "I'll have to get some bids to be sure, but looks like best we can do, ten thousand of these things, is about ninety-three, ninety-four, ninety-five cents a piece."

Ten grand. Where was ten grand supposed to come from? Maybe she could borrow it from her father. And then she'd never hear the end of it. "College degree, law degree, I'd of thought you'd have a decent job, a little money in the bank by now"—all that kind of thing.

"Nothing else you can think of to bring the price down?" she said.

"Not really."

She tried a joke. "Suppose I could supply you with counterfeit thirty-two-cent stamps."

Garry Hull stared at her for a minute. "I'd tell you the same thing I told a guy a couple months ago. Forget it."

"Are you serious?"

"Damn right. Mess with the post office, they'll put you in jail and throw away the key."

"No," Mae-mae said. "I mean, are you saying somebody wanted you to send out a mailing with counterfeit stamps?"

Hull studied her face for a minute, then nodded.

"Would you mind telling me who it was, Garry?"

He looked thoughtfully up at the wall, then shook his head. "No, I probably shouldn't do that. All I can say, a guy who does a lot of bulk mail said he knew a guy who knew a guy—that kind of thing—who could sell him postage stamps, any quantity he wanted, fifteen cents on the dollar. I told him it was a dumb idea and he didn't pursue it."

Mae-mae sat down in a seat and thought about it for a minute. That answered a lot of questions. At first she couldn't understand why anyone would bother to forge postage stamps. Who would you sell them to? How would you sell them? What would somebody do with them if they got hold of them in the first place? But all of a sudden it started to make sense.

"Follow along with me for a second," Mae-mae said.

"Okay."

"Let's say you're in the direct mail business, sending out mailings that cost a dollar a pop and your profit margin was ten percent. Is that a reasonable number, ten percent?"

"Sure."

"So you could cut fifteen, twenty percent of your marketing costs by using a fake stamp, right? Which means that in one fell swoop you're putting thousands more dollars in your pocket."

Garry Hull nodded.

"Okay, and there are probably dozens of companies in Atlanta alone that send out a couple million pieces of mail a year, right?"

"Easily."

"So counterfeit postage stamps could be worth, what, hundreds of thousands of dollars a year to each of them, couldn't they?"

Garry Hull was looking at her, his eyes huge and worried behind his thick glasses. "You aren't seriously considering this?"

"Garry," she said. "You mind if I use your phone?"

SEVENTEEN

$\mathbf{Y}$es, the receptionist said, Mr. Paris was in the office. Would Miss Cosgrove like to hold? No, Miss Cosgrove wouldn't, thanks. Mae-mae left Garry Hull to finish his *Bye-Bye Birdie* medley by himself and drove straight to Printmeister.

She wasn't sure what she was going to say to Paris until she was sitting across the desk from him. He was smiling at her, the same kind of bland smile you'd give to a pleasant but tedious child.

Mae-mae looked for a moment at the soft insincere smile, the soft insincere face and said, "How's the counterfeiting business?"

No change in the pleasant, patronizing look on his face. "Counterfeiting?" Lester Paris shifted forward in his chair and put his elbows on his desk. The way he said it, it was like he had read the word once or twice in a book but never quite figured out what it meant.

"Counter . . . feiting," Mae-mae said slowly.

Lester Paris tried a new approach, chuckling like she'd just told a slightly naughty joke. "I wish we *were* doing some of that. It'd sure make paying the light bill a lot less painful, wouldn't it?"

Mae-mae just looked at him.

Lester let the smile fade away, replacing it with a look

145

of presidential gravity. He touched an index finger and a thumb delicately to the corners of his mustache. "You're being serious?" he said.

"I saw you with the stamps," Mae-mae said. "I saw you pick them up from the guy down near Lakewood Freeway. I saw you burn them."

Lester's face twitched, once, a muscle somewhere near the eyes. Otherwise nothing changed. "I'm afraid I don't know what you're talking about. Are you saying you followed me yesterday?"

"Mm-hm."

"You saw me go to East Point?"

"Mm-hm."

"You saw me pick something up?"

"Mm-hm."

"You saw me take something out of my briefcase and burn it?"

"Right again."

"And for some reason you think I was burning—what?—some kind of counterfeit stamps or something. Is that what you're saying?"

"That's what I'm saying."

"I see." Lester Paris rocked back in his chair, stared at the ceiling, played with his mustache—tamping on it gently with the tips of his fingers. Finally he laughed a little, ho ho ho, like the Baptist preacher when he hears a joke that's just a teensy bit off-color.

Mae-mae decided to let him sit there, see what he'd come up with. After a while the off-color-joke face faded.

"This is some kind of negotiating ploy?" he said finally. "You want me to buy Myra's half of Printmeister, right?" Mae-mae didn't move. She could feel her heart going—*fip fip fip*—inside her rib cage. "You think if you threaten me, you can get some kind of sweetheart deal for Myra, is that it? Maybe a little side money, too, something to line your own pockets?" Lester smiled. "Be perfectly honest, I imagine the American Bar Association, I bet they kind of frown on this type of tactic.''

Mae-mae said. ''You think I'd make these accusations without proof? You think I'm that stupid?''

Lester digested this, eyes on the ceiling for a minute. ''So Candy told you more than you let on the other day, huh?'' Lester's lips curled like dried leaves, formed slowly into a thin, peevish smile. ''Such a shame about her accident. Anything she might have told you is pretty much hearsay now. Wouldn't amount to much in a court of law, would it?''

''I don't know if counterfeiting is what interests me most in the first place,'' Mae-mae said.

Lester's eyes narrowed. ''Oh?''

''Counterfeiting's a pretty bad thing.'' She crossed her arms, looked him in the eye, and tried out her own patronizing voice. ''But murder. Murder, Lester, that's a very, very bad thing.''

''Murder!'' Lester's eyes widened. It seemed like the first genuine expression she'd ever seen cross his face. ''What are you talking about, *murder*?''

''I'm talking about killing your partner to get his share of the profits of your counterfeiting venture. I'm also talking about killing Candy—running her off the road, whatever you did—so she wouldn't talk to me.''

Lester made a face like he was thinking. Then he said, ''You ever think to find out where I was on the night Charlie was murdered?''

Mae-mae hadn't.

''It just so happens I was on a fishing trip with my cousin Dale. Ask the police. They got like eight witnesses. Go ahead, the police are satisfied it wasn't me killed Charlie.''

''So you hired somebody,'' Mae-mae said. ''It's pretty much the same thing.''

''I'm tired of listening to this. Get out of here.'' Lester's voice had risen a little and his face had turned red. He stood up, pointed at the door. ''Get out of here right now! I've heard enough crazy bullshit for one after-noon.''

"I'm going to the police now, Lester."

"Go ahead! Go ahead!" Lester said. Then he laughed softly and sat back down in his big chair. The red slowly drained from his face. "You want murder, you got to have motive. The only way you could prove motive is if you could prove we were counterfeiting. And you can't prove that. You know why? Because there's no evidence. Not one shred." He seemed suddenly as calm and self-possessed as he'd been when Mae-mae first came into his office.

Mae-mae stood, opened the office door, and reached into her purse. With the door open, she could hear the printing machinery clearly now, thumping through the wall. "Motive?" she said. She pulled a partly burned set of thirty-two-cent stamps from her purse. "There's your motive."

Lester's face turned a jaundiced pale shade. "That's not possible," he said, his voice shriveled to a scratchy whine. "I burned them. I burned them! I poured half a can of lighter fluid on those goddamn things and I burned them *all*."

Mae-mae hoisted her eyebrows a little and said, "Maybe you should have used the whole can."

She turned quickly, glimpsed a flash of white face at the far end of the hallway, a face like a rotten fish. Ras-coe. Donald Rascoe, watching her.

And then she was walking down the hall as fast as she could. She felt the black fish eyes pinned to her back as she headed for the far door. She wondered if he had been listening to their conversation, then decided that, no, it had probably been too noisy out there in the hall-way for him to hear anything.

"Wait! Wait!" Lester's voice hurtled down the hall-way after her. "We can deal! We can make a . . ." But by the time she had reached the end of the hall, his voice was lost in the muffled clatter of machinery.

The thing that struck her when she got to her car—the whole time she'd been in there, Lester Paris hadn't looked at her boobs a single time. Not once.

EIGHTEEN

It occurred to Mae-mae that maybe she ought to put the stamps someplace safer than her purse, so she dropped by her house, slipped the stamps into the middle of an old legal textbook—Epstein's *Debtors and Creditors*—the tops of the stamps barely peeking out above the binding. Then she went back to work.

When she got to the office, she found a manila envelope propped against her door. It was addressed to Charles Towe, care of Colleen Mastronunzio, street address the same as her apartment. There was a Post-it note stuck on the outside that said:

> To Mae-mae Cosgrove,
>
> I got this in the mail a couple of days before Charlie was killed. Don't know what's in it. Maybe something related to the estate, maybe not. In any case if it's something Myra should have, I trust you'll handle it discreetly.

The note was signed, *Thanks (really), Colleen*. The envelope didn't appear to have been opened. Mae-mae looked at the envelope distractedly. Just as she was about to open it, the phone rang.

It was Dick Clark. After some preliminary chitchat, the detective said, "Tell you what, I'm on my way out to track down a witness, got something I need to mention to you. How about if I dropped by your office for a couple minutes?"

Mae-mae said that would be just fine.

Dick Clark came in smiling, too full of good cheer to be strictly believable. Mae-mae took him into her office and sat down. The detective stood by the window and looked out.

"Wow! What a *view*, huh?" Small horizontal wrinkles worked their way out from the vent on the back of his blue suit. He put his hands in his pockets, the white cuffs peeping out of his sleeves, and kept looking out the window.

"Pretty good view, yeah," Mae-mae said.

"Good day, I bet you can see Stone Mountain plain as day, huh?" His voice full of enthusiasm. "Can you see the carving on the side from here, General Lee and all? Probably read Stonewall Jackson's lips on a clear afternoon."

"Never tried. I get the impression the general doesn't say much anymore."

Dick Clark laughed dutifully. "Stonewall Jackson, quite a character. Quite a character. Battle of McDowell, I believe it was, this fellow comes up to him and says that a messenger—just a young kid—that this messenger boy's just been killed taking a message to one of the field officers. Jackson looks up and says, 'Very commendable, very commendable,' goes right back to what he's doing."

"War history," Mae-mae said, "that stuff never much appealed to me."

"Poor kid's just been shot out of his socks, all Jackson's got to say about it is 'very commendable.' " Still looking out the window. "You picture that? That's one tough bird."

"I assume since you're taking so long to get to the point that you're here as the bearer of some kind of bad news."

Dick Clark turned around and grinned, then sat down. "You're a smart girl, I'll say that. Sharp as a tack."

"Yeah, but sometimes I get impatient. Like when people seem to be jerking me around, for instance."

Dick Clark wrinkled his forehead. "Okay, okay. I get the point, counselor." He cleared his throat athletically, making several unusual noises, pulled on the crease of his right pants leg, and crossed his knees, right over left. "You remember what we were talking about the other day? About how I don't care if people go nosing around trying to help with an investigation? You remember that?"

Mae-mae nodded.

"Well, this time, I was a little off base. I shouldn't ought to told you that. I made a mistake." He raised his hands like he was surrendering to the enemy. "I made a mistake and I apologize."

Mae-mae looked at him. "You're saying you don't want me looking into this any further? That's what you're saying?"

"Well . . ." Dick Clark's throat seemed to be giving him trouble again, requiring some inventive throat-clearing noises, a couple of pained faces. He took a long breath after the throat-clearing exercises. "Bottom line, yeah."

"Leave it to the pros?"

"Leave it to the pros." Dick Clark nodded. "It's under control."

Mae-mae didn't get it. Why the turnaround? Why all of a sudden was she supposed to forget about the whole thing? It didn't make any sense.

Mae-mae shook her head. It all seemed kind of surreal. Murders, burning cars, counterfeit stamps, cops that changed their minds about what was a crime and what wasn't.

"Under control? In what sense?"

Dick Clark looked out the window, trying to see Stonewall Jackson again. Taking his time.

"You know," Dick Clark said finally. "I been in the department a few years now—going on twenty come next January—and one of the things I come to realize, sometimes you just got to let things go. Other people just got more expertise in some areas than I do. And bottom line, I just got to trust them. You understand where I'm coming from?"

"Go on," Mae-mae said.

"Tell you a little story," Dick Clark said. "I was just a little younger than you when I made detective. I was working VCU, vehicular crimes unit. Traffic inspector, real crappy work. Fatalities, hit-and-runs, that kind of thing, you interview everybody standing around the scene, you file a report, that's about all there is to it. Except for showing up at depositions, going to court about eighteen times, all the lawsuits. Rule of thumb when you're VCU—fifty percent of your life, you're waiting for lawyers. Naturally you're always looking for something high profile to come along, get you noticed so you can transfer to vice or robbery, move up to a better assignment."

Dick Clark smiled his television smile, like the T.V. camera's red light had blinked on.

"So anyway, one night I get a call, possible felony hit-and-run, down around Carver Homes. I climb out of the car and there's a half-dead black lady on the ground and this white fellow sitting in a Lincoln Mark VII acting all tore up about this terrible thing that's happened. The way he says it, she must of been drunk or something, just lurching out into the street from behind a parked car. He kept going on about how he'd been adjusting the radio and he'd looked up and *boom*, there she is, right? He tells me how guilty he feels because he was fiddling with the radio and if he'd just looked up a second earlier it wouldn't of happened, so on, so forth. And then he goes on about how she must have been blind drunk, looking right at him and not getting out of the way. He kept saying it: how drunk he figured she was.

"Next day the victim dies, so the case gets turned over to homicide. But homicide, hell, they don't give a hoot in hell about it. Since my name was on the initial paperwork, I end up getting the coroner's report by mistake. Well, turns out this lady *was* drunk, point oh two six blood alcohol. So I pull her sheet, find she's also a former heroin addict, done some county time for solicitation, and she's got a child abuse hearing pending. Model citizen. Now the guy in the Lincoln, he's deacon or elder or something at a big Methodist church up in Cobb County, treasurer of the Kiwanis Club, vice president of sales for some company makes electrical wire. Plus being a white man.

"But something about it, about this guy's story, rubs me the wrong way. Like, why's a Methodist deacon driving through Carver Homes at one o'clock on a Wednesday night? So I check into this and that, keep looking into it. I'm young, I'm gung ho, I got a gut feeling something's wrong, and if I figure it out, this could help bust me out of this stupid VCU assignment. So I con the homicide investigator into letting me follow up on the case a little. Come to find out I get a witness puts the white guy down there a couple weeks earlier, him and the dead lady. But it's a piss-poor witness, an old retarded man. Get another witness, puts the car—the Mark VII—puts it there a couple hours earlier. But no ID on the guy's face. Get another witness puts the guy with a black woman at his home when his wife was out of town. But no ID on the woman—and, hey, maybe it's mistaken identity, the person the witness saw was actually the cleaning lady or something.

"Well, anyway, a detective comes to me, fellow from the white collar crime unit, asks me to lay off this case for a little while. I ask why, he says, 'Just trust me; lay off it.' So I lay off it a while. Nothing happens. I get tired of waiting, I start asking around again, interviewing people, all kind of running around on my part. Cause, see, I'm sure by now this guy was getting some goodies on the side from the dead lady and for some reason it got inconvenient and so he decided to whack her. My theory, he figured he'd get her drunk, stand her up in the middle of the road, run over her. Maybe drag her forty, fifty feet down the street, see what happens.

"So anyway this guy, the white collar crimes lieutenant, he comes to me again, this time with the homicide guy who's handling the case, says, 'Hey, I thought we had an understanding.' I say, Well, maybe you got an understanding, but what I got is a murder. And I refused to back off, started pulling in his business associates, all this type stuff, putting some heat on my perp. You know what happened next?"

"No," Mae-mae said.

"Guy panics and disappears. Takes off for Honduras or someplace, never comes back. Turned out he was up to his eyeballs in some type of embezzlement scam, ripping off his company and his customers. Which, as it happens, this lieutenant was investigating. I blew his case, my case, the homicide guy's case, the whole thing shot to hell." Dick Clark laced his fingers together, then rapped on the edge of the desk with one knuckle. "But that's not the worst thing. You know what the worst thing was?"

Mae-mae shook her head.

"Worst thing was, I *never* would of caught that sumbitch. He killed her, sure as I'm sitting here, but I'd of never convinced the D.A. to indict. Never would of tied it all together."

Dick Clark put a self-satisfied look on his face and leaned back in his chair: The state rests, Your Honor.

"That's a nice story, detective."

"You understand what I'm saying? You got to just forget this whole thing. Let it go. We got people working on it."

"You?"

"People. We got *people* working on it." Dick Clark thumped on his knee with his little notebook. The black butt of his gun poked out of his jacket for a moment.

"By the way," he said. "You ever turn up these counterfeit stamps you were talking about last night?" Dick Clark took a Ziploc bag out of the inside pocket of his suit, flapped it in the air.

"They're at home."

"Oh." Dick Clark put the plastic bag back in his coat. "Well, I'd sure appreciate it if you'd turn those over to me. How about you bring them by first thing in the morning?"

"I could do it this evening if you want."

"Tomorrow's better. I'm gonna be tied up the rest of the day. Chain of custody issue. I don't want them sitting around on somebody's desk all night."

"Tomorrow morning then."

Dick Clark got up out of the chair, extended his hand. Mae-mae shook it.

"Well, I thank you," Dick Clark said, heading for the door. He stopped halfway out of the office and looked at her for a minute. "Now we got an understanding here, don't we? Leave it to the pros?"

Mae-mae nodded. "One question, though," she said. "Does Lester Paris have an alibi for the night of Charles Towe's death?"

Dick Clark said, "Do we have an understanding here or not?"

"Please . . ." Mae-mae wasn't above a little wheedling now and then. "Just answer me that one question."

Dick Clark folded his arms across his chest and leaned against the door frame, looking at her for a minute. "Yeah," he said finally, smiling. "Him and a cousin of his were fishing over in South Carolina, Lake Jocassee. Bunch of witnesses."

"So you're actually working on this now? It isn't just a random killing anymore?"

Dick Clark's smile went away. He said, "Now you're gonna be a good girl, right? Right?"

Good girl? *Good girl?* Mae-mae thought about that one for a minute.

Hell no, she was not. She was damned if she'd be a good *girl*. Life, man, sometimes you had to just take hold of it, forget about good and bad, just take hold and shake it. It was like climbing up that power pole, just deciding to do it and then doing it; it was something you couldn't let somebody do for you. He had almost had her—had almost lulled her into submission with his tedious cop story and his smile for the camera and his nice blue suit. He had almost, almost, almost had her.

But he blew it.

"Sure," she lied. "I'll be a good girl."

Dick Clark trotted out the American Bandstand smile, crinkling up his eyes. "Very commendable," he said. "Very commendable."

NINETEEN

After Dick Clark left, Mae-mae ate lunch and then had a couple of meetings with clients. Both of them were proctologists—patronizing, insufferable jerks who seemed to think the world was actually impressed by guys who spent their lives thumb-deep in other people's rectums. They had very complicated tax pictures, however, which allowed her to spend quite a few billable hours rendering opinions on the legality of the very aggressive games they wanted to play with the IRS. You just had to suck it up and think about paying that light bill.

As soon as proctologist number two had left, she typed up their bills, licked the stamps, made a special trip to the mail guy downstairs. She'd gotten one client's check that morning, deposited it before noon, so it would clear by tomorrow. How nice—to actually have money in the bank when you wrote a check. How refreshing.

She made out two checks—one for the mortgage on her house, one for the rent on her office—then balanced her checkbook. This left twelve dollars and ninety-four cents. That could be a problem; twelve dollars only buys so much Ragú Chunky Vegetable, so much Roman Meal bread.

Her mind drifted, different things flitting in and out

158

of her consciousness. Where was the missing twenty grand? And who had Paris and Towe been selling the bogus stamps to? (There had to be a buyer, right?) What had Rachel and her father argued about the night he was killed? What did Clay Wilder have against Charles Towe? How could she get more information out of Lester?

No answers presented themselves, so she let herself think about Chris Towe for a while. It gave her a nice hot goofy feeling, the kind of sweet glandular rush she associated with junior high and old Janis Joplin songs. She hadn't really felt that way in a long time. Without quite thinking about it, she'd started believing that maybe you just outgrew that feeling—that as you got older you just sort of dried out emotionally, settled into an arid, painless groove and never got too worked up, too enthusiastic about a man. But never got too disappointed when things didn't work out either. Easy come, easy go—like that.

But that was no way to live, your best moments manufactured all alone at the top of a power pole. A *power pole*, for Godsake—what kind of life was that? You needed connections. And not just polite ones, not just niceties and courtesies and favors. That was finger food, sandwiches with the crust cut off. There was no hope, finally, if life was nothing but one polite thing after another. You needed passion! You needed greasy tacos and rare steak and too much wine. You needed sweaty, aching, glandular *life*. It was time for that, dammit!

It was time to lie in bed next to a man, thinking about his voice and his skin and the lines of his jaw, consumed by that. Not just being *with* a man, but being on fire about him, burning up. It was time to love a man again.

Was Chris that man? You could wrestle with the question forever, intellectualize it to death. Because you never really knew, not utterly and completely. And if you let doubt or complacency or skepticism eat you up, then pretty soon you'd be up on top of a power pole again, alone, trying to scare up some fresh, real emotion. So, sure, why not? He seemed like a good guy. Funny, clever, kind of a wiseass. A little touchy maybe when it came to this thing with his dad—but basically a decent guy.

And anyway, what the hell, nobody's perfect. God knows she ought to be clear enough on *that* particular point by now.

When she pulled up at the curb in front of her house, Mae-mae thought she saw something out of the corner of her eye, like maybe someone had just turned out a light in the living room. But that wouldn't make sense: she never left the lights on when she wasn't home. It had always seemed like a waste of money.

As soon as she got inside, though, Mae-mae knew someone had been there. At first she couldn't place it. Not the mess, not the junk on the floor; that was always there. No, it was something else. She couldn't put her finger on it. Nothing broken, no furniture turned over, no lamps smashed. Something . . . Something . . . Some kind of funny smell. Like sulfur, like matches, like someone had just lit a gas stove. A burning smell.

She stood in the open front door and called out, "Anybody in here? Anybody in here?" She knew she should go next door, call the cops, do all that neighborhood watch stuff. But just thinking about it pissed her off, that somebody had been in there messing with *her* stuff, poking around in *her* things. She started to get hot under the arms, hot in the cheeks. Man! She was boiling mad. The hell with prudence.

And anyway, maybe she was making it up. Maybe the pilot light had just blown out on the stove or something.

She stomped back through the dark silent house, down the hall. When she got to the bedroom, she stopped in the dark hall, stood for a moment by the door. Calm down. Calm down. This could just be a figment of her imagination.

She turned on the light in the guest bedroom. One of the desk drawers was pulled out, the one where she kept her checks. Had she left it that way? No. Definitely not. But the box of checks was still sitting there, undisturbed. She pushed the drawer back in. It made a harsh squeak that filled the silent house for a moment. Then silence again. One of the filing cabinet drawers was open, too. She hadn't left that open either—though nothing appeared to have been disturbed.

And then she smelled it again, the smell of matches. Shit. Her skin started to feel a little numb, like she'd just climbed out of icy water. She ran into her bedroom.

All of her bureau drawers had been pulled out, the contents dumped on the floor. The clothes lay on the floor in neat heaps, one per drawer. The drawers were stacked on the bed. A neat burglar. Thank God for small favors.

Her jewelry! She dropped to her knees, pawed through the pile of bras and underwear. There it was, a small flat box in a faded cream color that her mother had brought back from Mexico back in the fifties. Please, not Grandma's engagement ring. *Please!* She opened the box. Cheap jewelry sparkled up at her. She pawed through the shiny bits of glass and metal—opal earrings Henry had given her the week before he got the Porsche (guilty son of a bitch, he knew even then), two small diamond studs her father had given her for her sixteenth birthday, a mood ring from 1974, a bracelet braided from links of hair-fine gold. But no engagement ring.

It was the only thing that meant anything to her and the bastard had taken it: an art deco pattern with a center stone and four smaller square chips set on each side. She squatted down on a pile of T-shirts and stared dumbly at the floor, remembering all the times she'd debated about getting a safe deposit box, hiding the thing safely away forever. And all the times she'd said: No, jewelry is for wearing, not just for having. She'd worn it every now and then, when she wanted to feel good.

Why did people do this kind of thing? It wasn't like the ring was worth a huge amount of money. It was just—

Wait a minute! Something sparkled in the middle of her bedraggled pile of bras. She plunged her hand into the rayon mess and pulled out . . . a shining white-gold ring with a fine round center stone and four smaller square chips set asymmetrically to each side.

Mae-mae blinked, thought for a minute. Wait a second, wait a second. If he didn't want the jewelry . . .

The thief wasn't after the jewels in the first place, wasn't after financial records or checkbooks. What an idiot! She jumped up and ran into the living room, pulled Epstein's *Debtors and Creditors* off the shelf, opened it to chapter nine, "Assignments for the Benefit of Creditors."

It was supposed to be right there, peeking out above the part about the adjudication and discharge provision of the Bankruptcy Act, all that junk about impecunious debtors and unsecured creditors.

But there was nothing there, no fake thirty-two-cent stamps with a hundred pictures of flags waving over a hundred Mount Rushmores, nothing at all.

Nothing, that is, but a thin film of black ash that had smeared itself into the pages and slid into the binding crease. Gone, burned up, nothing left but dust.

They had burned the stamps and left the ashes there in the book. Just to let her know that they could do it. Was it Lester Paris? No stamps, no motive. No motive, no murder. That was his chain of reasoning. It had to be Lester.

"Shit!" Mae-mae said, throwing the book on the couch. It made a soft thump. Then there was emptiness, no sound in the house at all. The numb, icy feeling hadn't gone away.

Behind her Mae-mae heard a noise, the soft creak of the front door. She turned and saw a dark shape, the silhouette of a man standing just outside the half-open door, his shoulder resting against the door frame. His face was hidden in shadow, but she could tell he was looking straight at her.

Mae-mae gasped, lungs sucking for air.

"Remember me?" the dark figure said.

Then he stepped into the light. Chris Towe.

"Chris! God, you scared the hell out of me."

"I'm sorry. The door was open," he said. "I heard you. . . ." Chris was looking at her intently. "Is something wrong?"

"I just got burglarized is all."

Chris looked around the living room, the pizza boxes and pantyhose on the floor, the furniture turned in all directions, the books scattered all over the place. He grimaced, shook his head. "Man. They really trashed this place."

Mae-mae colored. "Well, actually, no. It always looks like this."

Chris looked at her a second, then laughed. "Oops. Strike one."

Mae-mae shrugged. "I could hardly hold it against you. A mess is a mess, no getting around it."

"What did they steal?"

"Not much." Mae-mae thought about it. Did she want to get into the counterfeiting thing right now? Maybe it would be better to let it rest. Or maybe . . .

She went back to her bedroom, came out with a flashlight. "How'd you like to go on a little adventure?" she said.

"What kind of adventure?"

"That's the thing about adventures," she said. "You never know till you get there."

Fifteen minutes later they were heading down the Lakewood Freeway, taking a right on Sylvan, left under the bridge.

"Why do I have the feeling this has something to do

with Dad?" Chris said. They turned onto the street flanking the prisonlike warehouse.

"Let's just say it has something to do with Lester Paris." Mae-mae glanced at Chris. He looked uncomfortable, staring out the window. But he didn't say anything.

Mae-mae drove past the low brick building where Lester had picked up the bag full of stamps the night before. It was completely dark. She turned off her lights, pulled over to the side of the road.

"Nice neighborhood," Chris said.

"That's why I brought *you*," she said, smiling.

Chris laughed. "Thanks."

They got out of the car and walked over to the little building. Mae-mae approached the front door cautiously, peered through the dusty glass. It was so dark inside that she couldn't see anything. She rapped forcefully on the door with her knuckles and waited. Nothing happened.

"You ever jimmied a door lock?" she said.

"No," Chris said. He pulled on the handle of the door. It swung open. He smiled. "Will this do, though?"

Mae-mae smiled foolishly. "In a pinch, yeah, I guess so." She turned on her flashlight, waved it around the interior of the building. The floor was bare concrete, a big crack meandering like a map of the Amazon from one side of the room to the other; the walls were cinder block, painted a faded green.

"What are we looking for?" Chris said. His voice echoed in the big, empty room.

"Stamps, maybe. Maybe something else."

"Stamps?"

"Postage stamps."

"Oh."

Mae-mae shined her light around the room. It was completely empty. There weren't even any old boxes or boards or pieces of broken furniture. There was nothing at all, nothing but dust and the silent darkness. She walked to the back corner of the building where a small cubicle had been framed, a door built into one of its walls. She tried the door, but it was locked.

"You want to try your magic touch on this one?" she said.

"Why don't we get out of here?" Chris said. "I don't like this place. It gives me the creeps." His voice sounded hollow and spectral in the empty room.

"Just help me with the door and then we can go."

"Help you do what? It's locked."

"Well . . ." Mae-mae flushed. "Help me break it."

"Trespassing's not good enough, got to do a little breaking and entering, too?"

Mae-mae watched the beam of the flashlight wavering against the scratched doorknob.

"Okay," Chris said. He leaned against one side of the door, propped his foot against the door frame on the other side. "Jiggle and push."

"What?"

"This door frame looks kind of weak. Jiggle the knob while I try to push the door frame apart. Maybe we can open it without smashing the door."

Mae-mae reached underneath his heel. Chris grunted, and she jiggled the knob. Nothing happened.

Chris let his breath out. "One more time," he said.

More grunting. In the dim glow of the flashlight, she could see the cords standing out in his neck, his teeth bared with the strain. She jiggled and pushed, jiggled and pushed. Suddenly the door clicked and flew open.

Chris sighed. "Whew. I about had a brain aneurysm there."

"Thanks," Mae-mae said. "You're a genius." She gave him a little kiss on the cheek. Chris smiled shyly, looked surprised.

She walked through the door, waved the flashlight around the room. Again, nothing. It was just a small cubicle with a couple of bracket shelves bolted to the wall. Another door led out the back wall of the building. She tried the knob. Locked.

"What's that burning smell?" Chris said.

Mae-mae noticed it too. "Smells like cigarettes."

"Wait, no, it's *pipe* tobacco." Chris looked around the room. "Shine your light over there." He pointed at one of the bracket shelves.

Mae-mae pointed her flashlight at the shelf . . . and there it was. A short, crooked pipe. She picked it up, but it was so hot it burned her finger. "Ow!" The pipe fell to the floor with a crack, and a spray of glowing ashes sparkled momentarily against the floor. She stuck her burned fingers in her mouth. "It's still lit!"

"We better get the hell out," Chris said, "before the guy comes back for his pipe. It's obvious there aren't any counterfeit stamps here."

Mae-mae stared at him. She hadn't used the word counterfeit. Not once. "*What* did you say?"

Chris said, "I said, let's get the hell out before—"

"I heard you the first time."

Chris looked at her like she was crazy. Behind the building a car engine started up, roared around the side toward the street. They sprinted for the front door, but by the time they got there the car's taillights were disappearing into the distance.

"Okay, okay, I admit it," Chris said. "So I knew Dad was involved in this counterfeiting thing. Big deal." They were back at her house, sitting on the couch. "See, I don't think that had anything to do with Dad's death. I really don't."

"What do you think it was, then?"

Chris took off his glasses, wiped his eyes, stared blankly into the distance. "I don't know," he said. "I really don't know. But to be honest, I don't like thinking about it. The whole thing, it makes me sick."

Mae-mae watched the sad, empty look on his face. This whole thing sucked. Why couldn't she have met him under less complicated circumstances? "Fair enough," she said. "You want a drink?"

"I'll get it," he said, putting on his glasses.

"That's okay," she said.

She went into the kitchen, checked the refrigerator. Its contents: two Miller Lites, one head of lettuce. Perfect. She took out the beers, screwed the tops off, took two glasses out of the dishwasher, and went into the living room.

"We even get glasses?" Chris said. "You're really rolling out the red carpet."

"Matching, no less. You want Mickey or Daffy?"

"Your call."

"Here." She poured the beer, handed him the Mickey Mouse glass. "I'm fairly partial to Daffy myself."

Chris studied the scratched picture on the side of his glass like he was trying to figure out if it was really Mickey Mouse or just a blob of something that hadn't come off in the dishwasher. "Cheers," he said finally. "You never told me about this burglar. Have you called the police?"

"No," Mae-mae said. "The burglar didn't really get anything to speak of."

Chris raised his eyebrows. "You scare him off?"

"No. He just came for one thing."

A puzzled look crossed his face. "What was that?"

"A sheet of thirty-two-cent stamps," Mae-mae said.

Chris set his glass down for a minute, studied her face for a minute with his blue eyes, then shook his head. "I'm not even going to ask," he said.

"Probably just as well." She sighed. "And how was *your* day?"

"My day was fine. I have a nice day job. I show up, I do my job, I go home with a paycheck. Nobody hassles me too much. I make an honest living."

"And what *do* you do for a living?"

He shrugged, a tired look crossing his face. "It's a day job. You know, just a basic, decent day job. I don't talk about it a lot. I don't think about it when I go home.''

"Okay," Mae-mae said carefully.

Chris sipped his beer and stared at the floor. "I'm sorry, I'm not trying to be such a wet blanket. It's just . . ." He shrugged.

"I know."

"Look, while I'm on the subject of sorry, I want to apologize about the other night. I shouldn't have sung that stupid song about you. It was totally uncalled for and I apologize.''

Mae-mae smiled, raised her Daffy Duck glass, and said, "Well, here's to a man who's got the balls to apologize.''

Chris laughed and looked around the room. "Maybe it would be nice if you put some music on.''

"Something romantic?" Mae-mae said. She could feel the adrenaline numbness of the evening draining away from her skin, a warm, liquid sensation replacing it. It felt pretty good. "Emmy Lou Harris?"

"Emmy Lou? She's like the most depressing singer in the world.''

"You don't like Emmy Lou Harris?''

"She's great. Problem is, two or three songs into her albums, I start getting suicidal.''

"Okay, then who?''

"You remember Charlie Rich?''

"The Silver Fox!" Mae-mae smiled a little. "Oh, yeah. Daddy took me to see him one time at the Civic Center when I was a kid. It was him and Porter Wagoner, I think. Porter Wagoner and the Wagoneers.''
Charlie Rich. Boy, that was going back a ways. She remembered him sitting at the piano in his glittery suit with his black cowboy hat and his white zip-up boots and his long white sideburns. "He was terrible. Like Elvis—but with white hair and a string section.''

"Yeah." Chris laughed. "I always liked that one

song, though. 'The Most Beautiful Girl In the World,'
you remember that one?''

"It was okay. I probably have it somewhere, you
know, back in the dim recesses of my vinyl collection.''

He was looking at her, studying her like he didn't
really care about the song all that much. Like his mind
was elsewhere. Mae-mae looked away, feeling funny
suddenly.

"Play it,'' Chris said.

" 'The Most Beautiful Girl In the World'?''

It was embarrassing the way he was looking at her.
Embarrassing because his eyes, the way he was looking
at her, it was so nice—gentle but intense. Like she was
the only thing in the room, the only thing he could see.

" 'The Most Beautiful Girl In the World.' You got it,
play it.''

His eyes were on her, nothing but her, and he was
smiling, smiling a soft smile that she had never seen on
his face before. She felt like she was looking at him,
really *seeing* him, for the first time. There were deep
lines forming around his mouth, small wrinkles around
his blue eyes. It seemed like nobody she knew was
young anymore. Funny how that had happened. He had
his mother's eyes.

He reached out and put his hand on her shoulder. Oh
man, she felt it all over, everything lighting up and going
crazy inside. She leaned forward and kissed him, lightly.
Lightly lightly, just brushing his lips, feeling them trem-
ble once, feeling his breath.

Then there was no stopping it.

And somehow she never quite got around to playing
that awful old Charlie Rich record.

TWENTY

The next day she drove by the police station on the way to work. Dick Clark was in, but he wasn't at his desk; he was across the big room, sitting in front of a computer, his head thrust forward, squinting at the screen. She walked up behind him, watched him type things into the machine. He was the fastest two-finger typist she'd ever seen.

"What you doing?" she said.

Dick Clark swiveled around in his chair. "Oh, hi. Trying to chase down some dirtbags on the NCIC, the crime computer. This thing's got all the criminal records in the country on it. Type in a name, up she pops."

Mae-mae looked at the screen. There were blanks where you filled in with first name, last name, aliases, last known address, social security number, whatever. "Cool," Mae-mae said.

"So, you got those stamps for me?" Dick Clark said.

"That's why I came in," Mae-mae said. "Somebody broke into my house and burned them last night."

"*Burned* them?"

Mae-mae nodded.

Dick Clark sighed. "Do me a favor," he said. "Hold my place on the machine for a second. I need to run two more names and then I probably ought to get a quick statement from you about these stamps.''

''Hold your place?''

Dick Clark put an impatient look on his face. ''Just *sit* here like you're doing something. If I get up and walk off, somebody else'll sit down and I won't be able to use the damn thing again for another half hour.''

Mae-mae saluted. ''Yes, *sir!*'' she said.

Dick Clark looked at her. ''What?'' he said. ''Did I say something?'' Then he went away.

Mae-mae stared at the screen. It looked pretty simple. She wondered if her own name was in there. Why would it be? She'd never committed a crime. She'd done seventy-two in a thirty-five zone once, that was about it. She waited.

Dick Clark was taking his sweet time.

She swiveled around, looking for him, but he had disappeared. Nobody seemed to be paying her any attention.

Just for laughs she typed in her own name and social security number, then pressed enter. A message appeared on the screen: *Please Wait.* After a while a second message: *No Records Found.*

A thought occurred to her. She looked around the room again. Still no Dick Clark.

She started typing again.

Last Name: P-a-r-i-s.

First Name: L-e-s-t-e-r

Everything else she left blank. Would that make any difference? She hit enter.

Eventually a message came up: *One Record Found. Review Y/N?* She typed Y for yes.

According to the screen a guy named Lester Wayman Paris had been convicted three times for shoplifting, once for assault and battery, and once for solicitation of prostitution—all in Orange County, California. The charges were listed in date order—the latest charge was three months ago. All of which might have been interesting if Lester Wayman Paris hadn't been twenty-three years old.

Mae-mae tried another name. Charles Patrick Towe. *No Records Found.*

Mae-mae tried another name. Colleen Mastronunzio. *No Records Found.*

What was that guy's name, the fish-faced guy? R-a-s-c-o-e, D-o-n-a-l-d. *No Records Found.*

She tried Rachel Towe. *No Records Found.*

Christopher Towe. *No Records Found.*

Clay Wilder. The machine told her to wait for what seemed a long time. Finally a message. 3 *Records Found.* She dismissed the first one (*Race: black*), the second one (*Age: forty-seven*).

She tried the third name on the list. Clay James Wilder—a white man aged twenty-six, 5'9", 155 pounds, brown hair, brown eyes, no known aliases, small moon-shaped scar on face—had been convicted of one charge in Federal Circuit Court for the Northern District of Alabama at the age of nineteen. The charge: Violation of 18 U.S.C.A., Section 485. Whatever that meant.

That was him, though, it had to be. 18 U.S.C.A., Section 485.

"I didn't say look up all your friends," a voice behind her said. "I just said sit here." Mae-mae turned around and saw Dick Clark standing over her with his arms crossed.

"How's your knowledge of federal law?" she said.

"Depends," the detective said. "Why?"

"I'm a little rusty on my federal criminal code. If I were to say to you that somebody had violated 18 U.S.C.A., Section 485, would you know what I was talking about?"

Dick Clark had a funny look on his face. She saw him glance over her shoulder at the computer. "I thought we had an agreement here," he said.

"Eighteen U.S.C.A., Section Four Eight Five," she said. "You *do* know what it means, don't you?"

"As it happens, I do," he said. "I learned about that fairly recently."

"Okay," she said. "Educate me."

"Eighteen U.S.C.A., Section Four Eight Five." Dick Clark showed her his humorless American Bandstand teeth and said, "Counterfeiting."

When she got to work, there was a message on her machine from Judge Price, the probate judge. "Looking at my notes here, hon, we had something up in the air about this twenty-thousand-dollar mutual fund draft. I trust you've resolved this and merely neglected to contact me about it?"

Mae-mae drummed her fingers for a moment, hit the REWIND button, and sighed.

Sebastian looked terrible. His face was red and puffy and slick with antibiotic goo; his eyebrows and eyelashes were gone; the back of his left hand was an angry crimson. But it didn't seem to slow him down. He had already framed the Closterman, hung it over the fireplace in the room he called his parlor.

Mae-mae looked at the picture for a long time, the dead earl of Northumberland staring sadly back at her from inside his antique wood frame. "You've done well by him," she said finally.

Sebastian bowed, smiled slightly, then waved his hand toward the breakfast room. "Luncheon is served," he said.

When she had seated herself, Sebastian went into the kitchen, made some clattering noises, then carried out two plates. A starched towel hung from his arm, like he was trying out for a position as sommelier in a four star restaurant.

"In honor of the Closterman," he said, putting a steaming dish in front of her. "Cold trout in aspic, deep-fried soft-shell crab over angel hair pasta almondine, and a very rare *petit* fillet with a light bordelaise sauce."

"Surf and turf kind of thing," Mae-mae said. She snuck a look at Sebastian's face, hoping he'd be insulted. He pretended to ignore her. The fillet was buttersoft. "This is outrageous," she said. "This is amazing."

"I do wish you'd wait to speak until you've finished chewing," Sebastian said.

"This pasta—I can't believe this." Sinful, sinful. It was going to take a lot of bill basketball to shake this off her hips.

"And the wine . . ." Sebastian started to pour a red wine into her glass.

"Thanks, no." Mae-mae put her palm over her glass.

Sebastian looked pityingly down his long, red nose at her. "You *must* have the wine. It's a Clos de la Roche Domaine Armand Rousseau, the eighty-five, and it's been breathing since noon. Without it the entire meal will be defeated."

Mae-mae waited just long enough to make him squirm, then took her hand away. "For you, Sebastian. Just for you." He scrubbed her palm print off the rim of her glass with his starched cloth, let her taste, then filled her glass. She lifted her glass and said, "Here's to the Closterman."

"No." Sebastian stopped swirling the Clos de la Roche 1985 in his glass, looked her in the eye. "No, I think I'd like to toast something else." His face gleamed moistly, like something in the glass case at the meat counter. "Let us toast life. And the living. And those who make it worth something."

Mae-mae watched him, her glass poised in the air. There seemed to be something else he wanted to say.

"I should have let the Closterman burn," he said. "You were right, you know. I should have just let it go."

"But it's okay," Mae-mae said softly. "You got out okay. You got the picture . . ." But she could see that was not what he was driving at. "It really scared you, didn't it?"

He smiled a fragile smile, looked away for a moment, like he was thinking. "Life, you know, there's more to it than not being dead. It's harder, it's more elusive than that."

Mae-mae didn't say anything, wasn't sure what to do. She felt a rush of emotions, one barreling after another in quick succession.

Sebastian was still holding his glass in the air, his cuff links shining in the bright room. "I wish . . . I wish that I could—" He stopped for a minute and blinked, a confused look running across his face before he finally rallied and went on. "All I mean to say is that you bring life into my rather dry and tedious world. And for that I owe you a great, great deal."

Mae-mae frowned. It had always seemed kind of the other way around to her. Funny. Funny, how things work like that, going on right under your nose and still you never managed to figure them out.

Mae-mae's eyes felt wet. Why was it that some of the times you were closest to other people were also some of the times you felt most alone? It seemed like something was wrong with the math, like when you met someone halfway—really saw for a moment what they were all about—that everything was supposed to add up, all the figures were supposed to agree. Only it never seemed to work quite like that. Comradeship of the lonely, shit, maybe that's all it was, all that brought her and Sebastian together. But, no, that didn't seem right. There was more to it than that. There was more to it. There *was*.

She thought of the wind at the top of the pole, of being by herself up there with nothing but the darkness, the empty air, the fear of falling. It was so much simpler up there. She could almost feel the wind pushing her hair, pulling her skirt. Almost but not quite.

Mae-mae reached over and put her hand on top of Sebastian's. He winced, jerked his hand away.

"The burn," he said apologetically. He held up the

blistered hand for her to look at. It was slick, hairless, red skinned, blue veined, like the hand of a giant newborn child.

"Oh oh oh oh," Mae-mae said. "I didn't mean to do that!"

Later, after they had moved on to smaller things, Sebastian said, "So what's the latest on your investigation, my dear?"

Mae-mae told him everything that had happened since they had last spoken, about the break-in and the burning of the stamps, about Clay Wilder's criminal history, about the probate judge breathing down her neck about the missing money.

"Who do you think broke into your house?"

"My guess is that it was Lester. Or somebody he hired."

"And what about Rachel's swain—Clay, was that his name?—Where does he fit?"

Mae-mae shook her head. "I don't know. The more I find out, the more convoluted it gets. I can't figure out how it all fits together." Mae-mae swabbed at the juice on her plate with a piece of fresh bread. "This sauce is great. What's in here?"

"It's a bordelaise."

"Bordelaise—it's sure good. Anyway, I'm beginning to think that I'm just looking at the tip of the iceberg."

Sebastian made a sympathetic noise.

"It's obvious the police know something I don't," Mae-mae added. "The detective, this guy Dick Clark, first he goes, 'Oh, yeah, just nose around, see what you can find out.' And then yesterday he flip-flops, tells me I should forget about the whole thing."

"And have you?" Sebastian twirled precisely three strands of angel hair pasta on his fork, cupped his fingers under them, lifted them carefully to his mouth.

"No. I mean . . . I don't know. I'm beginning to think I'm wasting my time. Maybe Dick's right. Maybe I'll never get it sorted out." She took a sip of the wine. "There's also an ethical quandary here that I haven't really resolved."

"How so?"

"Okay, let's assume that I find out all about the counterfeiting. Let's say it was Lester who killed Charles Towe. Let's say that Printmeister is a mile deep in this counterfeiting thing. Let's say I figure the whole thing out and tell it all to the police. You know what happens then?"

"Tell me."

"What happens then is that Printmeister goes under and Myra Towe has a hell of a time getting her money out of the business. If she sold it today, it could be worth—I don't know—maybe half a million. So, if I dig up a bunch of dirt, I could be tossing away half a million bucks of my client's money."

Sebastian raised the portion of his blistered forehead where his eyebrows used to be.

"But on the other hand, I'm a sworn officer of the court. I'm obliged to report illegalities like this. . . ." She let her sentence drift off. "This is a hell of a dilemma."

"You'd best decide fairly soon, don't you think?"

Mae-mae nodded and sighed. "Maybe I should let the police worry about the counterfeiting and the murder. Then I can go ahead and cut a deal with Lester Paris, let him buy out Myra's half of the business, and then put the whole thing behind me."

The more she thought about it, the more it made sense. And it would sure make things less complicated with Chris. Whatever was going to happen there, it ought to be allowed to run its course without this screwy situation interfering. What was the harm in letting the police do their job?

"Would Paris agree to such an offer?" Sebastian said.

"I'd almost guarantee it. He pretty much said so yesterday when I showed him the stamps."

"Which you no longer have . . ."

"Damn. I hadn't thought about that."

Sebastian nodded, sliced his crab into several pieces, and ate them one after the other, English style, fork in the left hand. When he finished chewing, he reached into the pocket of his jacket, took out an envelope, and set it on the table. "I believe this might help," he said.

Mae-mae looked inside the envelope, looked at Sebastian, looked back into the envelope. It was a sheet of stamps, medium rare, singed slightly along one edge.

"Remember?" he said. "Before the Volvo blew up, you took two sets of stamps out of the fire. You gave the second to me."

"Sebastian," Mae-mae said. "Have I told you recently what a good guy you are?" She surveyed the wreckage of the meal. "Hey, and what happened to the thigh diet anyway?"

Sebastian smiled suddenly. "You're in love, my dear. I can see it in your face, in your cheeks, in your . . ." He waved two long fingers vaguely in her direction. "Dieting, my dear, is for the unhappy and the loveless. Dieting while one is in love—" Sebastian shuddered. "Why, that's simply pathological."

Mae-mae slathered butter across her last piece of homemade bread, stuffed it in her mouth. "You're right, Sebastian," she said, dribbling crumbs down her blouse. "You're absolutely right."

Sebastian smiled modestly. "Another glass of the Clos de la Roche, perhaps?"

Mae-mae shook her head. "Thanks, no. I think maybe I ought to call Lester, see if he's ready to play *Let's Make a Deal* with Myra Towe's relentless and hard-bitten lawyer."

TWENTY-ONE

Mae-mae drove back to the office and called Lester Paris.

"*Miz* Cosgrove," he said. "How we doing today?" His voice sounded creaky and nervous.

"Here's what I'd like to do," she said. "I think the best thing for everyone concerned is for you to buy out Myra Towe's interest in Printmeister. I'd like to discuss it with you. Today, if possible."

"I agree," Paris said. She could hear relief in his voice. "If we can get the right price, a fair price, okay, a *fair* price—then that's probably the way to go. Today, though? I mean I need to let my financial people help me out in terms of what's a reasonable price. I need a couple days."

"No you don't. We'll just sit down, go over some ground rules today, maybe toss out some ballpark figures." Mae-mae grinned into the phone. She was loving it.

After a moment Lester said, "You think you can just put the squeeze on me, is that it?"

"Nothing you can't live with," Mae-mae said pleasantly. "Say, four o'clock, my office?"

Lester sighed. "Four o'clock," he said.

* * *

Myra Towe led Mae-mae into her house, a brick ranch out in Dunwoody—no more than twenty-seven, twenty-eight hundred square feet, Mae-mae figured. It looked exactly the same as about ninety percent of the houses in Atlanta. A shade above average size, nice yard, a Lincoln Continental parked in the drive—but not the kind of house you'd naturally associate with millionaires.

Myra Towe was smiling politely. "Well," she said, "what a nice surprise."

Mae-mae smiled noncommittally. She was not looking forward to this conversation.

Myra led her into the living room. It was kind of haute funky—not the kind of decor she would have expected Myra Towe to have. Chrome and black leather chairs, an arrogantly striped black-and-cream couch, a coffee table made of rough-cut marble—white threaded with black. Ironically the room reminded Mae-mae of Colleen Mastronunzio's place. A couple of incongruously conventional pieces of needlepoint hung on the walls, along with an inexpert watercolor, a rural scene: a weatherworn barn with some horses out front, their heads buried in a corncrib.

"What do you think?" Myra said. "Rachel helped me pick everything out."

That explained it. "Very . . ." Mae-mae fished around for the right adjective. "Dramatic."

Myra smiled hesitantly. "Yes. Isn't it?" She didn't seem sure about it at all. "We used to have this awful living room suite, these brown plaid things that Charles and I picked out right after we bought the house. The more I lived with them, the more I hated them. So last week I had the Salvation Army come out, tote it all away. Every last stitch of that awful junk." She was still smiling her slight, ambivalent smile, as though she couldn't quite get used to what she had done. "Tea?"

"No, thank you."

Myra perched on the edge of the sofa, clasped her hands around her knees. She looked as though she were sitting in someone else's living room—someone she didn't know too well, for that matter. A half-full glass of iced tea sweated on a cork coaster near her hand. There was fresh mint in the tea, the sweet tang of it in the air. "So what can I do for you, Miss Cosgrove?"

"Please. Mae-mae is fine."

"Mae-mae!" Myra cocked her head like a bird.

"There are a couple of things I need to discuss with you," Mae-mae said. "First, the missing money."

Myra nodded slightly.

"Well, I found out where it all went," Mae-mae said. "All except for the last check, anyway."

Another small expectant nod.

"Myra, this is not easy for me to say, but that money was given to—" Mae-mae couldn't quite get the words to come out.

Something flashed across Myra Towe's face. Pain? Annoyance? It was hard to tell. The expectant look disappeared and Myra Towe sighed. She said, "I was afraid it was something like that."

Mae-mae looked at the floor.

"It *was* a woman, wasn't it?" Myra said.

Mae-mae nodded. "I could tell you her name if you want to know. If it means anything to you. I don't think you have any legal recourse to the money. . . ." The words sounded foolish. Legal recourse. They had the same bitter taste as things like fiduciary duty. The words to Chris's song in the bar came back to her: *Mae-mae Cosgrove, she was a cutie, couldn't get away from her fiduciary duty.* The law—it seemed like such a load of crap sometimes.

"Legal *re*course!" Myra laughed briefly, a high opera singer sound. There was still a smile sitting there on her face, but it didn't seem to be connected to anything. It reminded Mae-mae of a joke she'd heard once. The punch line (which you were supposed to deliver with a big smile and a drippy Southern accent) was: "What did Ah learn in finishin' school? Ah learned that Southuhn ladies don't say, 'Fuck you.' They say, 'Isn't that niiiiiice?' " Mae-mae couldn't remember the rest of the joke, though, the setup.

"I don't need, or *want*, that money, Mae-mae," Myra said. She was sitting up very straight, and the empty smile was still blazing away like a lonely lighthouse at the edge of some endless dark sea. "And all things considered I'd prefer that we not discuss it again."

Mae-mae nodded.

Myra leaned forward a little, her hands still clasped over her knees. Mae-mae noticed one of her wrists was shaking. In a soft voice Myra said, "But I appreciate your finding out for me. I always knew she was there, and that was enough. It's just—it's just that I don't want to know her name, or who she is, or anything else about her." Myra took a sip of her iced tea. "Was there anything else?"

"The business," Mae-mae said. "Printmeister. I think that you can get a good price for it right now. And I believe now's the time to do it."

Myra Towe's pale blue eyes watched her for a minute. After a few moments' thought, Myra said, "Do you mind my asking why right now? I mean as opposed to later?"

Mae-mae didn't say anything for a while. "This is kind of tricky," she said finally. "I think that Lester and your husband were doing something they shouldn't have been doing. I can use that knowledge to get you a good price. But the sooner I do it, the stronger the leverage will be."

"Something they shouldn't have been? I'm not sure . . ."

Mae-mae hesitated. "Something illegal, I'm afraid. It's probably just as well that I don't tell you anything about it. If I do, you become involved. Which could potentially cause problems for you later on."

An uncomprehending look crossed Myra Towe's face. "Problems. Like going to jail or something?"

Mae-mae smiled. "No. Nothing like that. But there might be tax problems or civil suits, who knows. Better to get shut of the whole thing as fast as possible."

"Tell me. What were they doing?"

"You sure you want to know?"

Myra nodded.

"It sounds strange," Mae-mae said. "But they were printing counterfeit postage stamps."

Myra slumped back in her brand-new black-on-cream couch and stared at something out the window. After a minute she picked up a black-on-cream pillow and hugged it to her chest like a baby. Mae-mae's stomach tightened and twisted. It seemed like every time she talked to Myra Towe, she dumped more foulness on the poor woman's head. Why did it have to be like this?

"Thirty-seven years," Myra said finally. Her voice was soft and dreamy, like a little girl's. "Thirty-seven years you live with a man, you think you know him, but the truth is . . ." She stopped and stared some more, a terribly sad look on her face. "Thirty-seven years! Thirty-seven years, Mae-mae. I envy you. A career . . . a life of your own. When you're my age you won't have to look back over the years and wonder where they all went, wonder if you made some terrible decision all those years ago and left yourself—your *real* self—back there in a patch of weeds by the side of some road you can't even remember the name of anymore."

Mae-mae didn't say anything. She wasn't so sure: did anybody hit sixty years old and not look back with some regrets? Hell, she only turned thirty-five a few days ago and already had more regrets than seemed strictly necessary.

"So now I'm all of a sudden supposed to have a life. My *own* life." She held out her arms, embracing the funky furniture, the room full of wrongly chosen things, and said, "Is this my life? Is it? I don't even know."

There was a long uncomfortable silence and then Myra Towe sat up straight, put the black-on-cream pillow back against the armrest of the couch, patted it neatly into place. She smiled a grim, humorless smile.

"Sell it," she said. "Sell it *now*."

On the way back to her office, Mae-mae put on a tape in her car, a singer named Lucinda Williams. Kind of country, kind of rock, pretty good stuff.

There was construction going on in the middle of Peachtree in front of the Nikko Hotel, the cars backed up all the way down past Piedmont. Mae-mae didn't really mind, though. Traffic jams, if you just relaxed and let them happen, were a great place to think.

Had she done the right thing? What she was doing, basically, was extorting money out of this guy in return for butting out of the counterfeiting thing. That's what it came down to. Well, the hell with it. Maybe it wouldn't pass muster in Business Ethics 101, but this was real life. She was in the middle of the thing and there was no good way to resolve it.

This great song called "Passionate Kisses" came on and Mae-mae sang with it, letting the words roll around in her mouth. It was a song that asked why couldn't you have the quotidian stuff in life, pens that didn't run out of ink, good food, a decent job—why couldn't you make those things happen and still be crazy in love at the same time? She thought about seeing Chris's long hair spread across the pillow on the bed next to her this morning. He had been so nice last night, so tender. They had made love and then just touched each other and talked and kissed and fooled around. It had been comfortable, comfortable and sweet, the way people were supposed to act when they really liked each other.

The song was saying, why couldn't you have all of the ordinary things and have the passionate kisses, too? Yes. Yes. Why not? Why the hell not? Mae-mae sang the chorus at the top of her lungs. Unbeatable! Absolutely unbeatable. She started laughing. Parked in the middle of Peachtree in her farting, dying Honda, waiting for some bored guy in an orange vest to flag her past the traffic, and she couldn't be happier, absolutely couldn't be a bit happier if she tried.

She had let herself get distracted, all this business about people getting killed and missing money—it just wasn't her business. That was for the police to figure out. It was time for her to concentrate on what she knew, be good lawyer, a faithful counselor, and let life run back into its familiar muddy channels.

When she finally made it to the office, she was still singing the song. It kept running through her head in the elevator up from the parking garage, running through her head in the big, pretentious lobby of her building, running through her head in the elevator up to the office. Humming the tune, singing bits and pieces of the chorus under her breath.

She tried to think about her meeting with Lester Paris, tried to make herself come up with a negotiating strategy—but it was impossible. Too much on her mind. Anyway, this was going to be a piece of cake. A walk in the park. She had all the cards, so it was just a matter of which way she wanted to play them. It was all under control.

She looked at her watch. Five till four. Just enough time to go freshen up, make sure she didn't have mustard stains on her blouse. Or that bordelaise sauce—which would never come out.

She unlocked her office door so Lester could get in if he showed up a few minutes early, then walked down the hall humming the Lucinda Williams tune. Make a deal, cut this thing loose, send Myra the bill, and be done with it. That was the way to fly. Definitely the way to fly. Then she could concentrate on Chris, concentrate on getting some new customers, maybe do something nice for Sebastian. Things were turning around.

Sell the company, get it done, get out. Face it, she was in over her head. Like Waylon and Willie said, time to get back to the basics of life. Basic passion, basic kisses. Basic, basic, basic things—that was what the situation called for.

In the bathroom she gave herself a long appraisal in the mirror. Hair: doing okay. Suit: fine. It was her Brooks Brothers power suit, the hardball negotiator suit that she only wore with her one precious pair of Joan & David pumps. Blouse: clean, starched, white as a Tide commercial. Amazing: she'd managed a whole meal without dripping anything on herself.

A little more eyeliner. Perfect. She studied the mirror, happy with the effect. Sometimes you just get on a roll and everything works out. Maybe she'd wrangle half a million out of old Lester. Was that possible? Why not. She was going to slay this guy, absolutely kill him.

Mae-mae went back to her office, sat at her desk and waited. After a couple minutes she noticed the big manila envelope sitting on her desk, the one addressed to Charles Towe that Colleen Mastronunzio had left at her door the other day. She opened the envelope, dumped the contents on the desk. There were several magazines inside, along with a cover letter that was paper clipped to the top of the pile. The message appeared to have been cut out of a book, taped onto a page, and Xeroxed.

It said: *One last warning. Don't quit now.* Scrawled underneath in magic marker was the message, *Installment # 2*.

"Jesus," she said. She felt something on the back of her neck, something crawling up her spine.

She looked underneath the letter. On the cover of the top magazine was a naked woman, extremely large bosomed, her thin witless face slathered with blush and eye paint. Printed in neon orange letters over her streaky blond hair was the name of the magazine: *Buxom*. A red silk bow the size of a hatbox covered the big-breasted woman's hips, like someone was giving her away as a present. It was the December issue, Mae-mae noticed. Cute: this year put white slavery on the list for that special person in your life.

She looked at the other three magazines: *Naughty Femmes*, *Tail*, and *Nasty Girls*. More naked women on the covers, insipidly posed, shoving various parts of their anatomy toward the camera. She leafed through one of the magazines, the one called *Tail*. There were some articles about sports, some movie reviews, a couple of dumb cartoons—but it was mostly just grainy pictures of women sticking their rumps in the air. Sometimes you saw their faces, sometimes you didn't; sometimes it was just a tanned, cellulite-free ass sticking up at the camera. Asses in the woods, asses on the beach, asses in elaborate bedrooms full of ruffles and throw pillows. It wasn't like pictures of women exactly. Not whole, living, breathing women; more like some kind of repetitious anatomy lesson—exotically produced so as to hold the attention of slow learners. Bums away, scholars!

Did guys really *like* this stuff? Obviously somebody did. Three dollars and ninety-five cents' worth. Supply and demand. Immutable laws. Mae-mae threw the magazines back on the desk, vaguely repulsed. She had never been one to get too worked up about pornography being an exploitation of women or any of that sort of thing, but this . . . a whole magazine full of asses? Couldn't they at least show these women's faces? Was that too much to ask?

The big question, though, was why had these magazines been sent to Charles Towe? It sure looked like the same person who'd sent the letter that Candy found. But what did it mean?

That was when Mae-mae noticed the paper clips. Each of the magazines had a couple of pages clipped together along the top. Maybe that was the answer. She opened the first magazine, *Buxom*. There was a black-and-white photo spread of a woman's torso, different angles. The woman's face wasn't visible in any of the pictures. Mae-mae noticed the pictures seemed more artfully photographed than most of the shots in the magazine.

Why had this spread been paper clipped? What was meaningful about these pictures?

She tried *Tail*, flipped through to the paper-clipped pages. Another spread—this one in color—featured a series of photos of a woman taking off a pair of lacy red panties in front of a big green garbage dumpster. Again, the photographs were nicely lit, well composed. Again, the woman's face was invisible, turned away from the camera. It seemed to be the same woman as before, though, a woman with long straight hair.

Mae-mae stared at the svelte bottom, the trim legs. She had a sudden bad feeling about where this was leading.

The next magazine, *Naughty Femmes*, promised—among other tantalizing features—a "wet and juicy mouth contest." Oh, goody. It was paper clipped right at the staples. Mae-mae turned the magazine sideways, pulled open the centerfold.

The woman in the picture wore a lace teddy, utterly sheer, one strap slipped off the shoulder, and was sitting in a bentwood chair with her right leg hooked over the armrest. She stared frankly at the camera, throwing out a kind of vague, naked challenge at the world. It was a stock provocative pose—and yet the way the woman had done it, it seemed somehow ugly, like she was ridiculing you for whatever prurient impulse had led you to that page. Shoving it in your face and saying, *It's just flesh; it doesn't count for anything, and you're a fool to even hope that it might.* Even if Mae-mae hadn't known the woman in the picture, it would have been scary. But knowing her, that made it worse somehow.

Rachel, Rachel, Rachel . . . It *does* count, damn it. Everything counts for something. Even big boobs and a flat stomach, things you lucked into and didn't have to work for or even want especially. It all counts.

Mae-mae stared at the picture for a long time, then folded it up. She didn't need to look at the other magazine. She knew what was there. Was this what Rachel and her father had argued about? Most likely. The message with it was labeled "installment number two," so he'd probably gotten some more of this crap sent to him. Why? Blackmail?

Before she closed the magazine, she flipped back a page. More pictures of Rachel. Rachel in a cowboy hat, boots, and a fringed leather G-string; Rachel holding a mug of root beer, a big white foam mustache dripping down over a smart ass smile. The title of the spread was *Sugar 'n' Spice* . . . Underneath the title were the words, *Photographs by Clay Wilder.*

"Uh-oh," Mae-mae said softly. She checked the other spreads. *Photos by Clay Wilder. Photographer: Clay Wilder. Pix by C. Wilder.*

Mae-mae's head felt gummed up, leaden. Too much information.

She jammed the magazines back into the manila folder, glanced at her watch. Ten after four, where was Lester anyway?

By four-thirty Mae-mae was getting nervous. Where the hell was he? She called Printmeister. The receptionist said Mr. Paris had left at twenty till four. *Did he say where he was going?* One moment, the receptionist had it written down. There it was. Cosgrave. Mae-mae Cosgrave, that was the name of the lady he was going to see.

"Cos*grove*," Mae-mae said. "With an 'o.' "

"Yeah, whatever," the receptionist said.

Mae-mae hung up. Weird. What was the deal? It was only a ten-minute drive. Even if he ran into traffic, he ought to have been here by now. She drummed her fingers on her desk for a minute, tried his home number. No answer.

Maybe he'd come by while she was in the bathroom. But she'd unlocked the door; there was nothing to stop him from coming in and waiting.

Maybe he had left a note on the receptionist's desk.

She went into the reception area, noticed the door to her conference room was closed. Well, that was the answer. She never closed her conference room. He must have left a note in the conference room. She turned the handle of the door and pushed. Something seemed to be wedged against the door.

She turned the handle again, shoved hard. The door opened about a foot and a half. The light in the conference room was off, but she could see a dim shape on the floor, leaning against the door.

Mae-mae reached inside and turned on the light.

Before she started screaming, a calm voice in her head said: *No wonder; he'd been here all along.* And sure enough he had. The thing wedged against the door was a corpse, a dead thing, its lifeless eyes scanning the ceiling for signs of impending redemption or damnation.

Signs that Lester Paris would never see.

✉

TWENTY-TWO

"**B**usted head," Dick Clark said, looking down at Lester's body through the door of the conference room. "Blunt trauma."

It hadn't taken him more than ten minutes to get there after Mae-mae put in the 911 call. The medical examiner and the fingerprint people and the photographer and a couple uniformed cops were all milling around, looking busy.

Mae-mae covered her face for a minute. Her muscles were trembling, like someone had hooked them to electric wires.

Dick Clark took out his notebook, the one with the rubber band around the pages he'd already written on. "You got it in you to talk for a minute, tell me why Lester was here?"

"Business. He was going to buy Myra Towe's half of Printmeister. We were going to talk about it."

Dick Clark scribbled, asked her some more questions, scribbled some more.

When he was through Mae-mae said, "It happened *here*? How could it have happened here?"

"Like you say, probably when you were freshening up."

"But . . . *here*?" Somehow she couldn't get the idea

191

into her head that he had actually been killed right here in her own office. Murdered somewhere else and dumped here, maybe. Here? It just seemed incomprehensible.

"Oh yeah. You can see on the ceiling, the blood where he was drawing his arm back." Dick Clark demonstrated, lifting his arm up and down like he was hitting somebody with a stick. "See? How the blood would sling off the hammer?"

She looked at him for a minute. "*Hammer*?"

"Whatever. The weapon, I mean."

"Yeah, but why did you say it was a hammer?"

Dick Clark called out to the medical examiner, a thin young man, balding, in a drab gray suit and a stained white apron, "Danny, what'd you think he got hit with?"

"Hard to say right now, but maybe some kind of thin hammer. Like a tack hammer."

Mae-mae said: "What about a ball peen hammer?"

The medical examiner shrugged. "It could be a ball peen hammer. Hard to say."

Dick Clark looked at her sharply, stroked his jaw. "Something going on here I ought to know about?"

"No," she said. "No. It was just something that crossed my mind."

She got all the way home, driving like a maniac, before she noticed the stain on her shoes.

They were blue shoes, so it was hard to see. But there was no mistaking it. She was walking into her house when she first noticed it—something smeared across the toe of the left shoe, a thick red-brown substance. She stared at it for a minute, horrified, then kicked the shoe savagely off her foot. It flew across the room, banged into the couch, skidded to a stop in the middle of the floor. Her one pair of Joan & Davids, those had to be the ones she got blood all over! Damn. Damn! Had she kicked him? Prodded him? Had he fallen against her when she pushed the conference room door open?

She couldn't remember. Couldn't remember at all. All she could remember were the dead eyes staring up at her, the blood caked across his forehead, his mouth, his nose. She had to clean herself off, clean herself off, clean herself off, clean herself . . .

Then she was in the shower, the water running down her naked body. She turned the water on so hot it hurt, seared her flesh, turned her skin red. The scalding water, the soap, the heat running through her hair and down her back, her breasts, her belly—eventually it started to calm her brain, and she began to wind down, the stream of thoughts and images slowing into some kind of sequence. Things started moving in order again. Mae-mae breathed deeply. In. Out. In. Out.

First things first. Take it one step at a time, work through it, think, think. Maybe she'd come up with something.

Who killed Charles Towe?

Don't know.

Who killed Lester Paris?

Don't know.

Was it the same person who killed Charles Towe?

Yes.

Why did this person kill them?

Counterfeiting.

Who else was involved in the counterfeiting?

Don't know.

Speculate.

Paris and Towe had to have been selling the stamps to someone. The buyer funneled the money to them through this offshore corporation, Janus Print Enterprises, under the guise of "consulting fees." Maybe Towe or Paris pissed off the buyers. So the buyers, the people behind Janus, then decided to kill Towe.

Pissed them off how?

Don't know.

Speculate.

Maybe Towe was stealing from them. Maybe he shipped them a load of bad stamps, ones with screwed-up registration, that were likely to be spotted by the postal inspectors. Or maybe Towe said he wouldn't print anymore, that he wanted to get out of the counterfeiting business. It could be a lot of things.

So who could he have sold them to?

Don't know. Maybe somebody who deals with little retail outfits like grocery stores, drugstores, check cashing stores, places where small lots could be sold without being detected. Maybe a client, somebody who does legitimate business with the company—but also wanted fake stamps. Maybe somebody in the direct mail business. Or some kind of Mafia type; or a fulfillment house, the ones Garry Hull called ''lickers and stickers''; or somebody in advertising. Or maybe just a big company that sends a lot of mail.

Anybody else?

Maybe somebody in the post office. After all, who'd be in a better position to run their own special discount program on postage stamps?

What about Clay Wilder—where does he fit in?

He obviously knew something about Towe. He's also a counterfeiter. Maybe he's the buyer. Or maybe he knows who the buyer is.

What about the porn magazines? Where are they coming from?

Somebody must have been trying to blackmail Towe with them. Maybe it was Clay. Maybe it was the buyer.

Okay, and what happened to Candy Frank?

Probably murdered. Two hours ago, I would have thought it was Lester who did it. But now? Hard to tell.

Who else could have done it? Rascoe?

He looks scary enough, but the FBI files didn't show anything on him. He's probably just a real ugly guy with weak social skills.

General conclusions?

Still confused. Need more information. The key is to find out who the buyer is.

Where can you get more information?

Clay Wilder. Rachel Towe.

And?

Chris?

What about Chris?

Don't know about Chris.

Come on, be brave. He had the opportunity, didn't he?

Probably.

Motive?

Don't know. He's not the buyer. He can't be. He'd have lots of money if he was the buyer, wouldn't he?

The hammer. What about the ball peen hammer? He supposedly threatened his wife with a ball peen hammer.

Don't know.

Speculate.

No.

Speculate.

No. Can't face that right now.

You better find something out about that hammer, don't you think? Don't you? Don't you? Don't you?

And then the water went stone cold.

When she finished dressing, Mae-mae called Sebastian. "Mae-mae?" he said. "What's wrong?"

"Something terrible has happened."

"What," said Sebastian, "is the problem with the shoe?"

He was standing in her living room. She had just finished telling him about the murder, and then she had noticed the shoe, the blue Joan & David with the red stain on the toe, lying on the middle of the rug.

She couldn't say anything, could only point at it. She wanted the shoe gone, wanted it taken away from her forever. "Get it away," she said finally. "Throw it away. Please. In the garbage."

Sebastian bent from the waist, picked up the shoe, examined it critically. "Joan and David, how nice. A bit worn, I'm afraid."

Mae-mae kept pointing, her finger only six inches from the stained toe of the shoe.

"Ah," Sebastian said. "A mess we've made." He squinted, peered at the stain distastefully. The shoe hung in front of his blistered, tomato-red face for a long time. Finally he brought it toward his nose and sniffed the toe. He raised his eyebrows slightly, slid an index finger through the congealed red-brown liquid, and then put his finger in his mouth.

"Bordelaise," Sebastian said. "You know, a dash more rosemary wouldn't have hurt a bit."

TWENTY-THREE

Mae-Mae spent most of the weekend with Chris. It didn't go well. She couldn't seem to locate the spark, couldn't make it happen. It was like they were forcing things.

It wasn't him, it wasn't her—it was these murders that were the problem. She kept having this nagging thought: the hammer, the opportunity, the argument between Rachel and Chris, the fact that Chris wanted her to stop looking for the missing money—it all . . . well, didn't exactly *point* right at him. Not directly. Not explicitly. He had no motive as far as she could tell. But something was off kilter. There was a reason Chris wouldn't talk about the murder, a reason beyond the mere avoidance of painful memories. But what was it?

Mae-mae didn't know. All she knew was that when she felt his skin, when she kissed him, when she held his hand, something tight and hard and cold ran through her. Doubt. It was doubt and there was nothing she could do to stop it.

Sunday morning they were sitting in the Majestyk Diner up on Ponce de Leon. Chris was scooping grape jelly out of the plastic package and then chopping it into his scrambled eggs with a knife. Halfway through the

197

eggs he looked up at Mae-mae and said, "What, you don't like jelly?"

But she wasn't thinking about jelly. She was thinking: What if? What if . . . Could this man kill his own father? Mae-mae refused to believe it. Not the tender man she'd spent three of the last four nights with. He wasn't a murderer. He couldn't be.

"Oh," Chris said. "That." He could tell she was thinking about the murders again.

"Yeah. That again."

Chris pushed his plate away, laid his forehead on the Formica tabletop, and stared down between his legs for a minute. When he looked up again, his eyes were wet.

"Why?" Mae-mae said. "Why can't you tell me?"

Chris shook his head, looked at the pile of purple eggs on his plate. "This isn't going to work, is it?"

"Not if—" Not if *what*? Not if he wouldn't talk to her, wouldn't tell her what was on his mind.

Chris took the paper napkin out of his lap, wiped his mouth, and then set the crumpled napkin on top of his unfinished breakfast. "I'm sorry," he said. "I'm so sorry. I just can't."

Then he stood, his eyes full of pale blue regret, and put on his coat.

Mae-mae went home, poured herself a giant glass of Mr. Pibb, and watched TV all afternoon. She learned a lot from TV. She learned about Liz Taylor on *Lifestyles of the Rich and Famous*, how many Rolls-Royces she owned. She also learned about porpoise communication; about the history of oil prospecting in the Austin Chalk; about William F. Buckley's views on high church liturgy; about the love life of Douglas Fairbanks, Jr.; about the Battle of Verdun, where blanched corpses, snagged in barbed wire, had heaped against the redoubts like drifting snow.

After a while she couldn't stand it anymore, so she called Clay Wilder, said she needed to talk. Clay said, yeah, sure, he didn't have a problem with that. What was on her mind? Mae-mae said she'd fill him in when she got there.

What was on her mind was: *who was the buyer?* Who bought the counterfeit stamps? Maybe he'd know something. If Chris couldn't deal with this, the hell with him. She'd handle it herself.

Clay's studio was in a semi-run-down area at the margins of the downtown skyscraper district. Mae-mae parked on the street, three-and four-story buildings of scarred and windburned brick rising all around her. It was a bleak place, the small businesses here hanging on by their fingernails behind a veil of rusting iron bars, dirty glass, steel mesh, burglar alarms, and triple-locked doors.

It was dusk by the time she got there. The neighborhood stayed in the gloomy shadow of the skyscrapers half the day, and when night finally came on, it did so with inevitability, the whole tired place resigning itself glumly to fate.

Clay Wilder's studio was at the top of a dark, brick-walled staircase. The words WILDER IMAGES were stenciled on the black door in fresh gold paint. Mae-mae pressed the bell, and when the lock buzzed she pushed the door open. The studio was a long, open space, an industrial loft with twelve-foot-high steel-trussed ceilings, bare brick walls, and a beautiful wooden floor.

In the center of the dark space stood a small table surrounded by gleaming photographic paraphernalia—tripods, umbrella flash reflectors, lights of various sizes and shapes, a metal stepladder, and several cameras. It reminded her of some kind of complicated NASA machine, antennas poking up at all angles. A dark figure with a ponytail leaned over one of the cameras.

"Be with you in a sec," he said.

Mae-mae walked over to the cluster of equipment. When she got close enough, she could make out Clay Wilder's face, the half-moon scar on his cheek shining in the dim glow of his photographic lamps. He was looking intently into the eyepiece of a Hasselblad, which pointed at a small object laid on the table.

"You ever tried to make a computer board look sexy?" Clay said.

"Sexy?" Mae-mae looked at the object on the table: a piece of green circuit board studded with microchips, lying on a bed of black velvet. A red plastic tape with a twenty-four-pin connector on the end curled around the side like a tail.

"I've tried putting it on blue silk, red velvet, black velvet, blue velvet, a drop cloth, and a white sheet; I've sprayed it with glycerine; I've put purple lights on it; I've stood it up, sat it down . . . and you know what?"

"What?"

"Still looks like a damn circuit board." He handed her a light meter. "Here. Hold that right there." He pointed at the circuit board. Mae-mae held the meter in front of the circuit board while Clay turned a knob, bringing the lights up all around her. For a moment she was blind.

Clay took a couple of pictures of the circuit board, the lights popping softly each time he pressed the trigger of his Hasselblad, then he flipped a light switch and the room was bathed in fluorescent light. Everything in the room seemed to be painted flat black. He led Mae-mae to a black card table in the corner. They sat down on black folding chairs.

Clay smiled sardonically. "To what do I owe the pleasure?" he said in his flat Texas drawl.

Mae-mae leaned her elbows on the table for a minute. "Tell me about counterfeiting," she said finally.

Clay squinted at her for a moment, then his eyebrows went up and down a couple of times. It reminded her of William F. Buckley on the TV program that morning, the way his eyebrows would shoot up for no particular reason while he was bullying some poor shill for the Democratic party.

"Oh, okay!" Clay said finally, a sort of bogus lightness in his voice. "What you want to know? Techniques? A little theory, a little practice? Legal aspects of same? I've got some expertise in all the above." The sardonic smile again, twisting the moon-shaped scar.

"How about telling me a story," she said. "Maybe drawing from personal experience."

Clay pulled a pack of Marlboros out of the pocket of his denim shirt, popped one out, lit it, blew some smoke into the air. "When I was seventeen years old, I quit high school six weeks before graduation, left my home in Texarkana, and went to work for my uncle over in Alabama. He was a printer. I was a real diligent kid, learned all kinds of stuff about printing—photographic techniques, lithography, offset, screen printing, you name it. Time I was nineteen, man, I knew it all. Thought I did, anyway. And I also thought the world was not rewarding me sufficiently for all this effort and diligence I was displaying. I mean I was driving a third-hand Plymouth, living in a broken-down old trailer, only making fourteen five a year. Didn't seem fair for a guy who was busting butt, knew everything in the world, right?"

He pulled on the cigarette, blew the smoke straight up in the air. "Me and this guy, Toby Lane—" He laughed suddenly. "Man, I hadn't thought about Toby in a long time. Me and this fool Toby, we thought we were smart as hell cause we'd figured out a way to print ten-dollar bills. Nothing to it. Cut us some plates, rigged up the press one night, by the time the sun came up, we had us a gym bag full of money, ten grand worth of bills." He smiled. "Every single one of them with the exact same serial number. Smart, huh? We take them home, run them through his cousin's washing machine to give them that nice wash-and-wear look, finish up about ten-thirty the next morning, go out for our triumphal breakfast. The Waffle House out on I-20. Damn Waffle House, man. I get two eggs over easy, hash browns—scattered, smothered, covered, if you ever had that—about eighteen cups of coffee. Oh yeah, and raisin toast.'' He smiled, thinking about the raisin toast, it looked like.

"When we're done, I say, 'This one's on me, Mr. Lane!' He goes, 'No no, Mr. Wilder, this one's on me.' 'No no, Mr. Lane.' We're having some fun. So ends up, I pay. I pass the cook a couple of these fake tens. This beat-up old guy, tattoos all over his arms, buck teeth, he stares at these bills about five minutes, then he takes out another ten, looks at it, puts the fake tens next to the one out of the drawer. 'You got anything else?' he says. 'This here's a counterfeit.' Old Toby, he starts edging over toward the door. I look at him, look at the cook, look at Toby. And then we make a run for the car. I guess we had the ink a couple shades too bright. Looking at it in the daytime, that damn stuff was glowing like a plastic Christmas tree.''

"So you got arrested?"

"Arrested, searched, convicted." He held the cigarette up to his face but then didn't put it in his mouth. "They took us down in no time flat. Sent us up to the federal camp at Talladega. My old bosom buddy Tobe told the court I was the ringleader, the big cheese, it was all my idea. Thanks to which I got an extra two years.'' He pulled on the cigarette and then laughed hard, the smoke drifting out of his mouth in small fuzzy balls. "He was right, too. Whole thing was my idea.''

Mae-mae drummed her fingers on the table. "Okay," she said finally. "That's fairly old news. Tell me something new. Tell me something relevant.''

Clay crushed his cigarette into the surface of the black table. "You want a beer, counselor?" he said.

"That might be good," she said.

Clay got up and walked across the room to a black partition. After a minute he came out from behind the partition with a couple of Michelobs, nice and cold. Mae-mae didn't realize how much she'd needed the beer until she started drinking it—her mind still unsettled, jittery, flying all over the place. She kept seeing Lester Paris's dead eyes staring up at her. They had had a milky look, like a gutted fish.

"Let me tell you what I learned over there at Talladega. I learned that criminals are fools." Clay looked steadily at her for a minute. "I mean really, they are just *dumb* people. You spend a few years in prison, you're constantly amazed what a bunch of idiots they got hanging around those places. It took me a while for it to sink in, but by the time I had served my four years and six months, I had realized something real, real interesting. I put two and two together and said, if criminals are dumb—and I'm a criminal—then I'm dumb."

He fiddled around with his Michelob, peeling the label off, folding it over and over until it had turned into an oozing square wad about the size of his fingernail.

"Prison," he said. Then he made a motion with his hand, a slow, straight chopping motion. "Prison either screws you up or it puts you on the straight and narrow. See . . . what happened to me, it made me realize that the only way for me to end my days as a dumb ass was to never, ever, ever, ever, *ever* again commit a crime. I mean, don't blow stop signs, don't jaywalk, don't play pool with your buddies that deal a little weed, don't steal, don't cheat at cards, man, don't even tell a *lie*!" He looked at Mae-mae for a while. "You understand what I'm saying?"

"Keep going."

"I'm saying Charles Towe hired me to work at Printmeister for one reason and one reason only. Cause on the application form, I checked the little box that said 'Yes, I have been convicted of a felony offense,' and then in the little blank I wrote in 'Counterfeiting.' That's why he hired me. I thought he believed me when I made my little speech about giving up my life of crime, all that hoo-ha. I thought he just wanted a good printer." Clay Wilder smiled bitterly, the half-moon on his cheek standing out white against his dark skin. "Only he didn't. The son of a bitch thought I was just slinging him some throwaway line. He thought he could *trust* me because I was a criminal. Can you believe that? Can you damn believe that?"

"So that's it?"

"Yeah. He was counterfeiting postage stamps. Thirty-two-cent stamps. One dollar stamps. I never heard of anything so dumb in my life. *Postage* stamps! Jesus." Clay drank some beer. "Five dollar stamps, you ever seen one of those? It's got a picture of a guy named Thurlow Weed on it."

"Who's Thurlow Weed?"

"I don't have the slightest idea." Clay drank slowly. "You know what it's like to decide that you're not going to give in to that kind of thing anymore? That you're going to be an absolutely honest guy? And every day when you apply for a job, or somebody asks you where you went to college or whatever, and you say, well actually I spent my college days in the penal fraternity down in Talladega—you have any idea what it's like seeing that expression on their face? The way their smile just freezes up and sits there, and they look at you like you're some kind of roach that just crawled out of the silverware drawer? You know what that's like?"

Mae-mae shook her head. "That's why you didn't like Rachel's father. That's why you quit the job at Printmeister."

Clay upended the beer, drained it, set it down carefully on the black table. "He presumed to *know* me. He presumed to *know* that I was a worthless piece of bug shit, and that anything I said to the contrary was just some kind of quaint little lie." He laughed harshly.

"So who killed him?" Mae-mae said.

He shrugged. "Who knows? Who cares? That guy meant nothing to me."

Mae-mae took another swallow of the beer. "Let's move on to pornography," she said.

"Pornography? That's one of those things, it's kind of in the eyes of the beholder, wouldn't you say?"

Mae-mae opened her briefcase, took out the envelope she'd gotten from Colleen Mastronunzio, spread the magazines across the table.

A tiny adolescent smirk worked its way into the edges of Clay's mouth. "I like *Tail* best. Intellectually, I mean. Can't beat that for conceptual elegance. Okay, babe, stick your butt in the air and say cheese."

"Am I supposed to be amused?" Mae-mae said.

"Hey, look, you can choose to get all worked up about how this stuff exploits women, sanctions the rapist mentality, objectifies women, whatever—or you can laugh at it. I choose to laugh." He picked up the Xeroxed message sitting on top of the magazines and read it. "Yeah, somebody had sent some stuff like this to him a couple days before he was killed. Rachel, she posed for a whole bunch of these things. It was her idea." He laughed. "Her dad, he chose to get pretty worked up about it. They had a fight after he got the first shipment of this stuff."

"And where did that lead?"

Clay looked around the room. "I guess you ought to ask her that." He didn't say anything else.

"Okay, then tell me about photography."

Clay shrugged. "I got into it in prison. My cell mate was photographer for the prison newspaper. He and another guy in the lunch line got in an argument over who got to have the last ham biscuit on the tray. The other guy beat him to death with a soup ladle. Prison, everything's kind of finders keepers. I got his camera, so I kind of fell into the job with the camp newspaper." He drank some beer. "Ever since I got out, I've been working toward this—getting myself set up so I could take pictures full-time."

"You make a decent living at it?"

"It's coming along," he said. His face took on a calm, satisfied look. "Coming along. I like taking pictures, so I don't resent doing the work. Even circuit boards. I could have let that thing alone a couple hours ago, but when you're trying to get something right, it's best to just keep at it.''

Mae-mae finished her beer. "Can I have another one of these?" she said. "Suddenly I feel like . . ." But she wasn't sure what she felt like.

"Help yourself," Clay said. "They're in the door of the refrigerator." He pointed at the black partition.

She got up and went around the partition. On the other side was a tiny makeshift room. There was a gas stove, a refrigerator, and a sink on one side of the room; on the other side, a bed, a desk, and a bookshelf. Everything was neat, squared away. A couple of amateurish conté crayon nudes were Scotch taped to the walls: both of them were women; neither of them Rachel. There was a book on the desk, *Let Us Now Praise Famous Men*, the one with the Walker Evans pictures in the front. The book was open to a photograph of a jug-eared man in overalls, a kind of stupid-faced guy with a look of beat-down sadness in his small, sweet eyes. His hands hung at his sides. There were tin pails sitting on a plank shelf behind his head.

Mae-mae got two beers out of the door of the refrigerator, walked out, and sat down again.

"Who do you think killed Lester Paris?"

He shook his head. "I'm serious," he said. "I don't know; I don't care."

"But Lester *was* involved in the counterfeiting, right?"

"Oh yeah. Definitely."

"Do you know who the buyer was?"

"Of the stamps?" He shook his head. "No idea. They didn't exactly advertise that around the shop. Lester would pack the stamps in a couple briefcases and off he'd go in his little Porsche. That was all there was to it."

Another dead end. With Lester Paris and Charles

Towe dead, who was going to point the way to the buyer? It occurred to Mae-mae that maybe that was why Lester and Charles were dead: The buyer had decided, for whatever reason, that it was time to erase his tracks. So maybe the things pointing to Chris were just distractions, coincidences.

"And Candy?" Mae-mae said. "Was that murder or was that a car wreck?"

Clay laughed. "Man, she'd been eating rye whiskey with her Wheaties since I started working there. The only wonder is it didn't happen sooner." Then his face fell. "She was okay, though. Nuts, but okay. It's a damn shame." He screwed the top off the bottle and then, with a look of puzzlement on his face, said, "Why's it so hard? I mean really, why is it so damn hard to just live a normal life, not hurt anybody, not raise your voice, not drink too much, not act like an asshole?"

Mae-mae didn't say anything for a while.

"So," he said suddenly, looking her in the eye. "I've bared my soul for you. What you gonna bare for me?"

"Not my fat butt, that's for sure." The beer was moving around in Mae-mae's veins. She wondered dreamily what it would be like to take her clothes off in front of a strange guy, lie down on the floor, let him take pictures of her. She imagined lying down on the floor like a corpse, her hands folded over her breasts. All in all it didn't seem real appealing.

"What's this about your ass? You've got a totally normal ass."

"Let's be honest. I have a very big butt."

"No, you don't." Clay showed a thin line of bunched-up teeth. "Trust me. I'm a professional."

That night Mae-mae couldn't sleep, so she turned on the television again and lay in bed, flipping the remote control. Kojak was grabbing a woman by her arm, squeezing it. David Letterman was listening to Reba McEntire tell a bad joke about redheads. A bunch of white boys in leather pants were making sex noises and thrashing their weird-shaped guitars. A French guy with a speech defect was whipping up puff pastry in a gleaming kitchen. Mae-mae kept pushing the remote control button.

She stopped at Channel thirty-seven. Well, look at that: it was Barry and June King. They were sitting in swoopy green chairs at a round green table interviewing an earnest looking young guy in a suit. The earnest stooge was clutching a scarlet book in his lap. It said I HURT! on the cover.

"Tell me," June was saying to the guy in the suit, "tell me what happened when you unlocked your rage." She seemed pretty interested in the answer, pretty intent on the stooge's face.

The guy frowned soberly and nodded his head. "You know, June, I just learned to stop defeating myself. That's what it comes down to. In the space of a single year I went from living in a four-hundred-square-foot apartment with a leaky roof, working sixty- and seventy-hour weeks, and making nineteen thousand dollars a year—"

"Yes?" June was nodding her head, her green eyes looking straight through the guy. She was desperate to hear the whole story. "Yes?"

"I went from a hand-to-mouth type life-style, to a point whereby in one year I was clearing over ten thousand dollars a month. After taxes!" He looked around like he was waiting for the studio audience to applaud. They didn't. "Now I'm living in a twenty-three-room home with a swimming pool and a cabana, and flying across the country in my own private plane." He smiled. Earnestly.

Barry King swung his swoopy chair around so he was facing a different camera and said, "Now that's a story." He stroked his gray beard sagely for a moment and told the home audience, "We'll be right back after a brief message explaining how this miracle mind technology can be put to work for *you*."

Mae-mae yawned. This was better than sleeping pills. "We're gonna lick this thing," she said. She didn't wait for the message about the miracle mind technology, just turned off the TV and burrowed into her pillow.

TWENTY-FOUR

"What a great view," Rachel Towe said. She was standing in the window of Mae-mae's office, looking down at the MARTA tracks. "I bet you can get a lot of thinking done up here."

"So everyone says," Mae-mae said. Rachel wore a paisley skirt, blue leather flats, and a blue bolero jacket over a silk blouse. Her hair was braided and pinned up on the back of her head. She seemed to be impersonating someone—God only knew who. "What's on your mind, Rachel?"

Rachel turned around and sat down. Her eyes were red, like she'd been crying. "Clay told me you came by last night. He told me you had seen me in the magazines, the ones they sent to Dad." She hesitated. "I figured you ought to know what that was all about."

"Okay," Mae-mae said.

"I mean the cops, they don't seem to be doing anything. You're the only one who seems to care." She stopped for a minute, then crossed her arms tightly over her chest. "Why is that, why do you care?"

"I'm just trying to look out for your mother's interests," she said, "like I'm paid to do." Which was not really it at all. The problem was Mae-mae didn't really know the answer to that herself.

Rachel looked down at the floor for a minute. "I'm not ashamed of the pictures. Okay? I don't think there's anything wrong with getting paid to take your clothes off. It's just not a big deal."

Mae-mae sipped her tepid coffee, waited.

"Dad and I had a real big fight about this stuff. The day he . . . died. I didn't tell you about it."

"Go on."

Rachel shrugged. "That's about it, really. See, somebody had sent a bunch of these magazines to Dad. Along with a note. I didn't see the note, but it was some kind of threat."

"What did they threaten to do?"

"I don't know. They were going to show the magazines to somebody—to Mom, I think—if he didn't do what they wanted him to do."

Mae-mae said, "What were they trying to make him do? Did he tell you?"

Rachel shook her head. "No. He just said that Mom would die if she found out. I mean, I'm thinking, hey, this is the twentieth century, right? Why would anybody get uptight just because their daughter's in a skin mag? I don't get it."

"*Would* your mother get uptight about it?"

Rachel shrugged. "Well . . . sure. But she'd get over it. She's tougher than she looks." She made a soft, breathy noise. "But I guess—I guess Dad never understood that."

Mae-mae finished her coffee, spat the dregs back into the cup. "Tell me about the fight."

Rachel shrugged again. "Not much to tell. I get this call from Dad that afternoon. He's all bent out of shape, telling me somebody sent him this . . . filth. That was his word. Filth. I'm thinking, you know, give me a break, but he tries to make a real big deal out of it. So I said screw it, it's time for him to get over this daddy's-little-girl crap. I mean I'd *had it*!" She looked quizzically around the room. "You mind if I smoke?"

"Go ahead." Mae-mae pushed her empty Styrofoam coffee cup across the table. "My only ashtray," she added.

Rachel took a cigarette out of a funny looking box and lit it. The musty, acrid odor of burned cloves filled the room. "So anyway, I got my stuff together, every nude shot I could find, threw it in the portfolio, and went over to the office. I figured I'd just have it out with him, because I was tired of him trying to run my life. We got there, I don't know, maybe six o'clock, and I went inside, dumped the stuff on his desk. It was like, here, look at this. Here's Daddy's girl. She's got tits, she's got an ass. If you can't live with that, hey, it's not my problem."

"How'd he take it?"

Rachel's face was cold, dismissive, all the strong emotions hiding somewhere. She shrugged. "He said I was, you know . . . a whore. Stuff like that. So we had a little argument, did a little yelling and screaming." Rachel said the words like none of it mattered much.

"And then?"

"And then we left."

"We?" Mae-mae said. "You and your father?"

"Oh. No. Me and Chris. My car was in the shop, so Chris had driven me over."

So that put Chris at the scene of the crime. Great. What a welcome surprise. "Did Chris go in, too?"

"No," Rachel said. Her face went blank, like she was remembering something. "Wait a sec. I take that back. He didn't go in with me, but when I got back in the car, I was crying and everything, I was a little upset. Anyway, I get back in the car and we drive off and then when I had told him what happened, Chris gets on his macho high horse and says he's going to go talk to him. I think he got worried because of all the bad things I said."

"Bad things?"

Rachel made a face. "I said I wanted to . . . kill him,

stuff like that." She made a thin, unconvincing noise that resembled a laugh. "Kind of ironic, huh?"

Mae-mae looked at her for a minute. "So Chris went in after you?"

"Yeah. Turned the car around, drove back. I kept telling him not to bother. . . ." She grimaced. "He was always defending me. Him and Dad got into it over me all the time."

"And he went in by himself?"

Rachel nodded.

For a second Mae-mae felt nauseated, like a hand had clenched around the base of her throat. "As I recall from the first time we talked," she said, "you said the Kings were there, too?"

"Yeah. But they were gone when I came out."

"And Donald Rascoe?"

Rachel shook her head. "Don't know. I couldn't really remember. I know I saw him when I went in, but he might have left."

"So conceivably your brother is the last person who saw your father alive?"

Rachel looked at Mae-mae sharply. "Besides the killer, you mean."

Mae-mae didn't say anything for a minute. The hand around her throat had started squeezing with a slow, steady throb. "How long was he in with your father?"

"Not long. Ten minutes maybe." Rachel stubbed out her clove cigarette. "Then he came back out and he wouldn't talk to me. Just got in the car and drove off. I remember his hands were shaking." She examined her cigarette butt minutely, like it was about to tell her something: an oracle scrutinizing the sheep's liver. "The way his face looked? Man, they must have really got into it."

Mae-mae got up and looked out the window. Maybe it did help you think, staring down at the little trees and the little train tracks. Things seemed more abstract when you were way up above the world. Like an architect's rendering. The things going on down there on the ground, though, there was no way of getting away from them. It just kept going on and on, no matter how much you tried to slink off, get some distance from it.

"Now about Chris . . ." Mae-mae said.

For a minute Rachel didn't say anything. She took out another cigarette, tapped it on the edge of the desk, and put it in her mouth—but didn't light it. When she spoke she didn't answer the question. "Hey, guess what, Mae-mae?" she said. Her voice was a little too girlish, a little too enthusiastic. "I got my big Hollywood break today. I'm going to be on TV."

"I didn't know," Mae-mae said dryly, "that you were an actress."

"I'm not. It's more like modeling, really. What I do, I have to lie on the floor in a red negligee with this fake blood all over my neck. These two guys come in and one of them, the fat guy in the raincoat, he looks down at me and says, 'What a hell of a waste, Cartwright.' Then they zip me up in a black plastic bag. We were supposed to finish shooting yesterday, but they had technical problems."

"Technical problems?" Mae-mae said politely.

"Yeah, the zipper kept sticking on the body bag."

Mae-mae kept staring out the window. Why did Rachel keep deflecting the conversation away from Chris? There could only be one answer to that: She must suspect him, too. But why would he have done it? Did it have something to do with Rachel? Had the whole counterfeiting thing been a smoke screen? He wasn't the buyer, Mae-mae had already dismissed that possibility: he didn't have enough money. The buyer had to have a lot of money. Maybe he worked for the buyer. Maybe he knew the buyer. So maybe the motive didn't have anything to do with the counterfeiting. But if that was true, then why kill Lester Paris?

It had to have something to do with the counterfeiting. Something was still missing.

The buyer. The buyer. Who the hell was the buyer? Some wiseguy from New Jersey? Somebody in the direct mail business? Somebody in the post office? Maybe it was time to confront him, to ask Chris flat out if he killed his father.

The hand, tightening and tightening. "Rachel, I hate to say this, but have you considered the possibility that Chris might have killed your father?"

Rachel looked at the floor. "Have I considered it? What's that supposed to mean?" Her voice tight and peevish.

"Rachel. Come on."

"What are you asking *me* for? You think Chris killed his own father, why don't you ask Chris?" She looked up from the floor, her eyes malevolent and blue. "Call him up. Ask him. I got no interest in that."

After a minute Mae-mae spoke quietly, "Where can I get hold of Chris during the day?"

"He's kind of hard to reach after ten or eleven o'clock," Rachel said. "He's usually out on his route."

"His route?" Mae-mae paused. "What does he do, drive a milk truck?"

"I thought you guys were getting to be . . ." Rachel smiled slightly. ". . . like, intimate."

"What kind of route, Rachel?"

"He's really a musician. It's just a day job."

"Rachel! What kind of route?"

"For Godsake, Mae-mae, I thought you knew. I thought you knew. He's a postman."

She must have seen the look on Mae-mae's face, must have sensed the numbness spreading through her skin, the hard hand tightening on her innards, because then Rachel Towe said: "No. No. No. It can't be. It can't. He's the most decent, gentle guy I know."

TWENTY-FIVE

Mae-mae went home for lunch, sat out on her back stoop, eating her cottage cheese and cucumber slices and staring into the air. The sky was a cloudless, vapid blue. The sun was bright and the air was crisp. It should have been a perfect day.

But she couldn't get her mind to track on anything. It was taking all her concentration just trying not to think about dead, staring eyes looking up from the floor of her office. The shadows of trees, tousled by the wind, danced in the scrubby grass of her backyard. A line of debris—leaves and pine needles from a recent rain—bisected the cracked concrete of her small patio, piles of dead earthworms curled up among the leaves. The rain had washed them up on the concrete and then when the storm was over the sun had killed them in droves.

When Mae-mae got back to the office there was a message on the machine. "Hi, this is Barry King from Motivational Techniques Research. It's very important that I reach you today. Please call me at my office."

She wished that there had been one from Chris. She played the tape over, as though it would conjure up a second message, some kind of reassurance from Chris. "Hi, this is Barry King . . ."

216

Mae-mae turned down the volume, walked into the conference room, and looked at the stain on the floor, the long thin splashes of blood across the ceiling. There was a bad smell in the room—a salty, meaty odor. The police had put a piece of yellow tape across the door. It seemed hard to believe someone had died in there only two days ago. She was going to have to call Dick Clark, find out when she could get the carpet cleaners and the painters in. Not that she could afford them. Maybe she'd have to do it herself. She sighed. When it rains it pours.

She went back into her office, picked up the phone, and called Barry King. "Miz Cosgrove!" he said. "How are *you* today?"

"I'm fine," Mae-mae said. "I've got a message here that you called."

"Right. Right. Absolutely." Barry King sounded like he was about to stick his foot in the door, try to sell her a vacuum cleaner or a magazine subscription. "I heard the terrible news about Lester Paris this morning. A real shocker. Right there in your office! Absolutely a devastating, devastating thing."

"Mm-hmm," Mae-mae said.

"Devastating."

"It was pretty frightening."

"Well that's not, frankly, why I called. We realize that Myra and Suzanne are in a real difficult position right now."

"Suzanne?"

"Suzanne Paris. Lester's wife."

"Oh."

"Point is, we realize that Printmeister is a valuable asset, real important thing to both of them. Now at this point in time we're big customers of theirs and, frankly, type of volume we produce, we've been giving a certain amount of thought to acquiring a printing plant ourselves." He paused, cleared his throat. "So this morning June and I are talking and it occurs to me, hey, maybe we've got some synergy here, right?"

"Synergy."

"Sure, sure," Barry King enthused. "We need a printing plant, and Suzanne and Myra need to realize some value in an asset which, correct me if I'm wrong, they aren't in a position to do much with themselves."

"You're saying you want to acquire Printmeister."

"Let's put it this way, we're interested in exploring our options. Now, reason I'm calling you, I contacted Myra this morning and she directed me to speak with you on the subject. Said you were representing her on this type thing."

Mae-mae fiddled with a hangnail, thinking about it. This was a good turn for Myra. With Charles and Lester dead, Printmeister was effectively gutted. No one to take client orders, no one to make bids, no one to control the flow of work. Which meant that the value of the business had fallen overnight to practically nothing. Printmeister wasn't even a business anymore: it was just a warehouse full of printing presses.

"I think we've got something to talk about," Mae-mae said. "When's a good time for you?"

"Sooner the better," Barry King said. "I called over there today and Donald Rascoe seems to have things under control—but let's face it, that won't last forever. He's not the guy you want to have calling on customers, huh?" Barry King laughed.

Mae-mae opened her calendar, flipped to the next day. "How about tomorrow, say . . . nine-ish?"

"Our office be okay?"

"Your office, nine o'clock."

Mae-mae set the phone in the cradle and wrote SNAKE OIL on the line next to nine o'clock, a big X through the next two and a half hours. That ought to be enough time to get this thing started.

Maybe she'd go over and talk to Rascoe this afternoon. He was the one person she hadn't had a chance to talk to at any length yet. She could find out when he left the building, what he'd seen the night Towe was killed.

Then tonight she'd talk to Chris.

In a public place. A *well-lit* public place. She wanted to trust him. She really did. But . . . God*damn*, thinking that way, it felt like poison running through her brain.

"Knock knock!" An enthusiastic voice from the reception room.

"Come on in," Mae-mae called.

A man in a postman's uniform filled the doorway. Only it wasn't her regular postman. It was Chris Towe.

"Special delivery," he said in a quiet voice.

"Chris," she said weakly.

He was smiling at her, his blue eyes lit up, bright but watchful behind his little round glasses. "Guess what I've got for you?" He was holding something behind his back.

The main thing she was conscious of was that she was alone. Alone, alone, alone. Keep calm. That was the key. Just keep calm, don't say anything, don't do anything stupid.

It was all mixed up—one part of her glad to see him, one part afraid, one part ashamed of being afraid, one part frustrated with her own confusion. Was he the one? Was he? She studied his face, looking for a clue. But there was just no knowing. You look at a person's face too carefully, you start to see irregularities, flaws—one eye higher than the other, lips a little too thin, wrinkles starting to pile up under the eyes. But truth? You don't see that. There's nothing written down there, nothing unambiguous or certain. Finally it's just flesh you see, the same collection of features, the same general arrangement as the dead thing she'd found in her conference room.

"Come on," he said insistently. "Guess."

Mae-mae shook her head. Her throat tight, dry.

"Okay, here's a hint." He was still smiling boyishly.

"I'm playing hooky from work. It's lunchtime. I'm coming to see you. It's a beautiful day . . ."

"I don't *know*."

He whipped his hand out from behind his back. He was holding a bottle of wine. "Finest wine available under a screw top," he said. "I've also got sandwiches—your choice of egg salad, tuna fish, or chicken dijon. Plus barbecue potato chips, pasta salad, and . . . the coup de grace . . ." He pulled something out from behind the door. A guitar. "Romantic music!"

"Chris . . ." Mae-mae said.

"Wait! Wait! I forgot the flowers!" He looked around like he was expecting flowers to pop up out of the floor. "Well, anyway I've got flowers down in the truck."

"We have to talk," Mae-mae said.

"I know." His smile went away. "I know."

"I already ate," she said. "But what the hell, let's go have a picnic anyway."

He had put on the dog. Flowers in a cut-glass vase, a blanket and pillows to sit on, glasses, real silver, the guitar, a picnic basket full of food, a decent Chianti (that did *not*, in fact, come in a screw top bottle). Under most circumstances it would have been really nice. The timing was bad, though: the whole thing had a kind of funereal quality to it.

They had gone down to Piedmont Park, set everything up on a hillock with a good view of the IBM Tower, the Driving Club, the pond, the grass sloping away down toward the water. There were some bushes around them, so it felt kind of private. People were walking dogs and holding hands all over the park.

Chris poured the wine intently, giving it more concentration than it really required. When he was done, he handed Mae-mae a glass. "I guess the chemistry's a little weak today," he said.

They tried to make small talk, but couldn't pull it off.

"You want to know why I brought you out here, Mae-mae?'' he said finally, blue eyes focused on her face. She didn't say anything. He looked down at himself, started flicking cracker crumbs off the front of his blue shirt. ''All this stuff going on, it makes you think about what's important, what's not.'' He looked away again. ''I feel like I need to be straight with you and so I wanted to bring you out here to say—'' He shook his head, looked down at his wineglass for a minute and then up at her again. ''I just wanted to say I'm crazy about you.''

''Thank you,'' Mae-mae said. What a lame thing to say. Goddamn, he just seemed só . . . *nice*. How do you handle *nice*?

''Thank you?'' Chris rested his chin on his hand for a minute. ''*Thank you* is the best I can get?''

Mae-mae took a deep breath. ''Okay, Chris,'' she said. ''Okay. We're being straight here, right?''

Chris set his glass on the blanket, dipped his finger in the wine, ran it once around the rim. It made a noise, a high crystalline sob. ''There's another guy. There's another guy, isn't there?''

''Chris, that's not the point.''

''It's not that guy Sebastian, is it? He's gay, isn't he? Isn't he gay? I thought he was gay.''

''No,'' Mae-mae said. ''There's no other guy. I'm not married, I'm not a lesbian, I don't have an incurable disease. That's not what I'm talking about.''

Chris stuck his finger in his mouth, sucked on it. ''Well,'' he said dryly. ''What a relief.''

''You said you want to be straight, right?''

Chris nodded.

''Okay, then you've got to promise me, right now, that you'll be straight with me. That you won't get up and stomp off in five minutes.''

''Done.''

Mae-mae fixed her gaze on his. ''It's about your father,'' she said. ''I know it's . . . painful for you. But we've got to talk about it. And I mean *right now*.''

Chris's face clouded for a minute, then he downed his entire glass of wine. "Fair enough," he said in a whisper. He poured until his wineglass was full again. "If it means that much to you."

"It does," Mae-mae said. "I just need to ask you some questions."

Chris nodded. His face was gray, pale crevices bracketing his mouth. His eyes were so blue that when she looked into them it was like she was looking through his head and into the empty sky beyond.

"Tell me what you know about the counterfeiting."

Chris wouldn't look her in the eye. He just stared down into his wine as though there were some kind of answer at the bottom of his glass. "I worked there on weekends sometimes, nights, whatever. Just helping out. I knew." His voice was low, hard to make out.

"Why did he do it?"

Chris smiled bitterly. "It was my fault."

"How so?"

"You want to know the truth? It wasn't the money. It was because he was a perfectionist."

Mae-mae made a quizzical face.

Chris held up three fingers, like an Eagle Scout. "Swear to God. My crazy old man was the world's most exacting printer. I mean printers, they're a stubborn, meticulous, pain in the ass breed of people, but he was the worst, the absolute worst of them." He smiled again, but this time it was a sad, fond smile. "What happened was Lester started printing these fake postage stamps, just a couple small lots, as a favor to some client. And he screwed them up—because, I mean, he didn't know jack about printing, not really. And so Dad found him one night printing this stuff and he flew off the handle. I can just see him, pissing and moaning about the colors being wrong, the ink smearing and all that." He laughed softly. "Man, I can just hear him."

"So he did the job over, did it right?" Mae-mae said wonderingly.

Chris nodded. "Just to prove that he wouldn't send out second-rate work." Chris drank some wine. "Unbelievable, isn't it? He said, 'Paris, you want to get us sent to jail, fine, but at least print the stamps right. At least do it right.'" He laughed again. "Crazy son of a bitch. Then once he'd thought about it, you know, decided maybe this wasn't such a great idea, well . . . it was too late. First, he was making piles of money, and second, he was in up to his eyeballs. They could threaten to roll him over to the cops if he backed out."

"They?"

Chris shrugged. "The buyers. Whoever they were."

"So did you have anything to do with the counterfeiting?"

Chris shook his head. "I knew it was happening. But I wasn't involved."

"Not with the printing?"

"No."

"Not with the sales, the distribution, nothing?"

"No. Lester handled that."

Mae-mae took a sip of her wine. It didn't seem to have a taste at all, just left a burning sensation down the center of her chest when she swallowed. "I thought you said it was your fault. I don't see the connection."

Chris tapped the patch on his sleeve, the U.S. Postal Service logo. "I was joking around once with Lester. I'd just read this thing in a post office newsletter, a story about a guy out in Wyoming who'd printed up like thirteen million dollars' worth of bogus stamps. You know, post office people were supposed to be on the lookout for them. Well, Lester asks me all these questions about how they can identify counterfeits: did they use ultraviolet dyes, special paper, all that kind of thing." He sipped his wine. "I thought he was just curious. Next thing I know he's in the business."

"What about Clay Wilder? Where's he fit?"

"Clay. He's a strange guy. You might not think it looking at him, but he's a real straight arrow in a lot of ways. Too straight, if you ask me. He went through some hard times early in his life and I guess it turned him into this tough . . . this completely uncompromising guy. All hard edges. That's why he quit working at the shop. Couldn't let himself be involved . . .'' Chris hesitated, like he was about to betray a confidence. ''He'd been in prison once and didn't want to go back.''

It all sounded plausible. But then why had he avoided talking about it all this time?

Mae-mae said, ''Do you know who killed Lester Paris?''

Chris's face was expressionless for a minute, like a mask, then he said, ''No. I don't have any knowledge about that.''

''Okay, what about this? Does this mean anything to you?'' She dropped the envelope that Candy Frank had given her into his lap.

He adjusted his glasses, looked closely at the stamp. ''Yeah, that's a counterfeit, alright.'' He took out the letter, read it, folded it back into the envelope, sighed. ''Dad was trying to get out of the business, I think. I know he was never comfortable with it. So it looks like they were threatening him, trying to force him into keeping the presses rolling.''

''Okay,'' Mae-mae said. ''Another question. Your dad apparently wrote a draft on a mutual fund he had. A draft for twenty thousand dollars. It was never cashed. Do you know anything about that?''

Chris shook his head. Again, just for a second, his face went completely expressionless. ''No.''

Again, Mae-mae tried to see what was going on in his head—but it was impossible to make out. Was he lying? Did he know something else, something connected, that he didn't want to volunteer? She felt like they were closing in on something, something terrible and unexpected. But what? She felt the fist tightening against her stomach again. That and a chilly numbness creeping into her fingers, her lips, her toes.

She had a sudden urge to just stand up and walk away, to be alone where nobody else's problems could intrude. Up on that pole again, maybe, just her and the sky. You could get addicted to that, to being isolated and not having to screw around with anybody else, not having deal with anybody else's wants and needs and pains. But it was no good, living that way. It was no good.

And besides, she could feel the tug of something, some force pulling them both toward a destination she couldn't make out. But what was it? Where were they headed? It was scaring the hell out of her, but she couldn't stop it.

"Let's talk about the day your father was killed." The words coming out almost despite her. "You and your sister went to Printmeister that night, didn't you?"

Chris was sinking into a ball, the wineglass clutched between his knees. "Yeah."

"What time?"

"Six, six-thirty, seven."

"Was anybody there while you were?"

"I told this stuff to the police."

"So tell me."

"Rascoe was there. The shop foreman. Also these two clients. Barry and June King?"

"I've heard of them. Anybody else?"

"Nope."

"Your sister went inside. What happened then?"

Chris sipped pensively, stared into the glass, then threw the rest of the red liquid away. The long thin red arc it traced through the air reminded Mae-mae of the bloodstains on the ceiling of her conference room. The fist was clenching and unclenching in her guts. It was hard to breathe.

It struck Mae-mae that they were isolated, more so than she had thought when they sat down. All the dog walkers and hand holders seemed to have disappeared from view, hidden by the bushes that flanked their picnic blanket.

"What happened then," Chris said, "is the Kings came out, hopped in their Jaguar, drove off." He looked away, down toward the still, black pond. "I think Rascoe must have come out after them and left, too. Yeah, he must have, because he wasn't there . . . later."

"And then?"

"Rachel came out. She'd had this argument with Dad and she was . . . she was really cut up." Something was boring out from behind his eyes, hollowing them out. He put his hands over his face for a minute. "If there's anything I hated my dad for, it was the way he unloaded on her. Her and Mom both."

"What did they argue about?"

Chris shrugged. "I don't know."

"Then what?"

"I went back in to talk to him."

"Immediately?" Mae-mae said. "Or did you drive off and then come back?"

Chris thought about it. He had a vacant look on his face, like his mind had been taken over by what had happened that night. "That's right. I forgot about that. We drove down Peachtree, and then I decided to go back. He was dumping on her because he was pissed off at himself—you know, because he was worried about other stuff." An angry look flashed through his eyes. "It wasn't fair. It just wasn't fair doing that to her."

"How long did it take for you to get back to the shop?"

"We were gone maybe ten, fifteen minutes."

"And when you got there?"

"I went in, had it out with him, told him . . . told him . . ." His face seemed to crumple.

"What?"

"Not to talk to her like that again."

"And then you left."

He nodded.

Again, it all seemed plausible. Mae-mae opened her purse, pulled out the manila folder with the porn magazines inside. She dumped the magazines out on the picnic blanket. "This mean anything to you?" she said.

Chris stared at the magazines for a long time. His face had gone gray-white again, a tiny blanched spot perching on each cheekbone.

Something about the look on his face scared her. She could feel it, the fear in him. No, not exactly fear. Dread. And it was in her, too. Dread—running hot in her stomach. Dread—stealing the sensation from her lips, her fingers. Dread of something terrible, unfathomable that was about to happen.

"Chris?" she said. The park was quiet now, deserted, like they were the only people there. Where were all the dogs? Where were all the kissy people, all the hand holders?

"Alright," he said finally. "Alright, the hell with it." He reached into his pocket, pulled out his wallet, took out a small folded piece of paper, and dropped it on the pile.

Mae-mae looked at the piece of paper. It was about the size of a check.

"Go ahead," Chris said.

She picked up the piece of paper, unfolded it, straightened it on her thigh. It was a draft on the Imperial Balanced Fund Number Two, check number 108, made out to cash in the amount of $20,000. Mae-mae turned the check over. It was endorsed by Charles Towe. His handwriting underneath it said, *Pay to the order of Christopher Towe.* There was no signature below that. Chris had never signed the check.

Mae-mae looked at him. "I don't understand," she said. "What does it mean?"

"You need answers so bad, there's your answer." Chris smiled coldly at her. "There's your answer."

"I don't understand."

"It was me," Chris said. He was still smiling the empty smile, his eyes still as blue and featureless as the sky. "I killed him. I killed my father."

* * *

Mae-mae stared off down the hill. They weren't alone anymore. A couple of college kids were kissing each other down on the jogging trail while a small, hairy dog ran around and around them in circles, yapping furiously. The sun was coming down on them, bright and pitiless, coming down on them all.

Now that he'd said it, Mae-mae didn't feel scared anymore, didn't feel sad or sick. There was just an ache, an empty, hungry sort of feeling like there was something important that she'd forgotten to do—but she couldn't even remember what the thing was she'd forgotten about. Just that vague, uneasy sense of loss.

"Why?" she said finally.

Chris looked up into the sky for a while, staring straight at the sun. "Oldest story in the book," he said. "Son wants a father's love; father won't give it, can't give it. Whatever. Complications ensue."

She watched him watch the sun. "Don't do that," she said finally.

"Do what?" Still staring.

"Look at the sun like that," Mae-mae said. "You'll go blind."

"Hardly matters, does it?" he said. But he looked away from it finally, his eyes brushing across her face, pupils hugely dilated, then sweeping out across the grass, across the whole green panorama. After a minute he said, "You know, he never encouraged either of us, always told us we were doing the wrong thing, wasting our time, on and on like that. But we never really listened. We were as stubborn as he was." He laughed, put his elbows around his knees, and clasped his hands together. His arms were full of veins, every thin strand of muscle visible under the skin.

"I bugged him, man, for two years to give me a stake so I could put together a good record—hire some really decent musicians, an engineer that knew what he was doing and everything. Just a loan, right? I mean, it had taken me years just to work up the courage to ask him for that sort of thing.'' He seemed very calm all of a sudden. ''How about a little more of that wine?''

Mae-mae poured him some more wine. He sipped it as though tasting it for the first time. ''Mmm. Not bad.'' He took another sip, set the glass down. ''So what happened, I drove back to the store—me and Rachel in the car—and I went inside by myself. Boy, I was really going to lay into him. I was going to chew his ass so he couldn't sit down for a week. So I walked in the door of the print shop and there he was fiddling around with the shrink-wrap machine. He sees me coming and he must have known exactly why I had come there, because he whips out his wallet and holds this thing up, this check. 'What do you think of that, Son?' he says. I say, 'What are you talking about?' He says, 'Twenty grand. For your music.' Well, I couldn't believe it. I'm speechless.''

He smiled with half his mouth. ''That's Dad. Always knew how to play the strings. Well, what could I do? My whole career—I mean, it's right there in front of my face. So I just stood there. He says, 'What's the problem, Son?' I finally say, 'You know damn well what the problem is. I don't like the way you've been treating Rachel.' Well...'' Chris made a breathy noise—not quite a laugh, not quite a sigh. ''He takes the check, folds it up nice and slow, making a big production out of it, puts it back in the wallet. 'It's signed over to you, Son,' he says. 'If you want it just say so. If you don't...' You know, and then he just kind of shrugs. So I say, 'Okay, I want it. Give me the check, Dad.' Well, I get another big show, him taking the check out, unfolding it, smoothing it out, the whole schmear. I reach for the check and he pulls it away—like you'd do out on the playground in school with some dorky kid who wants to read your comic book.''

Chris pantomimed, dangling the check, keeping it just out of reach. ''So finally he lets me have the check, and then he says, 'Make me proud, Son, okay?' Like the whole thing was his idea and he was the greatest dad in the world, like he's been backing me every step of the way. I mean it was the most humiliating thing that's ever happened to me.'' He stared sightlessly into his wine for a while. "So I just forgot all about Rachel and everything. I mean it just went right out of my head. I started to go, heading for the door, and Dad goes, 'Chris?' I turn around and look at him, and he says, 'I love my daughter, just like I love you.' And then he looks at me for a minute and says, 'But Son, she's still a whore.' ''

Chris shook his head, and water started to squeeze out of his eyes. "I've never been so mad in my life. It was like my vision closed in and all I could see was his face, this big obnoxious smile on his face. So I pick up this hammer—there's a hammer sitting there—and I go over to him and I say, 'You take it back. Take it back!' '' Chris raised his eyebrows sadly. "He just laughed. Laughed right in my face. 'What are you gonna do?' he says. 'Hit your old man? You're not that kind of guy.' And I said, 'What kind of guy am I, Dad?' He just laughed some more, like I was the biggest loser in the world, laughing and laughing and laughing.'' Chris shrugged. "And that was that.''

Mae-mae looked at him. "You hit him with the hammer?''

"Bang bang bang. Not that hard or anything. I only wanted to hurt him, I guess. Piss him off, show him I could stand up to him.'' Chris wiped his eyes. "As soon as I saw what I'd done, I went in the office, threw some junk on the floor, busted the petty cash box, figured they'd think it was some crack head looking to score his next hit.'' He smiled fondly at Mae-mae, like he was proud of her. "And they did, too, didn't they? Everyone but you.''

"And Lester Paris? What happened to Lester?''

Chris didn't answer.

"Candy?''

"It wasn't me." He shook his head. "She just drank too much, I guess, ran off the road."

"So what now?" Mae-mae said. "Turn yourself in to the police?"

"I guess that's the way act three ends." He looked around at the picnic, made a laughing noise. "This really didn't turn out the way I wanted it to, you know." He let all the air out of his lungs. They sat there in the bright sun for a long time, silently drinking their wine. It got a little chilly sometimes when the wind kicked up, but otherwise Mae-mae felt fine. The fist in her stomach, even that had gone away.

"Remember the day we met, we were talking about writing songs?" He said it suddenly, like it was something he had meant to say earlier but had forgotten about. "Remember I said I only wrote songs when I was sad, only wrote depressing songs? Well, that's not quite true. After I spent that first night with you, I felt happier than I've felt in a long, long time."

"So did I," she said softly.

Chris looked at her. He seemed fragile, embarrassed. "The next day I wrote you a song."

Mae-mae tried to give him a smile, a little reassurance, but her face didn't react in any particular way.

"I know you probably think I'm some kind of monster, but . . . it's not that way. Things happen sometimes. You know? Life just gets away from you." He paused, a plaintive childish look on his face, and said, "Can I sing it to you?"

"I'd like that." She didn't know what she was feeling now. Everything was murky. She didn't feel afraid anymore. There was no more dread, only a deep, dull sadness. All this time she had thought it would feel good, liberating, to get to the bottom of this thing, to find an *answer*, something she could take to Judge Price and drop on his desk and say, "Here you are, judge, mystery solved!" Funny, it hadn't worked that way at all. This particular answer, man, it really sucked.

Chris picked up his guitar, strummed a few chords, and then sang. It was a sweet, maudlin song about misunderstandings and love. Simple chords, simple sentiments, simple words. And yet somehow it worked better than any of the songs she'd heard him sing before. He wasn't trying so hard, wasn't so eager to show people how clever he was. The song said that life was tricky sometimes, and people were difficult—but that lovers could get over the obstacles if they really tried. In the end it was a hopeful song, a song about how love could overcome bad things in the world.

"Thank you," Mae-mae said as the last chord slowly faded away. "That was beautiful." She felt a soft smile on her face, and she wished that she could freeze this moment, make the rest of time go away, isolate it from everything that had happened before, from whatever would happen next.

Chris smiled softly back—his blue eyes clear, warm, tender, and full of regret. Because he knew better than anyone that you couldn't banish time. Things just kept happening, for good or ill, one event leading inexorably to the next.

And then Mae-mae found herself sobbing, not sure exactly why, whether it was relief or sadness or awkwardness or loss. She pressed her face into her hands and let the tears run down through her fingers, let her mind lose control of her body. She wanted to feel his hands on her skin, wanted to feel him comfort her and warm her and hold her. Whatever he was, whatever he had done, it didn't matter just then. She wanted him, wanted him to hold her, wanted nothing else in the world. But he couldn't and he didn't. She was alone. Alone, and had to take it by herself, had to make it on her own strength. God*damn* she was sick of being alone. Sick to death of it.

When she finally looked up again, Chris was gone.

Then she saw him, thirty yards away, standing at the top of the hill. He was holding his guitar by the neck, looking down at her. She couldn't make out the expression on his face.

He turned, tucked the guitar under his arm, and walked slowly over the crest of the hill.

TWENTY-SIX

Around three-thirty, Mae-mae put in a call to Judge Price, told him that she'd located the missing $20,000 bank draft. After she'd explained what had happened, the phone was silent for a while. She imagined Price sitting at his desk, his big domed head gleaming, getting ready to make a snide remark. But when he finally spoke, his voice was uncharacteristically soft. "What a tragedy," he said. "What a crying shame, see a boy and his daddy acting like that."

Mae-mae hung up the phone and decided to blow off work for the rest of the day. She had been sitting around all afternoon staring at a pile of recent tax-related Supreme Court opinions—unable to think, unable to work, unable even to get up the enthusiasm for a decent round of bill basketball. The whole thing seemed unreal and disconnected now that it was over, like a crazy movie where you'd slept through everything except the really disturbing parts.

She thought back to Chris's face, the sad look he'd had almost the whole time they were out there in the park—like he was resigned to taking his knocks. In retrospect, he had had that look of resignation even before he admitted killing his father, as though he was waiting for the inevitable. It was when she dumped the pornographic magazines out onto the blanket that he had finally cracked, though. Why then? Why not some other time? Why did the magazines set him off? Maybe there was no knowing. People just *did* things sometimes, and maybe there was no clear cause; pressure builds up and builds up and then finally it's the tiniest, most trivial jolt that sets off the explosion.

On the way home she decided she ought to stop off at the bookstore, pick up some thick, dumb novel, and try to forget about the world. While she was there, maybe she could find a copy of that book by Barry and June King, too. It might help her figure out what made them tick, give her a leg up in negotiating the sale of Printmeister. *I— Hurt!*—wasn't that the name?

She drove down to Oxford Books, found a big trough of them, gold stickers that said *Signed by Author* stuck on the covers. Twenty-six dollars and ninety-five cents. She put *I Hurt!* on the credit card, hoping it wouldn't set off the tilt alarm.

When she got home, she sank onto the couch and opened the book. On the dust jacket there were several testimonials: a former all-pro quarterback said their book *How to Stop Feeling Like Hell* had recharged his emotional batteries; a guy named Ron Begosian (author of *Cherish Your Inner Child*) said if you only bought one self-help book this year, let it be this one; and the president of Lucky Industries said that "Barry and June is the U.S.A.'s best in terms of dynamic mind power training." Quote unquote. Evidently all that dynamic mind power hadn't given him a shitload of help with his grammar.

Inside the flyleaf it said that Dr. June King had a Ph.D. in behavioral sciences from Texas Christian University and had written one book of her own called *Rage: Breaking the Cycle of Child Abuse*. Her life mission, it said, was to alleviate human suffering. Lots of luck, sister. Mae-mae skipped over the part about

Barry and his life mission. She was getting bored already.

Mae-mae leafed through the book, most of which seemed to be in the form of a dialogue between Barry and June. It was this kind of thing:

BARRY: What does it mean to *hurt*?

JUNE: Well, Barry, our team of highly trained scientific researchers have culled the scientific literature, conducted heaps of startling and innovative original research, and performed tests on thousands of human subjects—and do you know what we've found? We have found that the secrets of pleasure and pain can be unlocked with a very simple key.

BARRY: That's encouraging news!

JUNE: You bet it is. Hurting—what scientists call ''the pain response''—is simply one of four basic human responses to neurological stimuli. Once you've reached an understanding of the parameters of these physiological mechanisms, you're in the driver's seat.

BARRY: Wow! Neurological stimuli, physiological mechanisms—I'm afraid you lost me there.

JUNE: That's okay, Barry. The scientific details aren't that important. All we're saying is that your brain responds to influences in the outside world. Stroke me, I feel good; hit me, I hurt. Now using our research here at MTRI, we've developed an ultrasophisticated scientific technique called BIOVISUALIZATION THERAPY, which allows us to seize control of . . .

It was worse than she'd imagined, going on like that for 194 pages, fairly big print on fairly thick paper. The words ''biovisualization therapy'' were capitalized everywhere, jumping off the page at you. On the last page June and Barry's mantra was printed in glaring thirty-six-point type: *We're gonna lick this thing!*

There was also an appendix in the back, twenty-seven pages of crucial information about how you could sign up for Barry and June's seminars, how you could buy their instructional tapes and workbooks, how you could attend their focused retreats, etcetera.

Mae-mae felt stupid, her face turning red just sitting there, like she'd been taken in a game of three-card monte. Twenty-six ninety-five for this drivel! Even if she had gotten twenty-six ninety-five worth of insight into their characters, it still felt like a rip-off. She felt sorry for all the credulous goofs who had shelled out for this thing thinking it would change their lives.

About five-thirty she drank half a beer, couldn't stand being by herself, gave Sebastian a call. She didn't tell him what happened, not on the phone, but she couldn't keep the quavering out of her voice.

He had Willie Nelson playing on the stereo when she got there—an old song, "One Day At a Time."

"Willie Nelson?" Mae-mae said. "You're listening to Willie *Nelson*?"

Sebastian looked offended. "I was young once. Even a bit of a café bon vivant, if I may say so. Besides . . ." But he didn't say besides *what*. She noticed the wrapper of the Willie Nelson CD sitting in the trash. He'd gone out and bought it just to cheer her up. "Tell me what happened. Tell me what's wrong."

"You're a weird guy, you know that, Sebastian?" she said. "But you're really sweet." The quaver slipping back into her voice. She didn't want it this way, didn't want to lose control. "How's your face?"

His face had started to peel, giving the impression of a brick wall with some sort of dead foliage on it. "Still a bit tender," he said. "Now tell me what happened."

She handed him her copy of *I Hurt!*. "This won't heal your face," she said, "but I guarantee it'll keep you laughing so hard you won't notice the pain.''

Sebastian looked at the book for a minute, then set it gently on a chair. ''Tell me what happened.''

But she couldn't say anything for a while. ''It's Chris,'' she said finally. ''He's the one.''

Sebastian looked at her curiously, not understanding.

''He killed his father.''

Sebastian stood there for a moment, his bow tie twitching as he swallowed uncertainly. Then he reached out and wrapped her in his long arms.

For the second time that day, she sobbed without restraint.

TWENTY-SEVEN

Barry and June worked together in a huge office, probably 600 or 800 square feet, facing each other across twin teak desks the size of Lincoln Town Cars. Barry's desk spilled over with papers and computer equipment and books. June's gleamed spotlessly: one phone, one legal pad, one picture of her husband. Barry was on the phone, twirling around in his Eames chair. He waved pontifically at Mae-mae as she entered.

The thing that dominated the room, though, was a bank of television monitors covering the entire wall of the office behind the two desks. There must have been more than a hundred screens. And every one of them was playing the same thing: a Barry and June infomercial. There was no sound, just a hundred gesticulating Barrys in a hundred white suits; a hundred Junes looking sincere, rapt, and maybe a little too tightly wound. The televisions threw a stark bluish light through the entire room, silhouetting the real Barry and June in a flickering, flashing halo of their own images.

The whole scene was kind of hellish.

June stood and smiled, came around the desk and held out her hand. They shook. June's grip was firm, dry, strong. She wore a green silk outfit, a simple dress that hugged her body without making a big deal about it.

Businesslike but sensual. For a moment she turned to look at Barry, the light from the TV screens reflecting off her face, and her eyes went opaque, becoming blue white membranes, like the visual apparatus for some kind of animate machine. Then she looked back at Mae-mae, and her eyes were green and human again.

They sat across the table from each other on a set of matching leather sofas. "We heard the news," June said, "that Chris turned himself in to the police yesterday. How *is* Myra?" She had a dead serious look on her face.

"Bearing up," Mae-mae said. "I guess."

Barry put down the receiver, bounded out of his chair. "Dan Quayle!" he said, pointing at the phone. "Terrific guy, very underestimated by the media, you know. Big, big fan of ours."

Mae-mae smiled. Politely, she hoped.

Barry came over, spread himself across the sofa next to his wife, and clapped his hands. "So, counselor!" he said. "We gonna do a deal here or what?"

"That's what we're trying to find out," Mae-mae said.

"I like this gal," Barry enthused to his wife. June smiled, not parting her lips, the kind of smile that didn't give out the slightest clue as to what she was thinking.

The couches were set up so that Mae-mae was looking into the bank of screens. The dancing images of Barry and June moved their silent mouths endlessly. Mae-mae wondered if it was a negotiation ploy, making her stare into the great video maw until she rotted away into raw, quivering viscera.

"Tell you what," Mae-mae said. "Why don't you explain to me in a little greater detail what it is that you've got in mind."

Barry told Mae-mae that their organization not only published a number of manuals and seminar workbooks, but also did a substantial direct response business. While he talked, he ran his fingers slowly through his salt-and-pepper beard.

"Direct response?" Mae-mae said.

"Call it junk mail," Barry said. "We advertise our home-study kits, tapes, whatnot, through the mail. Anyway, over the past year, year and half, we've grown so fast that it's looking like it makes sense to invest in some plant and equipment instead of contracting out all the work. Our accounting people say it soaks up some extra cash, keeps the money out of the IRS's hands, plus we can depreciate the equipment here on out. Saves us some money on printing costs, gives us a little tax break at the same time."

That was good. If they were getting tax benefits from the purchase, maybe she could wring some more money out of them. Maybe she could even find some tax angles they hadn't thought of.

"My client is certainly willing to entertain bids for her fifty percent share of the business. As you know, I don't represent Mrs. Paris," Mae-mae said. "I spoke with Myra this morning, however, and she understands that Mrs. Paris is also amenable to selling."

"Any offer we make," June chimed in, "would be conditional upon sale by both parties."

"Fair enough," Mae-mae said. "Are you at a stage you'd like to make a bid?"

Barry looked sidewise at June, just a short glance. Mae-mae wondered what that was all about. She got the feeling, the more she was around them, that June was the brains of this operation and that Barry was just the mouthpiece.

"Yes, we are," Barry said.

"How much?"

"We're prepared to offer an even million."

A million. Did he mean for Myra's half interest . . . or for the whole thing? If it was for the whole business, it was a fairly reasonable offer. If it was for Myra's interest alone, it was time to start shoving contracts under their hands and hoping they'd sign before they came to their senses. Two million dollars for a business that earned only a hundred and forty grand last year was good money. Not outrageous, but good. Especially considering that the deaths of Towe and Paris had cut the heart out of the company. Two million for a metal building full of used printing presses. Not bad.

"A million," Mae-mae said, trying to get the rest of the sentence out in a casual tone. "That's for Myra's interest?"

"Right," Barry said.

"Two million for the business."

"Assuming we can make the same deal with Suzanne Paris, yes," Barry said.

"And," June said, "assuming no due diligence problems."

Due diligence.

That was the big bomb, the two words Mae-mae had been dreading. Due diligence is a lawyer's term that describes the process of poking around in a potential acquisition to make sure there aren't any skeletons in the closet—say, tax liabilities, pending litigation, major contracts up for cancellation, accounting discrepancies, upcoming write-offs: anything that could make a company worth less than it originally appeared to be.

Being at the center of a counterfeiting ring, for instance. That could be problematic.

Mae-mae had discussed the matter with Myra Towe the day before, and Myra was adamant: any potential buyer had to be informed about the counterfeiting.

"Well, I'll certainly be happy to convey your offer to Mrs. Towe. I think, however, I can say that it's in the ballpark." Mae-mae took a deep breath. "Speaking of due diligence . . ."

Two green eyes looking at her. "Yes?" June said finally.

"I think it's only fair for me to mention one significant item," Mae-mae said. "My client discovered, somewhat by accident, that her husband and Mr. Paris were engaged in . . . an illegal activity. That activity has

now ceased, but any buyer could conceivably be—"
how to phrase this? "—*concerned* about acquiring the
company for that reason."

Barry's black eyes took a sidelong glance at his wife
again, as though he was looking for some coaching.

"Like what kind of illegal activity?" he said.

"Counterfeiting," Mae-mae said.

"Counterfeiting!" Barry said finally. "Whoa!
Shocker! Charlie Towe was printing fake money back
there?" He ran his fingers through his beard. "I have a
hard time believing that."

"Not money," Mae-mae said. "Stamps. Postage
stamps."

Again the little glance.

"Stamps?" Barry said. "*Stamps!* I wouldn't think
there'd be much money in that."

"Look at it this way: what's your biggest single expense at this company?" Mae-mae said.

"Personnel," June said. "Thirty-one percent of
gross."

"Next?"

Barry made a thinking face. "Marketing expenses?"

"Next?"

Barry looked at his green-eyed partner for help.
"Postage and freight," June said. "Seven percent of
gross."

Mae-mae nodded. She was right; June *was* the brains
around here. Maybe the balls, too. As it were. "There's
your answer. If you gross, say, twenty million a year,
that's a million four in postage stamps."

"Stamps. Damn, I never heard of such a thing,"
Barry said.

Behind him on the video wall, a hundred versions of
June were talking insistently, voicelessly into a microphone. Her hair swung back and forth in a copper arc
as she talked, like a hypnotist's pendulum in an old B
movie.

Mae-mae took an envelope out of her briefcase, the

one Sebastian had given her the other night. She opened the envelope, dumped a few dozen singed stamps onto the desk. "Here's all that's left of the Printmeister counterfeiting business," she said.

Barry picked them up, squinted at them wonderingly. "These look just like regular stamps," he said.

"That's the *point*," June said dryly.

"Do you mind if we hold onto these?" Barry said. "We probably ought to have somebody take a look at them."

"I'd rather you not," Mae-mae said. "Not that I'm worried about indiscretion on your part. But—" She spread her hands apologetically. "They're all I've got. The last ones in existence."

Behind them, a barrage of video Barrys were grinning manfully into a hundred identical crowds. It was kind of nauseating. Maybe it was the flickering light of the screen, maybe it was all the motion. It was hard to tell.

Barry stared at the stamps for a while before handing them back. He leaned forward, drummed on the table with his thumbs while Mae-mae put the stamps back in her briefcase. "I guess we need to think about this a little, huh?" he said, looking at his wife.

"I'm afraid so," June said. "Conceivably this could affect our bid substantially. I hope you understand, Mae-mae."

"Of course," Mae-mae said. Oh, well. So much for the nice fat bid.

"May I ask what they did with the stamps?" June said.

"Sold them," Mae-mae said.

"To whom?"

"I don't know." Mae-mae shook her head. "But I'd sure like to find out."

They talked some more and then, as Mae-mae got up to leave, Barry said, "Strange, isn't it? Chris always seemed like a good guy."

Mae-mae nodded.

For the first time, Barry's eyes seemed to betray real emotion. But what was it? Confusion? Sadness? These were hard people to read.

He shrank within himself for a second, like Charles Towe's death had dropped onto his shoulders, weighing him down. Behind him a hundred electronic versions of his own bearded face grinned happily out from the video world. A message slithered across the screen in shining gold letters: *We're gonna lick this thing!*

TWENTY-EIGHT

Mae-mae sat in front of Dick Clark's desk, her hands folded together, sandwiched between her knees. A crying man was handcuffed to a chair in front of another detective's desk across the room. Every few minutes the crying man would start jerking his cuffs against the chair, and then the detective would look up from his computer and say, "Do me a favor, shut your lip." At which point the guy would calm down for a while. Near the main door a uniformed police officer inhaled some powdered sugar off the doughnut he was eating and went into a coughing fit.

Dick Clark was talking on the phone. He wore a starched white button-down and a yellow tie with small dots on it. If it weren't for the shoulder holster, he could have been some guy selling municipal bonds.

"Surprise development, huh?" he said after he hung up. "Never expected to solve this one with an easy confession."

"Some guys have all the luck," Mae-mae said glumly.

"I understand you convinced him to turn himself in," the detective said.

Mae-mae hunched up her shoulders. She didn't especially feel like chatting about it.

Dick Clark looked at her for a minute. "Last time I talked to you," he said, "you were all psyched up to find out who killed old Charles Towe. Seemed like it was top of your list. How come you don't look so happy?"

Mae-mae wanted to say, Well, because I was falling in love with the killer. Instead she just shrugged. No point in bringing that up. After she left he'd probably tell the cop with the doughnut about how another hypersensitive woman had let herself fall for a chump, and then the doughnut guy would choke again, laughing about it so hard.

Dick Clark took out his little notebook with the rubber band around it and asked her some questions. *When did Chris tell her he'd killed his father? How did he say he'd done it? Why had he killed him?* And that was about it. The detective closed his notebook, set it down on the desk, laced his fingers together behind his head, and stared up in the air for a minute.

"Fathers and sons," he said. "Fathers and sons. Oldest story in the book."

"His exact words."

"Kind of funny, isn't it? You finally had us convinced this stuff was all about counterfeiting and then up pops old Chris. Case closed. Isn't that nice? Isn't that convenient as all get-out?" Dick Clark kept staring up at the ceiling. "You got another couple minutes?" he said finally.

Mae-mae shrugged. "Sure."

Dick Clark waved at the uniformed cop over by the door, the one with the doughnut. "Hey, Bennie, where's that videotape player at?"

The doughnut guy shook his head vaguely.

"Well, hell, find it," Dick said.

"Then what?" The cop put a dumb look on his face. Dick just looked at him, let him know he didn't think the guy was so funny.

The uniform wandered out of the room, licking his

fingers. After a while he came back through the door pushing a black metal cart with a television on it. He pushed it over to the desk, making breathing noises with his mouth.

"You want me to plug it in, too?" There was a dim, truculent gleam in his eye. A slight dusting of powdered sugar clouded the front of his blue shirt.

"What, you going into doughnut withdrawal already?" Dick Clark said.

"Doughnuts? Who said anything about doughnuts?"

"Isn't that what you been spending all morning doing? Guarding that box of doughnuts?"

"Doughnuts? Those are chocolate *croy-sants*." The uniform sighed hollowly through his open mouth, sank to one knee, plugged the machine into a floor socket. "Godsake, everybody knows the difference between a croy-sant and a doughnut." He shambled back toward the door, spent a couple minutes staring into the orange and pink doughnut box, figuring out which croissant to eat next.

The television was stacked on top of a VCR. Dick Clark punched the ON button and while the television was warming up, he took a videotape out of the bottom drawer of his desk, opened the black tape case, and stuck it into the mouth of the VCR.

"What is it?" Mae-mae asked.

The detective picked up the box, read off the pink stick-on label: "Sworn videotape statement of Christopher P. Towe. Dated yesterday."

He pushed the fast-forward button, let the machine spin for a while, and then stopped. An image of Chris's face filled the screen. He looked frightened and pale, talking, but no sound coming out of his mouth. The detective hit the pause button; Chris's image froze on the screen. A jagged black line cutting across the screen made it look like a chunk of his head had been popped off with a saw.

"I want you to listen to this part of the statement,"

Dick Clark said, "tell me if it jibes with what he said to you."

"Okay," Mae-mae said.

Dick Clark turned up the volume, hit the pause button. On the screen Chris was nodding timidly. Helpless, defenseless, completely alone. It made her sick to see it. The first thing she heard was the off-camera voice of Dick Clark.

CLARK: And then what happened?

TOWE: That's when I hit him.

CLARK: With your fist?

TOWE: No. A hammer. I don't remember real clearly. It was, I guess it was sitting on the shrink-wrap machine next to him. I was so mad, I picked it up and I waved it at him and I said, "Don't say that again." And he just laughed at me and then I hit him. *Bam bam bam*, like that. I didn't mean—

CLARK: It's okay. It's okay. Here's a handkerchief.

TOWE: Thanks. It's just . . . I didn't mean to . . . I just wanted to show him, make him realize . . .

CLARK: Realize what?

TOWE: I don't know. Realize there're other people in the world, realize you can't walk all over everybody all the time.

CLARK: Okay. Okay. Now you said, like, *bam bam bam*. Right? Like you hit him three times. Is that correct?

TOWE: That's correct. I mean that's what I said. Three times? I don't know, it's hard to remember. It could have been more. I wasn't exactly thinking straight.

CLARK: Tell me about the hammer.

TOWE: It was . . . a ball peen hammer. The kind with the ball on one end and the regular hammer on the other.

CLARK: And what did you do with it?
TOWE: I, uh, I threw it in the reservoir down at—

Clark poked the pause button. Chris froze again, the black scanning bar tearing through his jaw this time. His eyes were closed, caught mid blink, giving him the look of an early Christian martyr, gagged and praying in the moments before his sacrifice. "Same story you heard?"

Mae-mae looked away, tears threatening to choke up her eyes so she couldn't see. When she got hold of herself, she said, "Basically, yeah, same story."

Dick Clark nodded. "Good. Let me read you something you might find interesting." He reached into his bottom drawer again, came out with a manila folder. "Medical examiner's report." He opened the jacket. "First thing we got is the initial autopsy report. Key item here, I'm reading, 'Cause of death: shock occasioned by blunt trauma to head.' Skipping down a little. 'Subject struck seven times in the head and neck. Four glancing blows causing only minor abrasions, three direct blows. Two of direct blows pierced cranium and entered the cerebellum, causing massive lesions and bleeding in left frontal and temporal lobes.' Goes on like that for a while. 'The third blow fractured the cranium three inches left of the midline but did not pierce. . . .' Okay, blah blah blah. 'All three direct blows caused semispherical punctures. See illustration.' " Dick Clark showed her his even teeth. "Got a couple of pretty little drawings here, then down at the bottom it says, 'Initial investigation suggests that trauma resulted from the blows of a hammerlike object.' "

"Okay," Mae-mae said. Where was he leading with all this?

"Thing to take note of," Dick Clark said, "is that he said, *semi*spherical. That means kind of like a half-moon. See?" He held up the picture drawn by the medical examiner: a shape like a half-moon, but turned sideways so the flat part faced down.

"Half-moon," Mae-mae said. So?

"See, the initial part of the postmortem, the canoe-maker saws you up, weighs your brain, that kind of thing. Then anything interesting he sends off to the pathology lab and they tell you, you know, did he have alcohol in his blood? Did she have semen in her mouth?—that type thing. Takes a week, couple weeks for that to come in."

Mae-mae nodded.

"So one of the samples he sends to the path folks was a piece of brain tissue, little hunk of stuff out of the bottom of one of these holes in Mr. Towe's head. Sometimes that helps determine the murder weapon, okay, because it might have had red paint on it or a certain type of metal might have flaked off. Whatever." Dick Clark flipped through the coroner's report. "Alright, here we go. Sample nineteen, control number 1047B."

Clark ran his finger down the page and started reading. " 'Sample composed primarily of brain tissue, dermis, and fragments of bone.' " Clark looked up. "Why they got to say 'dermis' when they mean *skin*? Never met a doctor who wouldn't use a twenty dollar word when a fifty cent word would do just as good."

Mae-mae was getting impatient. "So what's the point?"

Clark raised his eyebrows. "You're gonna like this. Here: 'Sample shows significant traces of two exogenous,'—good *Lord*, can't even pronounce these words!—'two exogenous substances. Substance one, three fragments of granular (point two millimeter diameter) synthetic rubber. Substance two, traces of mammamam—Let me try again, see if I can get this." He smiled like he was winding up to tell the punch line of a smutty joke. " 'Traces of mammalian fecal matter, probably of canine origin.' "

"Mammalian fecal matter?" Mae-mae said.

Dick Clark kept smiling. "Hand me your shoe," he said.

"What?"

"Your shoe. Hand me your shoe."

Mae-mae looked at him strangely, took off her left shoe, handed it to the detective. It was a blue pump with an inch-and-a-half heel. "Mammalian fecal matter," Mae-mae said again.

Dick Clark set the shoe down on a piece of white paper, traced around the heel with his pen. "Mammalian fecal matter, probably of canine origin," he said. "Where I grew up we called it dog shit. Two places you're liable to find it. First place is on your lawn. Second place—" He held up the piece of paper, revealing a small sideways half-moon outlined in the blue ink. "Second place is on your shoe."

"You're saying—" Mae-mae couldn't quite catch her breath for a second.

"I'm saying I never heard of dog doo on a ball peen hammer."

"Wait a minute. Wait a minute."

"I'm saying my captain, he likes confessions. He likes plea bargains. He likes everything nice and neat, no time wasted on messy bureaucratic hassles like jury trials."

Mae-mae was staring. "You think he didn't do it! You think he's covering up for somebody."

"I'm saying it wouldn't hurt to keep your eyes open." Dick Clark smiled coyly. "Hey, Bennie!" he called to the uniformed cop. "How bout bringing them doughnuts over here."

Across the room, Bennie was looking dolefully into the doughnut box. "How many times I got to tell him? The word is croy-sant. Croy. Sant."

Under her breath Mae-mae said, "Not croysant. Crois*sant*." Pronouncing it the French way.

"Who?" Dick Clark said.

* * *

Mae-mae drove straight over to Printmeister. On the way she thought about what Dick Clark had told her. A woman's shoe. Did that make the killer a woman? Could it have been Rachel? Hard to say. She remembered what June King had said about Rachel, that she was full of rage. Snake oil salesman or not, it was true. Rachel wasn't a happy young lady.

Or what about Colleen Mastronunzio? Or even Myra Towe? Any of them might have had reason—*good* reason, even—to lay into Charles Towe with the heel of a shoe.

Donald Rascoe was standing in the middle of the reception area of the print shop, wiping his hands on a long printer's apron. The apron had once been white, but now it was so covered with stains and splotches of color that it looked like a Jackson Pollock canvas. Rascoe was sweating hard, streams of liquid pouring down his rotted face. "What do you need?" he said. "I'm busy trying to do three people's jobs, so I'd appreciate your making it quick."

Mae-mae gave him a friendly smile. "You sure look like it," she said. "I don't envy you one bit."

"Save the friendly chitchat," he said.

"Okay," she said. "I'd like to know what you saw the night Charles Towe was killed."

He gave her his dead fish stare. "I told the cops already. Why should I tell you?"

"Because I don't think Chris did it."

He shrugged. "So? Is that my problem?"

Mae-mae paused. "Okay, let's try again. If you don't answer my question, I'll have you fired before the five o'clock whistle blows." She smiled blandly. "How's that for pleasant chitchat?"

"You can't do that and you know it," he said.

She put a little steel in her voice. "How bad do you want to find out, Rascoe?"

Rascoe thought about it, peering at her with his narrowed black eyes. "Okay," he said finally. "What happened, I was working back in the shop, finishing up a run on the forty-eight."

"The forty-eight?"

"Forty-eight-inch web press," he said, like any fool ought to have understood what he was talking about. "Computer manuals. I collated them, stacked them up. Charlie came back, said I could leave it and he'd do the shrink-wrapping. When I was through, I left."

"Did you see anybody besides Mr. Towe?"

"When I left he was in the office with the Kings, those morons off the TV."

"Did you see Rachel? Or Chris?"

"Yeah. Hold on. Okay, I remember. I left my coat inside, so I went out to my car then came back in for my coat. The Kings were leaving and Rachel was going into Charlie's office. When I came back out of the shop, they were yelling about something. I went out the front door, there's Chris sitting in his car. By then the Kings were gone."

"And that's it?"

"That's it."

"What did you do then?"

More malignant staring. "I don't see that's any of your business."

"Do I have to repeat myself?"

Rascoe looked away for a minute, then looked directly into her eyes. "Okay, I went down to a lingerie modeling place on Cheshire Bridge Road, paid some bimbo twenty-five bucks to dance around in a pair of black lace underpants. What else you want to know?"

Mae-mae didn't like the way he said it, so just to be obnoxious she said, "You know her name?"

"Nope." Rascoe smiled. It was a scary sight, teeth gleaming out of his ruined face. "But she had little pink scars in her armpits and the biggest titties money can buy.'' Then he turned around and walked off down the hall.

Sorry I asked, she was thinking.

Mae-mae sat in the parking lot for a while, thinking. Why did he do it? If he didn't really kill his father, why did he pretend he did?

She tried to come up with a scenario. Maybe Rachel flew off the handle and hit her father with her shoe and killed him. Then Chris came back and found his father dead on the floor. Realizing that Rachel had committed the crime, he faked the burglary of the office. Rachel might have hit her dad a couple of times with a shoe— but would she have beaten Lester Paris to death in cold blood? Or could Chris have done it, covering up for her? Dick Clark hadn't said anything about that.

So maybe Chris wasn't out of the woods yet.

Mae-mae slumped back in the seat of her Honda and stared across the parking lot, not looking at anything in particular. Suddenly she noticed the back door of the metal building opening, a man rushing out. It was Rascoe, grim faced, looking like there was someplace he needed to be in a hurry.

He walked quickly to an ugly tan Dodge, pulled off his abstract expressionist apron, threw it in the backseat, then climbed in the car. The engine started and Rascoe swung the car around toward the road, his tires spitting rocks and dust.

She cranked up her car and followed, the worn-out old Honda complaining and belching as she turned out of the parking lot.

Rascoe drove straight to Peachtree, headed downtown. Just as he was coming up on the Buckhead Ritz Carlton, he swung a hard right, pulling into the parking lot of the Phipps Plaza mall. Mae-mae followed, parked across the lot from Rascoe's car, and followed him into the mall. Phipps was one of these small, chic malls where most of the shops were too expensive, too hurtful on the credit cards for Mae-mae to visit very often.

Rascoe walked purposefully down the center of the mall, heading for Lord & Taylor. He had a liquid, athletic way of walking that didn't seem to go with his decayed face. When he reached the department store, he cut through the perfume section and headed for ladies' lingerie. None of the shellack-haired perfume ladies offered to let him try out their new line of fragrances. Mae-mae didn't blame them.

When he got to ladies' lingerie he stopped and stood for a while looking up at a mannequin wearing a quilted pink robe.

Mae-mae stood behind a pole in the executive ladies' section, pretending to be interested in a rack of Anne Klein suits. She lifted the arm on a beautiful red jacket, alpaca serge, looked at the price tag. It had been marked down to $695 for spring clearance. Originally eight and a quarter. It wasn't *that* beautiful.

When she glanced up again, two men were walking toward Rascoe. They both wore light gray suits and had the blocky physiques and hard, arrogant faces of ex–football players. They stopped in front of Donald Rascoe, looked around the store suspiciously. Mae-mae lifted the sleeve of the Anne Klein again. Still $695.

She leaned over, counted to thirty, then stuck her head up again. Rascoe and the hard-faced men were talking intently. One of the men shifted his weight and his coat opened, revealing a gun clipped to his belt. Rascoe talked some more.

"It's a lovely suit, isn't it?" a voice behind her said.

Mae-mae swung around. "Excuse me?"

An anorexic blond woman, her hair pulled back in a tight bun, smiled frigidly at Mae-mae with a pair of exceptionally red lips. "The Anne Klein," she said insistently. "Lovely suit, isn't it?"

"Right." Mae-mae said, trying to keep tabs on Rascoe out of the corner of her eye.

"Would you perhaps be interested in trying it on?"

"They don't have my size," Mae-mae said.

"I'm sure there's an eight in there somewhere." The red smile again. Goopy black eyelashes blinked several times at her.

"I wear a six, though, I'm afraid," Mae-mae said. *Bitch.*

The eyes went slowly up and down Mae-mae's body, appraising her ensemble—such as it was. "Perhaps something over here would be a little more suitable for the . . . modest budget." More blinking, more red lips.

Rascoe turned slightly. He was now facing in their general direction. Mae-mae tried to keep herself hidden behind the pole.

The skinny blonde was still standing there. Mae-mae recalled the main reason why she never shopped here. It wasn't just the money, it was these snotty sales clerks, always acting like working at Lord & Taylor was the next thing in line to being queen of England.

"All right," Mae-mae said. "Here's the deal. You see those three guys over there?"

The blonde looked over at Rascoe and his ex–football player friends. She didn't seem to think much about them one way or the other. They weren't prospects for a sales commission.

"As it happens," Mae-mae said, "they're three of the most powerful drug dealers in the tristate area. I'm a federal agent. Now if you don't get your skinny ass back over there to the cash register and start looking ex-*treme*ly busy, I'm going to haul you down to the regional office and book you."

"For what?"

Mae-mae seemed to remember seeing somebody do this in a movie once, and it had worked like a charm. Right now it didn't seem to be cutting the mustard, though. "Solicitation of prostitution, maybe—how's that sound?"

''That's not a federal offense,'' the blonde said. ''I think you're making this up.''

''Everybody's a lawyer,'' Mae-mae said. She tried to think of something else to get rid of the clerk.

The blonde just stood there, glaring at Rascoe and his two buddies. Suddenly her goopy eyes widened. ''They've got *guns*,'' the sales clerk said in a high voice.

''Yes, ma'am.'' Doing her best Jack Webb imitation. ''So do we. I just hope we don't have to use them. If it comes down to a hostage situation, though, don't worry. The SWAT team's in the parking lot.''

''SWAT team?'' The blonde looked back at the three men. ''My gosh,'' she said. ''Drug dealers . . . in Lord & Taylor. My . . . *gosh*.'' Her skin went ashy underneath all her foundation, and her red lips went slack and rubbery.

''Are you okay?'' Mae-mae said.

''I feel . . . I feel a little funny,'' the blonde said. Then her eyes rolled up into her head and she swayed, swayed and fell forward into the rack of Anne Kleins, bringing them down with a splintering, jangling crash.

Mae-mae tried to hide behind the pillar, but before she had a chance to duck, Rascoe had looked straight into her eyes. Did he recognize her? It was just a flash; maybe he was just looking for the source of the noise.

On the floor next to her the blonde was staring up at the ceiling muttering designer names over and over in a high, reedy voice. Her skirt was hiked up around her waist and she had put a huge run in her stocking.

By the time she had extricated the blonde from the rack of trashed Anne Kleins, Rascoe and the two men were gone.

On the way back to the office Mae-mae felt jittery, the adrenaline fluttering through her veins: she was on to something. Yeah, but *what*? Who were the guys in Lord & Taylor? And what was Rascoe's connection to them? Were they the stamp buyers—or someone connected to the buyers? Had Rascoe been their inside man all this time? Mae-mae couldn't think of anything else they could be. Unless Donald Rascoe made a habit of hanging around the ladies' lingerie section of Lord & Taylor, talking to guys with guns stuck in their pants.

But then there was a more important question: whatever Donald Rascoe was doing, did it have anything to do with the killing of Charles Towe? Hard to see how that could be. Not if Chris was, in fact, covering up for somebody. He wasn't likely to be covering up for Donald Rascoe: as far as she knew, they hardly talked to each other.

As she was pulling into the parking garage at her office, she thought she saw a junky tan car, a Dodge, swing around the corner of East Paces Ferry. But it was hard to tell. She waited for a moment in the bay of the garage to see if the car was going to pass her building or not, but then a bright red Jeep Cherokee pulled in behind her and blocked her view.

Rascoe must have seen her. He *must* have.

The shrimpy, shystery looking guy driving the big Jeep started laying on the horn. She vaguely recalled having seen him once at a bar association meeting. It was guys like that who gave lawyers a bad name.

Where was the tan Dodge? Damn it. She couldn't see a thing.

TWENTY-NINE

At six-thirty Mae-mae hung up the phone and ticked the last item off the "to do" list in her pocket calendar. She had been talking to Myra, trying to figure out what to do with Printmeister if the Kings didn't want to buy the plant. They had pretty much resolved to try a few small business brokers, see if somebody could dig up a buyer. And if that didn't work, they'd lock the front door, send everybody home, and sell off the presses. Mae-mae hoped it didn't come to that.

At the end of their conversation Mae-mae told Myra about her conversation with Dick Clark that morning. "So if Chris didn't do it," she had said, "who do you think might have?"

Myra didn't know.

"I hate to ask you this," Mae-mae had said. "Do you think Rachel could have done it?"

There was a long pause. "Rachel?" Myra said finally. "No. No, I don't think either one of them could have. Maybe *I* could have." She laughed bitterly, a soft, hissing sound in the phone. "But not them."

Mae-mae wasn't sure quite how to take that.

"That's not a confession," Myra said softly. "I mean . . . if that's what you were thinking."

"No, I wasn't thinking that," Mae-mae said.

But after she had hung up, she was still wondering. Could Chris be covering up for his mother?

A few minutes later, the phone rang. Mae-mae answered it and heard Barry King's voice on the other end.

"Mae-mae! Glad I caught you."

"Hi, Barry."

"Given it some hard thought," Barry King said, "and we'd like to stay in the ball game."

"That's great. I hoped you would."

"We just thought it was only fair you give us a little leeway with the price I quoted. We need to reevaluate this, run it past our legal people, whatnot. So before we go to all that trouble I want to find out if you're, that is, if Myra's going to hold us to the kind of price that we talked about this morning. I mean this thing about the counterfeiting—wow!—that's kind of a curveball, you know what I'm saying?"

"Sure," Mae-mae said. "Naturally you understand that I can't speak for Mrs. Towe right now. Of course I'll be happy to pass that on to her and see what she says. Between you and me, I think if your next offer is reasonable, it'll be given due consideration." Mae-mae smiled to herself.

"Any more news on Chris?" Barry said. "I feel sorry as hell about this whole thing. Horrifying, really, isn't it?"

"Well. I did find out something. . . ." Mae-mae said. After she said it, she realized she probably shouldn't have.

"Oh?"

"Well . . ." Mae-mae hesitated to say anything, but somehow she couldn't help herself. "There's some evidence to suggest he didn't do it."

Barry didn't say anything for a minute. "You're kidding," he said finally.

"Nope," Mae-mae said. "New evidence. According to the forensic pathology people, Charles was killed with

a woman's shoe. Evidently Chris was covering up for
somebody.''

"Is that right? A woman's shoe. But who's the
woman?''

"Nobody knows—except maybe Chris. I'd sure like
to find out, though.'' Mae-mae decided she was running
her mouth too much. "Anyway, I'll be in touch with
Myra and let you know her feelings about your bid.''

After work Mae-mae drove to Little Five Points, Rachel's neighborhood. The Honda coughed and farted every
time she shifted, and then finally died at the corner of
Euclid. She managed to get it started again, but not without some laughing and finger pointing from the black T-
shirt and funny haircut types on the corner. Mae-mae
parked on the street in front of Rachel's house and the
engine expired again with a colicky rumble.

Mae-mae knocked, and after a while Rachel swung
the door open. "Oh, it's you,'' she said unenthusiasti-
cally. "Hi.'' The low sound of music came through the
door, a whiny woman singing with a band that sounded
like it should still be rehearsing in Dad's garage.

"How you doing?'' Mae-mae said.

"Hey, guess what?'' Rachel said. "They let Chris out
on bond today.''

"When?''

"Late this afternoon. I was going to go see him, but
I had to be at a shoot till six.''

"Can I sit down?'' Mae-mae said.

"Sure.'' Rachel waved her hand vaguely at the jumble of furniture that was her living room.

Mae-mae sat. Besides the patchouli and cigarettes,
there was a vague smell of unwashed bodies in the room.

"You want a beer?'' Rachel said. "I got a couple
sixes to celebrate Chris getting out of jail.''

"Sure.'' Rachel came back with the beer and sat
down on the dirty rug in the middle of the room. Her
thick-soled Dr. Martens poked out from under a puddle

of tie-dyed skirt. Mae-mae tried the beer. It was luke-warm. "Refrigerator's busted. Sorry. Landlord's too cheap to fix it."

There was an awkward pause while Mae-mae tried to think of something to say. Rachel was squatting on the floor, looking at her.

"I talked to Mom today," Rachel said. "She said you're helping sell the shop?"

Mae-mae nodded and drank some of her warm beer. It foamed up and a stream of thick bubbles ran down the side of the bottle. "Rachel," Mae-mae said. "Did you tell me everything about your argument with your father? Everything?"

Rachel looked down at the threadbare rug, found an especially interesting thread, and started pulling on it. It came away from the rug, inch by inch, working its way across the rug and leaving a tiny white streak where it pulled free from the fabric.

"Sure," Rachel said. "I didn't lie about anything."

"Okay, but did you leave anything out?"

Rachel jerked the thread, pulling the whole thing free. The thread dangled in her hand for a minute, then she wadded it up and threw it into a dusty nook beside a shelf jammed with paperback books. "You don't think Chris did it," she said finally.

"No, I don't."

"He *confessed*," Rachel said. "He *said* he goddamn did it!"

"Yeah, but I talked to the police. The forensic evidence says that he's lying."

Rachel cocked her head to the side and looked at Mae-mae for a minute.

"The medical examiner thinks your dad was killed by a woman."

A look of understanding started spreading down Rachel's face, her eyes widening for a moment. Her surprise was quickly replaced by the flush of anger. "What is it with you?" she said, spitting the words out between clenched teeth. "What is it? Every time you come here you do this stupid Columbo routine, beating around the bush, asking all these sneaky questions. Why don't you just come right out and ask the question? Huh? Just ask the question."

But Mae-mae couldn't say it.

Rachel's eyes were blazing. "Come on, Mae-mae, *say* it! Say, 'Hey, Rachel, did you fucking whack your old man?' "

"Okay," Mae-mae said finally. "Okay. Did you kill your father?"

Rachel produced a wild parody of a smile, twisting her clean features into an ugly knot. "No! No, I did not kill my father. I wish it had been me instead of Chris, but it wasn't." She paused and her voice softened. "I know you like Chris. I love him, too. He's probably the best guy I've ever known. But *he* killed Dad. *He* killed Dad and I know he did it. I've got proof." She hammered herself on the thighs, twice, with her fists. A line of tears squeezed out of one eye.

"What do you mean, proof?"

Rachel got up and walked across the room to a coat closet, turned the chipped white porcelain knob, and opened the door. She got on her knees and lifted something up out of a hole in the baseboards at the back of the closet. When she stood, she had a heavy paper bag in her hands.

She walked back and sat down on the edge of the other couch, knees together, the paper bag sitting on her lap under her hands. Mae-mae had a vision of Rachel's mother, the first time she had come to Mae-mae's office, sitting the same way. Only it was a blue clutch that she had been resting her hands on. "This was what you left out of your story?" Mae-mae said.

Rachel nodded. "When Chris came back to the car, he had this paper bag in his hands." She patted the bag on her lap. "I sort of forgot about it at the time. But a couple days later he gave it to Clay, told Clay to get rid of it.''

''Why didn't he do it himself?''

Rachel shook her head. ''I don't know. But Clay, he's real rigid about things like this; he knew there was something . . . bad . . . in here. He decided he wouldn't have anything to do with it, so he gave it to me. I was going to burn it, but—''

''But what?''

''I don't know. I was scared to or something.'' Her face crumpled. ''I just didn't know what to do. I've never had anything like this happen before.'' She wiped some tears off her nose with the ham of her hand, then she gave Mae-mae the paper bag.

It was like a grocery bag but wider, made from brown kraft paper folded into a packet the size of a small purse. The Printmeister logo was stamped on the paper in red letters. Mae-mae had a hunch she knew what was in it.

She unfolded the bag and dumped the contents on the couch. A bundle of crumpled butcher paper fell onto the cushion.

''What is it?'' Rachel said.

Mae-mae started peeling back the layers of butcher paper, some of which was stained brown and stuck together, to see the thing inside. It took a while, spreading the paper out like the petals of a flower. And at the center of the flower, there it was: a woman's shoe.

Two-inch heel, size seven and a half, stained with splotches of brown.

Rachel made a brief hissing noise, a gasp. ''A shoe?'' she said. ''He used a shoe?''

''That's the point,'' Mae-mae said. ''He told me that he killed your dad with a hammer. That's what he told the police, too. But this is the real weapon.'' They stared at the shoe for a minute and then Mae-mae started wrapping it up again. ''Is it your shoe?'' she said.

Rachel's face had gone pale, her skin translucent. Her eyes seemed very large. She sat down, took off one of her ungainly Dr. Martens, and held it up so Mae-mae could see inside. There was a little silver circle inside the heel with the size printed inside it: eight and a half.

"Do you know whose it is?"

Rachel shook her head again, a bewildered look on her face.

Mae-mae put the stained pump back in the bag, folded it up. "I'd better take this to the police," she said.

Rachel sat limply on the floor. "Okay," she said plaintively. Then she looked up at Mae-mae, a childlike expression in her eyes. "Chris didn't do it? You really think Chris didn't do it?"

The Honda shuddered, squealed, and finally came to life. As she was about to pull out a car materialized out of the darkness behind her and stopped. She could see the smoke from her ailing engine curl and twist inside the cones of its headlights. Mae-mae waited for the car to go by, but it didn't. Maybe they wanted the parking space.

She pulled out and drove off down Colquitt, turned left on Euclid. The headlights behind her, she noticed, hadn't pulled into the parking space, but instead followed her onto Euclid and then onto Moreland.

The Honda bucked and stalled at the next light. The car from Colquitt was still behind her. Under the yellow streetlights she couldn't tell what color it was. It might have been tan, it might have been brown. Hard to tell. This time when she restarted the engine, the car refused to settle into its old steady hum. It jerked all the way up Moreland, turned flatulently onto Ponce de Leon, getting worse as she hung a right onto North Highland. She was passing the St. Charles Deli when the engine sighed, rattled, died. Mae-mae coasted the car into the parking lot, set the hand brake and tried to start the engine again.

There was no point, though: it had ceased to be an engine anymore. The thing had irrevocably passed over the threshold that separates machine from scrap metal.

One hundred and seventy-eight thousand, three hundred and thirty-seven miles into its life, her 1978 Honda Accord had given up the ghost.

"Yee-hah," she said to the empty car. "Car payments. Just what I need." She sat for a while, listening to country music on the radio. After a while Hank Williams, Jr., came on. Hank Junior pretty much sucked, so she picked up the brown paper bag off the seat, got out, slammed the door without locking it. Even left the radio on. Maybe some friendly ghetto entrepreneur would figure out a way to steal the car and then she wouldn't have to pay fifty bucks to some jerk with a tow truck. She started walking down North Highland. It was lucky she was only about half a mile from home.

As she walked, she thought about what to do next. Give Dick Clark the shoe, obviously. Maybe it would have the fingerprints of the real killer on it—whoever that might be. Colleen? Myra? The list was starting to close in. Or what about Rascoe? There was something screwy about that guy. What if he was the one and had done it with a woman's shoe on purpose, thinking that it would point the finger in some other direction?

When she reached Lanier, she turned right. It was a dark street, full of trees that waved slowly under the sodium street lamps, throwing undulating shadows across the dark pavement. It was a little spooky—but the walking felt nice.

Mae-mae had never really liked cars in the first place. They were nothing but hassle after hassle, like little jealous gods, capriciously screwing up your life if you didn't stack new brake lines and alternators and mufflers onto the altar with pretty fair regularity. The hell with cars. Who needed them anyway?

As she turned the corner of Bellvue, she looked around to her left and saw a man behind her. He was about a block behind her, though. Not close enough to worry about. She listened for his footsteps, seeing if he'd turned the corner. There were some freaks and winos in the neighborhood, of course, this close to Ponce. They were mostly harmless, but it never hurt to keep your eyes open. A car came by, engine roaring, its lights shining in her eyes.

When it was gone she thought she heard footsteps but wasn't sure. She turned around to look, but there was nobody on the sidewalk behind her. There was a dark, faceless figure on the other side of the road, though. He had a smooth way of walking, like mercury on glass. The same guy? Or was it even a man? Too dark to tell.

Mae-mae kept walking. Above her the moon slipped behind a cloud. Each time Mae-mae left the puddle of light under a street lamp, she looked longingly up at the warm yellow lights in the houses, feeling her heart pick up a little speed.

Come on, Mae-mae, she thought. *Just enjoy the walk and quit making things up. If the guy was planning to waylay you or something, he'd have stayed on the same side of the road you're on.* Besides, it was a public street. People had a right to walk on public streets. It was no big deal.

At the next cross street she looked back again. The man—it was definitely a man—was still walking in the same direction as she was, still on the other side of the road, his head shadowed, so he seemed to have no face at all. Gliding, gliding. Mae-mae clutched her purse and the paper bag tighter to her side. There was something familiar about the man—the way he walked, maybe— but she couldn't quite place him.

Then it came to her, where she'd seen the walk. A smooth, floating sort of walk. It was at Phipps Plaza today, watching Donald Rascoe in Lord & Taylor. The man behind her was Rascoe. It had to be. She started walking faster, listening for footsteps. When she got to the next corner she turned, looked back again.

The faceless man was gone.

Thank God. So maybe it wasn't Rascoe at all. Maybe she *was* just being paranoid. Carrying around a murder

weapon, thinking about death and violence all week—
you started getting nervous about everything, jumpy, assuming the worst. Hell, you could let it creep into your
life until everything else had been squeezed out, until all
you could think about was death and mayhem and cra-
ziness, your head full of rottenness and fear. That was
no good. You had to resist that, try to keep yourself on
an even keel.

The rest of the walk home was uneventful. The air
was crisp. The moon came out again, a big white joke
of a moon. Dog-walking yuppies hustled by, polite and
smiling, wearing sweatshirts painted with the names of
famous universities they hadn't attended. Somehow they
seemed like her friends, even though she didn't know
any of them.

Not bad, Mae-mae thought. It wasn't bad out here at
all—once you got rid of your paranoia. Her feet started
to get a little sore, so she sat down on a set of concrete
steps, pulled off her shoes, looked furtively up and down
the street—to hell with it—then yanked off her pantyhose. The cool, dry concrete felt good under her toes,
reminding Mae-mae of her old tomboy childhood days.
Man, those days seemed a long way away. She wadded
up the panty hose, stuffed them into the toe of her shoe,
put the shoes in her purse, started walking again.

Much better. She started to smile. Maybe it was the
relief of feeling—finally—that Chris hadn't done this
terrible thing. You could get emotional whiplash with
all that had been going on lately. By the time she was
a block from her house, she was humming an old Willie
Nelson song, "Good-Hearted Woman," the one about
the good-hearted woman who was in love with a good-
timing man. She sang part of it out loud, the part about
how she loved him in spite of his wicked ways. And
then she laughed, laughed a big hyena laugh right in the
middle of the road. It all seemed kind of funny now. A
dog walker, a guy in horn-rimmed glasses and a Harvard

Business School sweatshirt, came around the corner and gave her a funny look.

Mae-mae didn't care. Everything was okay. It was all going to be okay. She could feel it. It was just a matter of time. They'd figure out why Chris was doing what he was doing, they'd let him go. Everything would be okay. She walked down the block, stones and moss and dirt underfoot, and stood at the edge of her yard. The ancient, bent dogwood on the sloping lawn had just started to blossom, its flowers floating in the dark air like blobs of melting butter.

Life was good.

Mae-mae walked up to the front door and stopped. For some reason, a cold, prickly sensation had just run up the back of her neck. What was it? She turned around and looked out at the street. She had seen something. But what? There was nobody on the street, nobody lurking in the yard, no weird noises. . . .

Then she saw it: a junky tan Dodge parked about half a block down the street.

Rascoe. It *had* been Rascoe! Shit. He must have circled back, picked up his car, and driven over. But where was he now?

She took her key out of her purse, started to slide it into the door. What if he was inside the house? Maybe he was the one who had burned the stamps. The damn back door, she had never fixed it after the break-in. He could just reach through the burglar-friendly plastic wrap she put over the broken pane of glass, twist the knob, walk right in.

She backed away from the door, past the ragged pink azaleas, down to the splintered concrete of her driveway. There was no light around the side of the house, nothing there but darkness. The moon had slid behind a cloud again. She peered around the corner, letting her eyes adjust to the nothingness. All she could see were dark ill-defined shapes, different shades of gray black.

She inched forward, feeling the sharp concrete under

her bare feet. She stumbled once, catching her toes on something. It hurt like hell, but she was afraid to make a sound. When she got around to the back, she stuck her head out past the branches of an unruly holly bush and scanned the backyard. The back porch bug light was on, spreading its mustardy glow across the small, sparse lawn. Nobody there as far as she could see. It didn't look like the plastic wrap on the door had been torn— but it was hard to tell from the angle she was looking at it.

She stood there for a minute, head craning out around the bush, trying to think what to do next. Nothing left to do but go inside.

Then she heard a noise behind her, the sound of shoes scraping on pavement. She whirled and there he was, the faceless man, walking toward her. For a moment everything in her body shut down, like someone had pulled the plug.

The faceless man stopped five feet from her, his black, empty face aimed at her. "Time for me and you to have a little heart to heart," he said.

Then the moon came out from behind the cloud, the light spilling down on his rotten skin, and he wasn't faceless anymore.

Donald Rascoe. It had been Rascoe all along.

THIRTY

She stood for a moment, nothing happening but her breathing, staring at the black eyes, empty as death in the moon's pallid light.

He raised an index finger to his lips. "Take it easy." He leered at her. "Easy does it, sweetheart."

Without thinking, without willing herself to do anything in particular, Mae-mae found herself jumping toward him. She lifted her only weapon, the paper bag with the shoe in it, cocked it over her shoulder like a softball bat, and whacked Donald Rascoe across the face.

"Wait," he said. He stared at her, like he hadn't expected any resistance. "You don't—"

Mae-mae hit him again.

"God damn you!" There was blood on his cheek. Rascoe reached for her.

She jumped back, gripped the toe of the shoe through the paper bag, waited. He hesitated then slid toward her, grabbing her blouse. She swung as hard as she could. Rascoe let go of the blouse, put his hand up to ward off the shoe. He was too late: it glanced off his forearm and smacked the side of his head with a satisfying crunch.

Rascoe staggered, a welt opening up near his temple. A tiny trickle of blood ran down the side of his wrecked face. "Wait," he said again. His legs seemed rubbery and he dropped to his knees for a moment, shook his head, then struggled to his feet again, moving slowly toward her. Mae-mae had a sinking feeling that it was all over now. It had taken surprise and luck to hit him the first three times. Even with Rascoe hurt he was still big enough and strong enough and quick enough to overpower her if he wanted to.

"I'll scream," Mae-mae said.

"You bitch," Rascoe whispered. "Don't scream." He was bent over, grimacing, one hand held against his temple.

"Get out of here," Mae-mae said. "Now! I'll scream!"

Rascoe held out his hand like he was a cop stopping traffic, then he backed slowly away. The moon went behind a cloud, and his face went black again as he scurried backward down the sloping drive. She watched until he had hobbled back to his car, turned on the lights, and driven away.

Her hands were shaking so hard she could hardly get the key in the door. When she finally got inside, she locked the dead bolt and headed straight for the cabinet underneath the sink where she kept her seldom-used quart of Jim Beam. A healthy dose of bourbon in a coffee cup, a splash of tap water; she drank it down in one pull. It didn't do a damn bit of good, didn't stop the hammering of her heart.

She went back into the living room, dumped the shoe out of the torn Printmeister bag, unfurled the butcher paper, and looked at it. Green leather. A Joan & David: a very pretty shoe. Too bad it had dried blood all over it. Whose shoe was it? Size seven and a half. Her own size. That ruled out Colleen Mastronunzio—she was too tiny. What about Myra?

With a sweep of her arm, she scraped everything off her coffee table, heaping it all on the floor, and set the shoe back on the empty surface. Next she took the fake stamps out of her purse, dropped them beside the shoe. What was the connection? Mae-mae couldn't think of a damn thing. She took the letter out of her purse, the porn magazines out of her briefcase, set them in the middle of the coffee table, too.

Connections. Connections. What did Donald Rascoe have to do with counterfeiting, pornography, and women's shoes? Why did Chris make up a story about killing his father?

She stood there staring at the stuff for a long time, but nothing came.

Well, forget it. She needed to give Dick Clark a call. If nothing else, Rascoe might come back. She got up, went to the phone. The message light was blinking.

Just as she was about to push the playback button, the doorbell rang. Somewhere just under her sternum, a fist began tightening around her stomach. Rascoe again? She picked up the phone. She better make the call. Now.

The doorbell rang again. But what if it was Chris? Or Sebastian?

She set the receiver down, went to the door, and looked through the peephole. It wasn't Rascoe. Thank God. It was June and Barry King. Mae-mae's heart slowed; the fist eased its grip on her innards. What did they want at this time of day?

She opened the door.

"Hi!" Barry said, smiling through his beard. June had a smile on, too. "Sorry to interrupt your evening, but we've got a proposition for you. Mind if we come in?" He was wearing a maroon cashmere sweater, a heavy gold chain around his wrist, a pair of one-size-too-small white cotton twill pants, and shiny shoes made from some kind of dead lizard. The outfit made him look like a car dealer on winter vacation in Boca Raton. June wore a green silk dress, double-breasted with big white buttons. It seemed like June always wore green. It went so nicely with her hair.

"I was just cleaning up," Mae-mae gestured around the living room. "If you don't mind the horrific mess . . ."

Barry didn't mind at all. She showed them inside. "Make yourselves comfortable," she said. "I've got to make a phone call."

"Who you calling?" Barry said. He and June were both scrutinizing the stack of magazines in the middle of the coffee table. Barry had a funny look on his face. Maybe it was all those bare bosoms staring up at him.

"I'm calling the police," Mae-mae said.

"The police," Barry said.

"Yeah." She went into the hallway and pressed the playback button on the phone.

The first message was from Chris: "I just called to say I got out on bail today. Can I come and see you? I'd understand if you didn't want to see me . . . Well . . ." There was a long pause and then he hung up.

Second message: "It's Sebastian, my dear. The book you gave me, the one by Dr. and Mr. King, made quite interesting reading. It's rubbish, of course, but I found something I thought might rather prick your fancy. As I was skimming this charming piece of charlatanry, a sentence on page thirty-one leaped out at me. I'll read it to you: 'Once you make a decision, the key to success lies in sticking with your original conception through thick and through thin.' " Sebastian gave it a dramatic pause. " 'The danger? The greatest danger of all is weak follow-through.' Recognize that, my dear? It piqued my curiosity, so I read on. You'll never guess what I found on page eighty-eight." Sebastian's flat electronic voice paused, then answered itself: " 'This stage of BIOVISUALIZATION THERAPY will be the hardest. *A final warning. Don't quit now.*' " Another pause. "Now there's food for thought," he said. The electronic hum of a dead line followed, then the answering machine clicked off.

"Holy shit," Mae-mae said.

"Food for thought indeed," Barry said. His voice was

close behind her. "I wouldn't make that call to the police just yet if I were you."

Mae-mae turned, stared into the barrel of a small, shiny automatic pistol. In the other room, she saw June examining the shoe in the middle of the table. The *green* shoe. June always wore green. June looked up at Mae-mae and said calmly, "How did you find out?"

THIRTY-ONE

"**H**ow did I find out what?" Mae-mae said.

Barry laughed cheerfully. "You could save us all some time, spare us the dumb act," he said, still wearing his biggest salesman smile. "Why don't you pull up a chair?"

Mae-mae looked at him, then at the tiny black hole that pointed at her. For a minute, nothing moved. Then June took out a pistol, too.

"Matching pistols," Mae-mae said. "That's cute."

"I do know how to use this," June said. She sounded nice and calm, like a meditation instructor or a t'ai chi master. "Just in case you were wondering."

"I'll bet you do," Mae-mae said. She took a Le Menu plate off the seat of the wing chair, threw it on the floor, and sat down. Her legs had gone soft and watery. Her stomach wasn't feeling so great either.

Barry pointed at the shoe in June's lap. "You know, we were wondering all along what happened to that shoe. About an hour after it happened we realized, all the excitement, we'd left it there. We went back to pick it up, but you know what?—it was gone."

"Meaning an hour after you killed Charles Towe."

"Well, it wasn't me exactly. Every now and then the missus gets a little overexcited." Barry shrugged. "It was bad luck, could have happened to anybody.''

"You want to tell me what happened?" Mae-mae said.

"No," June said.

But Barry was already talking. "Charlie was always a problem." He looked at June. "Always a problem, wasn't he, hon?"

June looked at him the way you would look at a TV when you wanted to change the channel but somebody else had the remote control.

"Charlie was just never . . . how should I put it? Enthusiastic. Never was a team player," Barry said. He shook his head like a father lamenting a kid who wasn't doing real well in school. "We had a great arrangement, but he just kept trying to back out."

"Which is why you sent the letter. And the porn magazines and stuff?"

Barry shrugged.

"And when that didn't work?"

"That's the funny thing about a guy like Charlie." Barry looked mystified by something. "The crotch shots of his virginal daughter. I think we almost got him with that. Not that it was such a big deal to him personally. He just didn't want his *wife* to know!" Barry burst into laughter. "Isn't that a hoot? He didn't mind catting around, rubbing his wife's nose in that particular pile of nuptial doo doo—but by God he wasn't going to put her through the agony of seeing pictures of her daughter in a satin G string. No, sir! That wouldn't be *right*!"

"Isn't that a hoot," Mae-mae said.

"Well, you may not think it's funny, but I think it's fascinating. Being a student of human nature, I mean."

Mae-mae glared at him.

"Anyway," Barry said. "He kept trying to weasel out of our arrangement. Well, that last night, things just got out of hand."

"Got out of hand? Killing somebody with a shoe, that's getting out of hand?"

Before Barry could respond, the doorbell rang.

"I don't see any particular need to answer the door," Barry said. They waited for a while. Barry yawned and put his lizard-skin loafers up on the coffee table. He wasn't wearing socks.

The doorbell rang again. Mae-mae looked nervously at the door, but Barry just shook his head.

A third ring. Then Chris's voice. "Mae-mae! I know you're in there. I saw the light come on. Mae-mae!"

The bell again.

Barry turned to June, looking for instruction. June said, "Make him go away, Mae-mae." She made a subtle gesture with the gun to let her know what would happen if she didn't.

Mae-mae got up, pulled the dead bolt, opened the door about six inches. Chris was standing on the porch in his leather jacket and white T-shirt, looking bedraggled and tired.

"It's a bad time, Chris," Mae-mae said. Her voice came out in a soft, lisping croak.

"A bad time." He looked at her for a minute, then blinked and looked out into the dark yard. He had a look of weariness and vast disappointment in his eyes.

"I don't know," she said. "I mean . . . later."

Chris turned his eyes back to her face after a few seconds, a deep crease forming just above the bridge of his nose. "Something's wrong, isn't it?" he said, his voice dropping.

Mae-mae nodded as subtly as she could, hoping the Kings wouldn't see it. Then after a second: "No."

"Are you sure?"

She flicked her eyes hard to the left, hoping he'd catch on: there's somebody in here. He was staring at her like she was nuts. She turned her head a little, just enough so the Kings couldn't see her lips, and mouthed the words: *Help me*.

"What?"

HELP ME! He was looking at her, and it was clear he didn't understand.

June cleared her throat softly behind her.

"Is somebody in there? Are you okay?"

"I have to go," Mae-mae said. *HELP ME!* She closed the door and sat down again.

There was no more doorbell ringing. The fist had begun to squeeze and squeeze under her breastbone again.

"Well, now we got that out of the way," Barry said, "let's get down to the point of why we're here." He had picked up the stamps off the table.

"I can't wait," Mae-mae said.

"So these are the only ones left, huh?"

Mae-mae nodded.

"How nice." He took a Bic lighter out of his pocket, lit the end of the stamps, held them up so the flames spread across one sheet, then set the burning paper down next to the bloodstained shoe. "Going, going, gone. No more counterfeiting."

They watched the stamps burn. The little fire leapt, sputtered, died, leaving a black curl of ash on the table. A couple of the stamps hadn't quite burned, but Barry didn't seem to care.

"Well, now you can take the shoe and say bye-bye," Mae-mae said—hoping that was all they wanted.

Barry didn't fall for it. "Unfortunately that's not the main thing. See we had a couple plans, a couple alternatives in mind when we came here. One scenario, you were onto us, the other you weren't." He poked up the green shoe with his gun. "Now we pretty much know which plan we got to go with."

Mae-mae was going to ask what the gist of Plan B was, but then she heard a noise on the back porch. They all heard it. It sounded like someone tearing the plastic wrap off a casserole dish.

"What was that?" Barry said.

Mae-mae did her best to look stupid. "What was what?"

Then they heard the snap—the sound of a dead bolt being opened. Then the creak of a door.

Barry motioned to June to stay where she was, then he retreated into the hallway across the room. From where Mae-mae was, he was easy to see. But to someone coming in from the dining room he would be invisible. Until too late.

Mae-mae sat stiffly, staring into the blind eye of June King's silver automatic. Was it Chris? Had he understood what she was saying? Or maybe Rascoe had come back. The back door closed with a soft click. The floor creaked.

A shadow lengthened in the doorway. Nothing else moved. Mae-mae's heart was beating hard.

And then there he was: Chris.

He was holding an electric guitar on his shoulder, both hands wrapped around the neck like it was an ax or a maul. He looked into the room, his pale eyes widening when he saw the gun in June King's hand. He stood flat-footed for a moment. "I don't get it," he said.

"Behind you!" Mae-mae screamed.

Barry King's maroon sweater was looming in the hallway behind him. Chris must have seen the gun as he turned: he swung frantically, slamming the electric guitar into Barry King's arm. The arm made a woody snapping sound and the gun flew across the room. Barry King yelped and clutched his wrist. Chris grabbed King by the collar of his sweater and hurled him to the floor.

On the other side of the room, June King was on her feet. "Don't move," she said to Mae-mae.

Mae-mae didn't. The little silver gun had taken all the life out of her legs.

Chris crashed down on top of Barry King and they rolled over and over into the middle of the rug, knocking over a plate of last night's supper. Chris righted himself and grabbed Barry's neck.

"Don't hurt me!" Barry squealed. He was clutching one hand against his chest, pushing feebly at Chris's arms with the other. "June, do something! Don't let him hurt me!"

"He won't," June said calmly.

Chris turned, looked into the muzzle of her silver automatic. His head sagged, and then he got up slowly, holding his hands out from his sides, chest level, like he was imitating a very fat man. His face didn't look frightened so much as disgusted. Or maybe disappointed.

"Sorry," he said to Mae-mae. "I guess I was a little short on firepower."

"He broke my wrist," Barry King said. "He broke my goddamn wrist." He was clutching his arm, staring at it like he'd never seen a wrist before.

"Sit down over there, hero," June said, pointing her gun at the couch. Chris sat down next to Mae-mae.

"Thanks for trying," Mae-mae said softly.

Chris shrugged. "Mind my asking what's going on here?" he said.

"Look at my goddamn wrist," Barry King said. He held up his arm. It had a little twist in it, kind of like a metal coat hanger where the two ends join together.

"Barry, please quit whining," June said. She hadn't once raised her voice.

Barry looked at her meekly, then stood up. There was a smear of day-old Budget Gourmet vegetable stroganoff on his sweater. "Look at this. This is a four hundred fifty dollar sweater. Look at this!" He picked up his gun off the floor with his good hand, his black eyes burning, went over to Chris and pointed the gun at his head. "Say you're sorry, you piece of—"

"Sit down, Barry," his wife interrupted.

"First he breaks my arm, then he gets stroganoff on my four hundred and fifty fucking dollar sweater. I'm gonna—"

"Sit *down*, Barry." Like you'd say it to a seven-year-old.

Barry sat down, put the gun in his crotch, and stared balefully at his wrist.

"Can you satisfy my curiosity," Chris said, "and at least tell me what's going on here?"

"Barry was getting ready to explain why they killed your father."

Chris looked at Barry, looked at June, looked at Barry again. It all seemed to be beyond his comprehension.

"It was *her* that did it," Barry said. Still peevish. "Don't blame me."

"Go on."

"We were there that day—as you know, Mae-mae. Charlie was doing a little printing job for us."

"Counterfeit stamps," Mae-mae said.

Barry shrugged, went on with his story. "We take delivery of the print job and drive off. Now halfway to Norcross, we look at the printing job and find out it's messed up, the registration's all screwed up, the whole thing looks like crap. So we drive back and Charlie says, 'Yeah, I did it on purpose. I'm tired of you people. You can show your dirty pictures to my wife, you can send me to jail, I don't care, because I've had enough.' That type of thing, right? Well, June says something to him, I forget what, and he just walks up to her and says, 'Little woman, I don't give a damn for you.' And then he takes her arm and tries to push her over toward the door. She doesn't want to go, he kind of jerks her, she falls down. That's when her shoe came off. So he just looks down at her and starts giving her more of this 'little woman' this and 'little woman' that. Wrong move. Wrong move. Cause then she stands up with the shoe in her hand and . . ." A tired expression ran across his face.

"And then she killed him," Mae-mae supplied the end of the sentence.

"It's starting to swell up, June," Barry said. He was squeezing his wrist, his face pale underneath his car dealer tan. "We got to do something here."

Then Mae-mae noticed June. She was trembling and her eyes were gleaming and spots of red had formed on her cheekbones, fighting for control of herself.

"You don't under*stand*!" June spit the words out. "You don't understand *anything*. None of you do!" Her voice had risen way out of its usual yoga teacher contralto, into a shrill, awful screech.

"See, June had a very hard childhood. Her father was—"

"Shut up, Barry! You don't understand what it's like to . . ." She tried again. "My father . . . My father . . ." Suddenly she froze, and—as though a veil had been dropped across her eyes—all expression drained from her face. She stared out across the room, breathing deeply a few times.

"Easy there, babe," Barry said. "Easy." There was suddenly a soft, tender look on his face. My God, Mae-mae realized, he really loves her. The poor fool loves this reptile, not even knowing her for what she is. Or, maybe, knowing her and loving her still. Mae-mae wasn't sure which was worse.

But June didn't need Barry right then; she was already back under the ironfisted control of her own will. It was horrifying to watch, like seeing someone turn from a human to a monster and back in the space of a few seconds—or maybe from monster to human to monster; it was hard to say which described it better.

"I think it works even better this way," June said in her calmest contralto. "We'll handle them both. We barely even have to change the plan."

"What do you mean—*handle*?" Mae-mae said.

Barry looked at her apprehensively, as though he didn't especially like the idea of whatever was about to happen. "Okay," he said slowly. "I can see how that might work."

"Mae-mae," June said. "Please get a piece of paper and a pen. It's time to take a little dictation."

There was a legal pad on the floor next to the coffee table, a pen in her purse. Mae-mae could hardly hold the pen, her hands were shaking so hard.

"Write down exactly what I tell you," June said. The

gun was pointing straight at Mae-mae's face. "Word for word."

Mae-mae lifted her pen to the paper.

June dictated: "It was just an accident."

It was just an accident. The letters were wobbly, jerky. Mae-mae's hand wasn't working right. She heard the scratch of the pen on the paper, heard the steam train roar of blood in her ears. Everything seemed to be insignificant and faraway.

"I did not mean to kill Charles Towe. On the night of June twenty-first we got into an argument about . . ." June was thinking, trying to come up with a suitable excuse for murder.

"His financial affairs." Barry filled in the blank, his voice tired and flat.

Mae-mae wrote it down.

"Stop it!" Chris said. "Don't do it!" He shook Mae-mae by the shoulders. She felt his hands on her, his distant touch. "Stop writing, Mae-mae!"

She didn't listen. Everything was faraway. Nothing mattered. She was all alone inside her head and nothing mattered.

June went on: "He assaulted me. In a moment of anger, I hit him with a shoe, and then he fell down and I hit him again. Before I realized what I was doing, I had killed him. I was appalled by what I had done, but I was afraid, too, so I ran away."

In a moment of anger . . .

"In my capacity as legal adviser to Charles Towe, I met his son Chris. We have been involved romantically for some time. Lester Paris discovered evidence about what I did. Chris killed him in order to protect me. Later, fearing that I would be caught anyway, he claimed to have killed his father in order to protect me."

Mae-mae kept writing.

June paused, thinking. "Chris and I are sorry for the pain we have caused. We have decided to end the horror."

Writing. Writing. The blood roaring. Vision narrowing into a gray tunnel, nothing in the world but the contralto voice and the pen and the yellow paper. *Chris and I are sorry for the pain we have caused. We have decided to end the horror.*

"Now sign it, both of you."

Mae-mae signed. Chris hesitated, the pen trembling in his hand. June raised her gun, put the barrel right up against his left eye. You could see the tension in her finger, the pressure on the trigger.

Chris signed.

The fog began to blow free of Mae-mae's mind. It occurred to her for the first time in a clear, hard, unimpeachable way that if something didn't happen very soon, they would be dead within a couple of minutes.

"What I still don't understand," she said finally, "is why you people went into counterfeiting in the first place."

"Barry," June said. "Point your gun at Mae-mae."

Barry did as he was told.

"I mean, weren't you doing well enough with your little new age medicine show?" Mae-mae pursued.

"Chris," June said. "Pick up the shoe and put it on Mae-mae's foot."

He picked up the green shoe, knelt, put it on Mae-mae's foot. It was too tight, but he managed to squeeze it on. Then he sat down again.

June let her little automatic trail slowly down Chris's face until it was touching his upper lip. Mae-mae's mouth went dry. She tried to swallow but couldn't.

"Here's what you're going to do, Chris," June said. "Put your hand around the gun, your finger on the trigger. Don't try anything funny or Barry kills Mae-mae first. Painfully. The reason we have to do it this way, we need the powder marks on your hand. There's a forensic test they do and we need them to be satisfied that you pulled the trigger." The voice—calm, like she was explaining biovisualization therapy to an especially dumb audience.

"See, what happened," Barry said. "We had a little cash flow problem, couple years ago. Which we solved by, among other things, getting Lester to print us up some fake stamps. Well, eventually we got around this little kink in our bankroll, but by then we figured out we could make a nice profit with this stuff. We don't use them ourselves anymore. What we did, we found a few buyers here and there—a couple Italian guys from New Orleans, some marginal direct mail types, a post-master down in Florida who has a little cocaine problem. Whatever. We make the sales, funnel the money off-shore, one piece goes to us, one goes to Towe and Paris. If Towe hadn't had his panties hitched so tight, every-body'd still be happy, nobody'd be getting hurt."

"Shut up, Barry," June said. Then to Chris: "I'm sorry it has to be this way." There was nothing in her eyes to indicate she actually *was* sorry. But then she didn't look happy about it either. It didn't seem to matter one way or the other.

Chris turned his head and looked at Mae-mae. His eyes were very blue and bright. "Whatever happens," he said. "I just want you to know . . ."

June's finger tightened on the trigger. Mae-mae couldn't watch. She closed her eyes. A loud bang re-verberated in her ears.

Chris never had a chance to finish his sentence.

THIRTY-TWO

The silence that followed seemed to last forever.

"The fuck was that?" Barry said.

Mae-mae opened her eyes. The explosion—it wasn't the sound of the gun going off, it was the sound of someone blowing up the front door, shattering the jambs, driving it off its hinges.

The door fell facedown in a cloud of blue smoke, and four men followed it into the room, running, four men with blue windbreakers and baseball caps. Four men with guns.

The first man through the door was Donald Rascoe.

"Donald?" Barry said.

Rascoe was holding a wallet sort of thing out in front of him, the kind with a little gold shield in it. "Federal agents!" he said. "Put the guns down!"

Barry King stared at them, dumbstruck. June's gun was still pointed at Chris's mouth.

"Now!" Rascoe said. He had a bloody welt on his temple and he didn't look like he was in a particularly good mood. His gun was aimed straight at the jade pin on June's left breast.

Barry set his gun slowly, carefully on the coffee table. June didn't move.

"Now!" Rascoe said again. He had a glazed, trigger-happy sheen in his eyes. There were big yellow letters stenciled on the blue windbreakers: POSTAL INSPECTOR. Jesus, she'd never thought of that before. If she had ever imagined postal inspectors (which she hadn't especially), they would have been little guys in brown suits sorting through the mail in a cheap paneled office in Washington. Not undercover cops with huge guns and explosives that blew your door off the hinges.

"June," Barry said. "Please, June." He had a pleading note in his voice, expecting the worst.

June's hand slowly dropped, till her gun was pointing at the floor.

"That's good," Rascoe said. "That's nice. Now let go."

"For Godsake, babe. Do what he says!"

But she didn't do it; she just stood there rooted in the middle of Mae-mae's disaster of a living room, staring at the men in the blue windbreakers. There was no expression on her face at all.

One of the ex–football players said, "Honey, you don't put that gun down by the count of three, we just might have to manhandle you a little." Not smiling, but like he thought he was pretty funny. A man who loved his work, manhandling people.

June just looked at him, studying his face while he counted out loud.

"ONE!"

She didn't seem to care. Wherever her mind was, it wasn't in that room.

"Please! June! Babe!" Barry had slipped down on his knees, holding his good hand up to her like some hack Shakespearean actor.

"TWO!"

"June, for chrissake . . ."

She swayed slightly, as though listening to distant music, her hard little body moving gently under the green silk dress. When the cop got to THREE! she smiled, a sweet, true smile, like she had finally reached a place she'd been searching a long time for, finally found some kind of clear information about the nature of things. And once she reached that point, there was no place else to go. She lifted her gun as though to fire.

Four police issue nine-millimeter automatics responded, ending all debate.

The slugs tore through the green silk, leaving six or eight small holes in her chest, and June King pitched over onto the coffee table, then slid off onto the floor, stretched out full-length on her back. She struggled for a second, like she was trying to kick herself free of a net.

"June!" Barry King screamed. "No!" He dove onto the floor and put his arms around her, an inarticulate screech coming out of his mouth.

June's lips moved and her eyes looked sightlessly around the room. A gasping, bubbling noise came out of her mouth. She was trying to say something, but Maemae couldn't make out the words. After a minute she slumped onto the floor, her head hitting the floor with a soft bump, her copper hair splaying across the carpet.

"What'd she say?" one of the ex-footballers said.

The bearded man on the floor wiped his face, a smear of his wife's blood appearing on his cheek. He shook his head sharply like he was trying to get something clear in his mind—but the thing just wouldn't resolve.

"What'd she say, huh?" The cop again.

She looked about the same dead as alive: calm, almost beautiful, her eyes fixed on the distance, her face not giving out much that you could hold onto. Her hands lay open at her side. The only other thing worth noticing, there was something nestled in her left palm, a small gray wisp of something. They must have stuck to her hand as she fell against the table—half burned, barely recognizable: the last two stamps, the only ones that hadn't burned. Fakes, both of them.

"What'd she say, King? What'd she say?"

Barry King's head sank onto his wife's bloodstained chest.

THIRTY-THREE

"**W**e're gonna lick this thing," Rascoe said. "Get it?"

They were standing around in Mae-mae's kitchen, winding things up. Dick Clark had come in a few minutes earlier, started explaining everything that had just happened.

"Get what?" Dick Clark said.

"Her last words," Rascoe said. "That's my prediction, what she said: We're gonna lick this thing. Stamps, get it?"

Dick Clark didn't laugh. He didn't seem to get on real well with Rascoe. He went back to explaining things to Mae-mae and Chris. Rascoe had been working undercover for the past six months trying to find out who was buying the counterfeit stamps. He had started closing in on the Kings right before Towe and Paris had been killed. "King's name used to be Katz. He sold penny stocks, oil syndications, stuff like that, out in Dallas. Then he ran into some trouble with the SEC, skipped town, changed his name. That was about the time he and June met." Dick Clark picked some lint off his spiffy suit, looked at it, flicked it in Rascoe's general direction. "One thing led to another."

"Sorry about the shoe," Mae-mae said to Rascoe.

"Shoe?"

"That's what I hit you with."

"Damn," he said. "I was wondering what that was." He laughed—like it was no big deal getting knocked in the head.

"What were you following me for, anyway?" she said.

"Long story. After Towe was killed, we went to Paris, told him we'd cut him a deal. He gives us the buyers, we give him a reduced sentence. He goes, 'Counterfeiting? What counterfeiting?' He must have told the Kings we were after him, maybe tried to lean on them. We figure they got nervous, whacked him.

"After that my whole case was shot to hell. I had a suspicion the Kings were the buyers. But no direct evidence. The only person I could think of who might be able to stumble on something was you. So I followed you home today. I was going to come by and ask if you'd wear a wire for us, help us bust Barry and June." He took out a pack of Winstons, went through some rigamarole firing one up. "Only you didn't give me a chance."

Mae-mae played the scene over in her head. "Why didn't you show me your badge or something?"

Rascoe had a sly look in his eyes. "We were tapping the King's car phone, so we knew they were on the way over. I didn't want you to scream because then the city cops would show up, maybe scare Barry and June off. See, whether you said yes or no, we planned to have a microphone truck set up across the street. I figured we could just listen to what was going on here, see if anything developed."

"You've been out there the whole time," Chris said, "listening to us with microphones?"

"Laser mikes. Digital technology, my friend. Picks up the vibrations of the window."

Chris looked at him for a minute. "You're saying you

knew she had a gun in my mouth the whole time? And you just sat there?''

Rascoe shrugged. "You can't just bust down doors and come in shooting without good reason," he said. He ran a finger across the raw looking place on his forehead where an eyebrow ought to have been growing. "Besides, we were recording everything. They didn't admit to the counterfeiting until the last few seconds. We needed a confession on tape." He winked at Mae-mae. "You should know that, counselor. Got to have something we can take into a court of law."

"You just sat there." Chris said wonderingly. "You just *sat* there."

"I wasn't going to blow six months' work just to keep your pecker hard." He held up a cassette tape, waved it in front of them.

"Keep my . . ." Chris stared at him. "She could have shot me. That woman could have killed me!"

"She didn't though, did she? Must've been your lucky day." Rascoe smirked, walked out of the room thumping the cassette against his leg. It didn't matter to him. He had what he wanted.

After a while Mae-mae started to feel a little claustrophobic, all the cops and forensic people and paramedics tromping around her house. She took Chris by the hand and they walked silently out into the moonlight. There was no point in saying anything. It was all too close. The light smell of the azaleas filled the yard. Dogwood blossoms floated in the air. Chris put his arm around her and they walked up the street. They walked for a long time.

There were no thoughts, really—just the feel of breathing, of muscles moving, of Chris's warmth next to her.

"You thought it was Rachel?" Mae-mae said finally.

"Yeah. I thought she was the one. I guess the Kings must have come back and . . . done it . . . right after we left that night. I came back and there he was on the floor. I figured, you know, it had to have been her.''

"And you never asked her if she did it?''

After a minute he said, "I guess I should have asked. I guess I should have trusted her that much.''

And they left it at that.

When they got to the parking lot of the A&P up on North Highland, Mae-mae stopped and looked up. There was a big power pole next to the road, sticking way up in the air. She felt confused for a minute, not sure whether she wanted to be with Chris or whether she wanted to be alone.

Everything was so intense and crazy. It was hard enough dealing with things like this when you were alone. How were you supposed to handle it with other people, other people who were as fragile and uncertain and mortal as you were?

"What are you looking at?" Chris said finally.

Mae-mae stared up at the pole. "You mind if I climb up it?''

Chris put a finger on his glasses, blinked once. "You're serious," he said.

Mae-mae nodded.

Chris looked up at the pole for a while, then looked back down at her like she was out of her mind. But he didn't say anything.

Mae-mae spit on her hands, rubbed them together, just like back in elementary school. She hugged the cold galvanized pole, wrapped her legs around it, started slowly inching her way up toward the first handhold. It was real work. Her breath was coming hard when she finally reached the first steel peg.

She looked down. Chris's eyes were distressed.

"It's amazing once you get up there," Mae-mae said.

"I'm scared of heights.''

"Just try it.''

"Seriously. I'm scared.''

Mae-mae grabbed the second peg and pulled, worked

her right foot up to the first peg. From there it wasn't too hard: one peg after another—right hand, right foot, left hand, left foot—the pegs splayed out at ninety degree angles. When she reached treetop level, a soft breeze caught her, pulling at her clothes. The adrenaline started to kick in and she felt scared and high and wonderfully forgetful.

The clouds were low overhead, moving slowly in the breeze, tinted at the edges with silver moonlight. Down on the ground, Chris had his hands in his pockets. He walked around, looked up at her, looked away.

Mae-mae kept climbing, the rough steel pegs chafing her hands. She could hear the high tension wires humming now, a low, unvarying musical tone. Sixty cycle hum. The lights of the city revealed themselves over the trees, the skyscrapers downtown throwing blots of yellow light up into the shifting sky.

When she got to the top, she could feel the pole sway in the wind, a magnificently vertiginous feeling. Threads of light shot out in all directions below her, their feeble energy running swift and nervous across the dark ground.

What the hell was she doing up here? Why wasn't she down there with him? You can't do it all yourself. You just can't.

Below her Chris still had his hands in his pockets, his head hunched over like he was afraid even to look at her.

She called down to him. "Back there—what was it you were going to say?" Meaning, just as June was about to shoot him.

Chris looked up for a minute, a sweet and frightened light in his eyes. He understood what she meant. "I'm not sure," he called back. "Something about you. Something about love, I think."

"And you were serious?"

"Never been more serious in my life."

Mae-mae smiled and looked out at the lights shining

up against the darkness, the empty earth, the mottled sky. The lines were humming, her body alive with their sound. And for the first time in a long, long string of years she wished she could share this thing, share herself *exactly*, let someone else feel the same pure and resonant tone.

When she looked down again, Chris was halfway up the pole, climbing slowly toward her, hand over hand, body tight to the steel. He was afraid to look up.

But that was okay—he was almost there.